Two Wicked Desserts

TWO WICKED DESSERTS

LYNN CAHOON

WHEELER PUBLISHING
A part of Gale, a Cengage Company

Copyright © 2021 by Lynn Cahoon.
A Kitchen Witch Mystery.
Wheeler Publishing, a part of Gale, a Cengage Company.

**LIBRARY OF CONGRESS CIP DATA ON FILE.
CATALOGUING IN PUBLICATION FOR THIS BOOK
IS AVAILABLE FROM THE LIBRARY OF CONGRESS.**

ISBN-13: 978-1-4328-9664-5 (softcover alk. paper)

Published in 2022 by arrangement with Kensington Books, an imprint of Kensington Publishing Corp.

Printed in the United States of America
1 2 3 4 5   26 25 24 23 22

To the creators of magic out there who keep us entertained and our imaginations working overtime.

ACKNOWLEDGMENTS

I talk about the writing process on my Facebook page, but a lot of times I leave out the daily boring activities that all authors have to work with. The creating — the writing — the world building, the traveling to events and meeting readers, that's the fun stuff. The edits, the proofreading until your eyes bleed (and then still missing an obvious typo), the bookkeeping, the accounting, the scheduling — well, sometimes this stuff can be overwhelming. At least that's the stuff that wears on this author. So thanks to all the people on my team who make these days easier. From my husband, who takes giveaway packets to the post office, to my editor, who challenges my mix of magic and mystery, to my agent, who helps me negotiate the business side. And all the others who touch my books and make them better. One step at a time. You guys rock.

CHAPTER 1

Mia Malone watched as her grandmother, Mary Alice Carpenter, stared at the notes from her grimoire. The book's pages were that lovely cream color old books get, but the ink used to write the spells ranged from standard black or blue to the more recent ones in colored ink. Where her grandmother had found the glitter pens Mia didn't know. Her own grimoire was out on the large desk in the room. She didn't have half as many spells as her grandmother, but hers were neat and tidy in the large book. Even from the beginning.

"I'm certain I have the ingredients right. This spell should have worked." Grans peered at Mia over her round, wire-rimmed glasses. Mr. Darcy sat on the large bench in the middle of what used to be a chemistry lab before the school had closed. Mia had purchased the school to save it from being torn down for a strip mall, as well as give her a space to open her own catering company and cooking school in Magic Springs, Idaho.

So far, the catering jobs and takeout business she'd snagged had kept the large, empty building heated and food on the table, but Mia hoped the classes would start to put her monthly profit-and-loss statement in the green. She needed a slush fund for slow times. But she'd worry about that later.

Today they were trying to help her cat. Mr. Darcy had taken on an unexpected visitor when he interrupted one of Grans's spells after her beau, Dorian Alexander, had been killed by a rival coven leader. Mr. Darcy had been host to Dorian's spirit for several months now, and even if he wasn't Mia's familiar, she'd be able to see he was tired of sharing his body.

Right now, he stared at Grans, waiting for her to put things back. He tapped his left foot twice, a signal he was getting impatient.

"She's doing the best she can." Mia stroked his fur, and he nuzzled his face into her hand. Then he gave Mary Alice one last stare, let out a loud meow, and jumped off the bench. He ran to the closet, where the secret outdoor passage hid, pawed it open, and disappeared. Mia stared after him. "I guess he was done talking."

"He's probably out hunting moles in the yard. Dorian always did like the outdoors. Although he used to hunt deer and use a rifle or a bow rather than his teeth." Grans pushed a strand of hair from her face. "I really am trying. I love having Dorian around, but I know Mr. Darcy deserves his body back. Maybe I could transfer Dorian into that grandfather clock in my living room."

"If we're doing that, shouldn't we be performing this spell at your place?" Mia wasn't sure her grandmother really wanted to release Dorian. While he was in Mr. Darcy, she could park him here at the school with Mia. If she released him into the clock, he'd be with her twenty-four seven.

"Dear, Dorian and I were just beginning our courtship. Don't you think it's too early for him to be moving in?" Grans closed the grimoire and glanced around the room. "Do you think I need to take the book upstairs while we have dinner? Or will it be safe here?"

"With half the town knowing where the secret entrance is and the fact that I can't seem to keep a lock on that closet door, you should bring it upstairs." She grabbed the book and then walked over for her own, carefully holding them separate. The books fought when they touched each other, a situation that her grandmother couldn't explain. "Come on and let's cook."

It was a pretty spring day in Magic Springs. Mia stared out the large windows looking out over the mountain range the town had been named for and wished she was outside with Mr. Darcy. Wildflowers had begun to bloom out in the woods past the grassy backyard and she wanted to walk the back area so she could figure out where she was putting her garden plot.

"Aren't you working tomorrow? If not, you could invite Trent over and he could help you plan the landscaping." Grans followed her out of the chemistry lab and to the stairs that would take them from the second-floor classrooms to her apartment on the third floor. "Maybe he could devise a plan to block the secret entrance as well. The man seems very versatile."

Mia slowly climbed the stairs, keeping her pace even so her grandmother wouldn't hurry to keep up. "Trent's tried. He says the house is preventing anyone from closing it off. He thinks there's a ward on the entrance, but he hasn't figured it out yet. Do you think someone added in some magical additions when they built the school?"

Her grandmother didn't answer until she was on the landing in front of the apartment door. There were only three doors on this floor. One to Mia's apartment. One to a storage room. And one that was locked, and Mia couldn't find the key. Trent thought it led to a widow's walk on the top of the building. She glanced at the locked door as she unlocked the apartment and waited while Grans stepped in ahead of her. Finally, she sat down in the kitchen and motioned Mia to set her grimoire on the table.

"Are you okay? I can get a contractor in here to install an elevator if the stairs are too much." Mia set Grans's grimoire in front of her, then returned her own to its spot on the kitchen bookshelf. The book shared its shelf with Gloria, Mia's kitchen witch, and a few crystals.

Her grandmother looked up from scanning the book's pages. "Why on earth would I need an elevator?"

"You didn't say anything. I thought you were winded." Mia dropped into the chair near her fridge and wondered if there was any sun tea left.

"I was thinking. You asked me a question and I was trying to remember if I had any notes in the grimoire about spell work done

13

when the school was built. If I remember right, the school was built in 1940. My mother might have been part of the construction crew." She flipped through the pages as she talked. "Our family's magical history is in my grimoire. Someday, because your mother has passed on the opportunity to learn the craft, the history will all move to your book."

Mia frowned as she looked at her book on the shelf. "Maybe I should have gotten a bigger one. Or you could just will me that book and I can keep it as well as my own. Kind of like volumes."

Grans shook her head. "It doesn't work like that. When I pass on, the spells our family of witches has developed over the years will move into your book. My book will die with me. Most witches have their books buried with them, but really, it's just a shell by the time of the ceremony. The spells will pass as soon as my tie to the earthly plain is broken."

Mia thought about this new bit of magical family history she hadn't known. "So what happened to Dorian's book? Because he's still here and all."

"His physical tie has been broken. He's only here in spirit." Grans shrugged. "I assume his daughter got the new book delivered to her place in Hollywood. I'm sure she'll try to use the spells to further her career, which, of course, will ruin the book and all his lovely spells. I really hope Dorian talked to her about the power she now wields. I tried to talk to her at the funeral, but she looked at me like I was a crazy old woman. Can you make me a cup of tea?"

Mia stood and filled the teakettle, putting it on the stove to heat up. "I thought we'd have roasted pork and vegetables tonight. I have some apple pie for dessert."

"Is Christina joining us?" Grans kept slowly turning pages.

Christina was the only employee of Mia's Morsels, as well as Mia's almost-sister-in-law and now roommate. Or would you call the sister of the jerk you were once engaged to an ex-almost-sister-in-law? Either way, she was turning into an amazing chef, even though her career goals were focused more on the hospitality side of the business. More than that, she had become a good friend.

Mia got out cups and tea bags. She would have her own herbs this year to dry for tea mixtures this summer. As soon as she got the garden planned and planted. There was a lot of work to be done before she'd be sipping a cup of her own brew next fall. "Christina's returning home this weekend from her birthday trip. She spent the week with her parents and Isaac in Bermuda, at their vacation place."

"When I turned twenty-one, no one sent me on an all-expenses Caribbean trip. We were just adults." Grans studied a spell in the grimoire, then shook her head and turned the page. "How did school go for her this term? Does she like the business classes?"

"Now that she's in charge of her future, school feels different now. And she's loving the hospitality program. She's a natural, but her heart is in event planning. She's probably going to open her own shop as soon as she gets the degree." Mia poured the water over the bags and brought the steaming cups to the table. "I'm glad she finally found her passion."

"I'm surprised she's still living here with you. I would have thought that she'd have gone home to stay with her folks." This time Grans did glance up, watching Mia's reaction.

"I'm not sure, but I believe she's here because she needs connection. Being home would have been miserable for her. Her mother would have pushed her into law or pre-med, something that Christina didn't want." Mia played with the bag, not letting

16

it steep on its own. "I know she's not really related to me, but I like playing big sister. And she does a lot for the catering company."

"You could hire someone with fewer issues." Grans refocused on the book. "But I understand your concern about the girl. She's special."

Mia stood and grabbed her laptop. As she booted it up, she grinned at her grandmother. "Maybe I can find some information about the builders and who was involved in the school planning."

"How will that help? They're probably all dead by now."

She stood and got a notebook from her desk drawer. "Probably, but maybe you'll recognize some of the names from the coven. And if they were in the coven, maybe they passed on their spells to someone in the family."

Grans nodded. "That's brilliant. I wouldn't have thought of it."

"I only just did. Probably because of your explanation about how the family grimoires work. All we have to do is find the witch or witches who were part of the development of the school." She keyed information into her search engine and went to find the information.

Two hours later, her stomach was growling and she had three names: Charles Silas Miller, Andrew Nathan McDonald, and Horace James Blough.

Her grandmother looked at the names as Mia pulled out the sheet pan where she'd roasted dinner. The roast felt done, but she put a meat thermometer inside just in case. Perfect temperature, she thought as the digital readout blinked.

"I don't know any of these men. Of course, I was just a little girl when the school was built. I wasn't even in school yet." Grans put the laptop and notebook on Mia's desk, along with her grimoire. "Don't let me forget this when you drive me home."

"I won't. Believe me, I don't want to deal with the problems." Mia got out plates and served the meal. After a few bites she set down her fork and smiled. "I love this kitchen. It's not as high tech as the one in my house in Boise, but it feels good. The school feels comfortable. Even the places I haven't had time to clean and organize."

"I'm glad you feel at home. That's important to your ability to be happy. You kept too busy in Boise to even breathe, let alone figure out what your heart was telling you." Grans sipped from her water. "Speaking of your heart, how are you and Trent doing?"

"We're fine." Trent was the owner/manager of Majors Grocery and Mia's boyfriend. He was also a reluctant witch, not like his little brother, who enjoyed magic and its benefits. Mia figured that Levi's living here was the real reason Christina had stayed in town, but he was a good guy and she didn't mind having him and his brother over most nights. "He's been getting some flak from John Louis about selling again. I guess John thinks if Majors closes, he can get a bigger grocery to come into town."

"I can't believe he isn't still in jail for what he did to you. Holding a gun on someone just isn't a joke in my mind." Grans's lips pursed together. She didn't like talking about John Louis, not at all.

"Apparently it wasn't loaded, and John has friends in the county government. Anyway, he's supposed to stay away from me, so that's a win at least. I haven't seen him since he came back from his trip to Boise when he did his 'time.' " Mia used air quotes. "He must have some really powerful friends to just get six weeks in the low-security prison section. I heard he was still running his realty business while he was in lockup. I hate to see him actually make money by ripping Majors Grocery out of Magic Springs."

"That's not going to happen. Albertsons already opened a small store in Sun Valley. There's no way they'd open a second one so close. Besides, all the one in Sun Valley carries is prepared foods and gourmet items. I stopped in for a few items the other day and couldn't even find regular flour. Rice flour, yes, but not all-purpose." Grans glanced around the room. "It's feeling chilly in here. Do you have the heat on?"

"Yes, but only in the apartment." Mia glanced around the room, hoping she wouldn't find Dorothy Purcell. The local ghost had expanded her haunting spots from the nursing home and the hospital to the school Mia had bought. She guessed she should feel grateful the ghost liked her enough to visit, but sometimes it wigged her out. Like the whole Mr. Darcy and Dorian thing.

A slight tapping echoed through the apartment.

"What is that?"

Mia got up and walked to the living room. "Mr. Darcy. He's started pawing at the door when he wants in. I'm not sure if he came up with the idea or if it's Dorian being polite."

Her grandmother stirred her tea and looked up when Mia returned from letting

Mr. Darcy into the apartment.

"I think it's time to talk a little more about the history of our family grimoire." Grans cleared the table of plates. Then she sat back down. "Do you have any whiskey, dear? This is going to be a little bit of a shock."

CHAPTER 2

Mia made coffee, poured two shots of whiskey for her grandmother, and checked not only the apartment door but also the downstairs door to make sure they were locked before Mary Alice would talk. Finally, Mia sat at the table and stared her down. She sipped her coffee while she watched her grandmother wrestle with whatever it was she needed to tell her.

"This is why I like being a kitchen witch. There's no drama. No transferring and stealing powers or books. We're just here dealing with the positive vibes of the world." She glanced at her familiar, Gloria, but the doll was turned away from her too. Something was definitely wrong. "Okay, now you all are scaring me. What's going on?"

Grans looked at the empty shot glass, then at the bottle. She shook her head, obviously deciding that another drink wouldn't help. Instead, she sipped her coffee. "Mia dear. I told you today that the spells a family owns pass from one witch to another. One that is bone of my bone. Blood of my blood."

"Related, you mean." Mia clarified for her grandmother.

She shook her head. "Yes and no. It's more than just related. My sister wouldn't get the spells when I die; you would. You're my descendant. The only way the spells would go to someone else is if I didn't have children or grandchildren."

Mia didn't know where this was going, but she felt her grandmother was taking the long way around to giving her an answer. "Okay, I get it. What am I supposed to know?"

"The spells from our family go back a long way. To the beginning of the Americas and even before that. But I believe, well, the book says, we are Bishops." Grans pushed out the words as if they'd been burning a hole in her throat. She sipped the coffee.

"Okay." Mia still didn't know why the spirit was mad at all. "Forgive me for asking the obvious, but who are the Bishops?"

"I think we'll stop here. We can talk more later." Grans glanced at the clock. "Do you mind taking me home? I'm tired."

"Of course." Mia stood and grabbed her keys while her grandmother picked up her purse. "Watch the house, Mr. Darcy. I'll be right back."

The cat jumped up on the wingback chair that was facing the front door. He circled into a ball on the seat, but his gaze never left the door.

Mia and Grans left the apartment and walked toward Mia's van. The vehicle didn't look great, but it worked well for deliveries and catering gigs, so she didn't care that it wasn't as pretty as the new ones owned by the Lodge for their events.

As they drove the few minutes to Grans's place, Mia tried to get her grandmother to tell her more about her heritage, but her grandmother kept waving the questions away.

"I'm sorry, Mia. I need to make sure I'm telling you things the right way."

Mia pulled the van into Grans's driveway. As soon as the van stopped, Grans hurried out and to her front door, not waiting for Mia to get out. Something had her spooked, and Mia was going to find out what it was.

Mia was back home and unlocking the front door when she realized that Grans had left her grimoire here at the house. "I even told her I wouldn't forget. I guess I'll just lock it in my safe. I'll leave mine out on the shelf."

It wasn't the best plan, but it was the only one she had. She couldn't lock both of them up in the same space; they'd fight to the death. Besides, she wasn't going anywhere, so no one would have a chance to get into the apartment. She relocked the door and headed upstairs. She was beat.

Her cell rang just as she was settling into her bedroom with a book to read. Seeing the display, she smiled as she answered. "Hey, Trent. I was thinking about you tonight."

"Really? Tell me more. Especially the dirty parts." He chuckled over the line.

She had to grin. It *was* about the dirty parts that she needed his help. Just not what he was thinking. "Okay, then. Can you come over here about ten tomorrow morning? I'll cook you a late breakfast."

"You know the way to my heart, but you still haven't told me what you need exactly. I'd enjoy hearing the details, especially from you." His voice was deep and husky. "Maybe I should come over now?"

"I'm tired. Grans was over all day and we were trying to find a spell to free Dorian. Tomorrow will have to do. You don't have to work, do you?" She lay on the bed and plumped up her pillow, then turned on the reading light.

"It's my day off. I guess I'll see you then, if you're not going to talk dirty to me," he said, trying to persuade her.

She yawned. "There will be plenty of dirt tomorrow, I promise."

"Good to know. Good night, Mia."

"Good night, Trent." Mia hung up the phone and set it on her wireless charger. Then she opened her book and started reading. It was long after midnight when she finally turned off the light. She'd be cutting it close to her getting eight hours of sleep before Trent arrived, but the story had been so worth it.

The next morning sunlight streamed into her bedroom, waking her along with the birdsong that came from the surrounding trees. She loved getting up when her body told her it was time rather than for some artificial clock so she could go work for someone else. In Boise she'd been the head of catering for the hotel, but because her ex-boyfriend, Isaac, had also been her boss, he'd scheduled planning meetings at six every Monday morning. Even if she'd catered an event the night before. One more reason she was glad she was out of the relationship and her own boss now.

She got ready for her day, and by the time

she'd reached the kitchen, Mr. Darcy was in the laundry room, waiting to be fed. She took a can of wet cat food and put some in his bowl. The look on the cat's face was one of pure disgust. "Sorry, Dorian, but you know Mr. Darcy loves his turkey and liver."

The cat dug into the food and she went to the counter to make a cup of coffee. She had an expensive coffee maker, but most days she used the one-cup model she'd bought for her work office. She grabbed a carton of yogurt and a banana, and once the coffee was done, she started eating. She'd cook eggs and toast for Trent when he arrived, but she liked lighter fare.

Noticing her grimoire, she crossed the room to move it to the table. She opened the cover and studied the page where her first spell was written. Small, tiny handwriting with a ruler line drawn below the words. She remembered asking Grans to draw the pencil lines so she wouldn't go crooked on the spell. She'd wanted her book to be nice and neat. She flipped through the pages, and as she did, she remembered each of the situations concerning the spells. She wondered how the book would feel with the family's spells added. Hopefully, she wouldn't find out for a long time.

The main-door doorbell rang and she

27

glanced at the video feed of Trent waving at her. She stood and buzzed him in. She'd replaced the original system with a higher-tech one a few months ago, after someone had broken into her house. The upgrade had been expensive, but it had been worth it. She must have saved a ton of trips down the stairs, and she could totally ignore door-to-door salesmen. Who made a living like that anymore anyway?

Instead of sitting down, she went to meet him and unlock the apartment door. Trent was finishing the last set of stairs and held a card out to her. "Looks like you had a visitor last night or this morning."

She took the business card. It was John Louis's, and it had a note scribbled on the back. She read it aloud. " 'Call me when you decide to sell. Sooner than later and you'll get a bonus from me.' I can't believe this. Man, he's persistent."

"Do you want me to talk to him?" He shut the door and locked it, then followed her into the kitchen. "I could take a bat with me to help him understand the words coming out of my mouth."

"My luck, he'd say something totally stupid and you'd be tempted to use your prop." She nodded to the coffee maker. "Tell me what you want for breakfast and you can make your coffee to get you by while I cook."

He stepped over to the counter and took out a cup. "Actually, I had to run out to see my folks, so my mom made me biscuits and gravy. So just coffee's fine."

"Everything okay at the farm?" Mia had met his folks once at a community dinner and auction. His dad was the jovial type who loved everyone. His mom? She was more reserved. More watchful. Mia couldn't tell if they approved of her dating their son or not.

Trent watched his coffee finish brewing and brought it over to the table. He glanced at her grimoire but didn't say anything about it. "Everything's fine. They updated the will and wanted me to know the changes. Boring estate stuff."

"That's funny. I had a chat with Grans yesterday about the way our family passes down spells and such. I didn't realize spell books were a historical record of the family tree." She eyed her spell book and laid her hand over the top of it. "Maybe that's why my book and Grans don't get along. Her book sees us as their replacement."

Trent shifted in his chair, focusing on his coffee. Then he changed the subject. "What's on the agenda today?"

She studied him. There was definitely something he wasn't saying. "Okay, spill. What do you know about passing down grimoires?"

"Mostly that they're a pain in the butt." He set aside his coffee. "I don't *know* this, but I've heard stories that sometimes books can start fighting between themselves. Throwing a revolution of sorts. I think it's more likely that the descendants decided it was their time to shine and took out their elders. Either way, the coven has a history of early ascension of powerful leaders after the accidental death of their elder."

"Wow." She stood and put her spell book back on the shelf. "Sometimes I forget that a lot of witchcraft isn't as warm and cozy as the kitchen witch branch. I just want the world to be a happy, safe place to live. What about the rule of three?"

"That's only a limitation on human witches. If a familiar or an object does the act, it doesn't have a body to bounce back to." He reached down and scratched Mr. Darcy on the head. "I see you weren't effective in freeing Dorian yesterday."

Mia shook her head. "No, we weren't, and I'm beginning to think Grans's heart isn't in the reversal spell."

Mr. Darcy made a noise, then ran from

the kitchen.

"Sounds like Dorian has been thinking along the same lines. I'll ask Mom if she knows of any spells. Maybe she's seen it happen before." He glanced at his watch. "Time is ticking; why did you want me to come over today?"

She pulled out a notebook in which she'd drawn the starting of a landscape design. She didn't have any measurements or utility markers, but it was a beginning. She tapped her pencil on the page. "I want you to help me set up an herb garden over here, near the back fence."

He took the notebook, then went to the window. "You want it on the left of the willow?"

She followed him and pointed out the markers. "It's going to be crazy big, but I need a place where I can grow herbs to dry and package for the winter. Sometimes your provider doesn't carry what I need to make certain dishes. And I'd love to maintain a small vegetable garden for my own kitchen."

He compared the drawing to the landscape outside and then set it down. "We can't dig until we get the utilities marked. I'll call that in now and we can go out and set it up so when they get paint down, we're ready."

"So you're going to help?" Excitement over the possibilities of the garden almost made her words more of a shriek. "Thank you so much."

"It will be a fun project. Besides, we can see how well we work together. Sometimes that's the Achilles heel for couples. Dating's fine, but you put them into a project and add some stress and they fall apart." He turned to study her. "Are you sure we're ready for something like this?"

"Heck, I know we are." She stepped away from him and grabbed two bottles of water from the fridge. "And if we're not? I'll still have my garden."

"Pure evil, that's what you are." He nodded to the door. "Ready to get this thing started?"

"Definitely." She grabbed gardening gloves from the washer, where she'd tucked them so she would remember. "I've got my watch alarm set for five, just in case we go crazy and lose track of time. I told Grans I'd bring dinner over to her when I returned her grimoire."

As they worked, Mia was acutely aware of the comfort level between them. No one raised their voice or argued for their point. Decisions were made fairly and in a calm manner. This really was different from her last relationship, when if Isaac didn't get his way, he pouted for days. This was really a different world.

By the end of the day they sat under the willow and studied their progress. She took out her notebook and penciled in the changes they'd made during the day.

Trent watched her as she drew and nodded. "As long as the underground utilities are where they're supposed to be, you'll be fine."

She leaned back on the tree trunk and sighed. The school was starting to look more like her house. Her business. Her life.

He took her in his arms and scooted between the tree and her back. Then he leaned her back. "It's a really nice place, Miss Mia. You need to stop worrying about things so much. Relax and let the day shine for you."

"If you say so." She closed her eyes and released a long breath. All was good with her soul at that specific moment. She didn't really know what the phrase meant, but she'd learned the song in vacation Bible school, and when things were on a roll, it came to her. And relaxed her.

She opened her eyes again and took in the scene. This was what she'd imagined when she'd thought of home. The building was a little larger than the one in her daydreams, but the feeling was solid. It felt like home. And she hadn't had a place like that for a long, long time.

CHAPTER 3

The next morning Mia taught her first small class in the downstairs kitchen. Brunch Basics. She'd hoped to have Christina here to help during classes, but she wouldn't be able to make it back until that weekend. Ten students had signed up and paid in advance for the class. She had just finished with the demonstrations and was handing out the recipe book for people to take home when she realized she knew one of the students.

"You're Bethanie Miller, right?" Mia handed her the class book. The last name Miller had been on the builder list. Mia wondered if Bethanie was part of that line of Millers. She'd have to do some research before she brought the question up to the girl. The last time she'd seen Bethanie she'd been dressed in a full white-satin suit at a chili contest. Mia was glad she'd made sure Mr. Darcy was locked up in the apartment.

Dorian might have a few issues with seeing her since Bethanie's family had been involved in Dorian's demise. The spirit in her cat might just hold a grudge against all the Millers. Today Bethanie had gone away from the all-white look and was dressed in jeans and a T-shirt that proclaimed that Magic Springs really was magical.

"Hi, Ms. Malone." She took the book. "I hope it's all right I took your class. I'd understand if you didn't want me here, but Christina said it would be fine. That you were cool."

Mia studied the formerly rich coven princess of Magic Springs. "It's a small town. I was going to run into you sooner or later. I didn't know you and Christina hung out."

Bethanie bobbed her head. "Yes. She's so much fun. And she's been teaching me jazz dance. I took ballet as a kid, but jazz is really fun."

The rest of the class had already left the kitchen. A few were with Grans, making an order for carryout. Mia realized that Bethanie had waited to approach her, probably so that they could talk without causing a scene. "I'm glad you two are bonding. Christina needs more local people to hang out with."

"Her boyfriend is ultracool too." She smiled, and for the first time Mia could see the young woman behind the walls she always seemed to have up. "Anyway, I'd better get going. I took the morning off from the real estate office to come here. My boss hates anything fun, so I told him I had a dentist appointment."

"What office do you work for?" Mia started walking out with her. There were lots of real estate offices nearby, especially ones that specialized in high-end homes for the rich who enjoyed owning their own ski lodge for winter vacations.

"I work for John Louis. He sells commercial real estate." She flipped back her hair as she tucked the recipe book into her tote. "He's a real tool, and he's always trying to get me to go out with him, even though he's married, but he pays well, so there's that."

Mia paused at the cash register and watched out the window. She could see the front walkway. A man stood waiting at the corner of the property. Bethanie met up with him, took his arm, and pointed toward town. Then they disappeared down the road. Maybe someone else had Bethanie's heart.

Grans finished packing up a few premade

casseroles and a salad for one of the class members.

Mia waited for the last person to leave, then sank into a chair. "Teaching people to cook is really hard work."

"I don't see how. You just stand up there and tell them how you do it. Add in some funny stories and you're good. You sold over three hundred dollars in carryout this morning, so you did something right." Grans looked around the now-empty lobby. "I'm going upstairs to put up my feet. Why don't you bring up one of those pans of chicken enchiladas for lunch? I can make a salad to go with it."

"Sounds good. I'll clean up down here, then I'll be up." She glanced at the door through which Bethanie had disappeared. "Silas Miller's daughter came to the class today."

Grans paused at the bottom of the stairs. "Bethanie? I didn't see her."

"She was the last one to leave the classroom. You might not have recognized her because she was wearing normal clothes. I bet her budget for designer duds tanked when her dad went to jail." Mia tucked the leftover recipe books into a box to put in her business office. "Weird thing was, she said she was hanging out with Christina."

Grans shrugged. "They're the same age; I would be shocked if they didn't run in the same circles. It's a small town, Mia. There aren't a lot of options in the friend pool in a small town."

"I know, but wow. It kind of took me off guard."

Grans pushed a lock of hair back into place, off Mia's face. "You worry too much. Sometimes people can change. You just have to give them a chance."

"Okay, okay. I get it." She nodded to the stairs. "Go watch your shows. I'll get the place back in shape."

Grans made her way to the bottom of the stairs. "When were they coming to check for lines? Maybe you could have them look at that plug outside that doesn't work."

"Not the same people, Grans. I need to call in an electrician for that. I'll go out to see if they've been here yet. I'd like to be spending the weekend digging up a garden spot. And I think I'm going to hire someone to put in some flower beds, especially around the front of the house. It needs some color."

"Make sure to check your color listing for the right mix." Grans started upstairs as Mia went back into the kitchen to clean up after the class.

The phone rang and Mia picked up the kitchen extension. She also had the ability to transfer the business's calls to her cell so she didn't have to be near the office all the time. "Mia's Morsels, what can I make to delight you for tonight's dinner?"

"Mia? Is that you?"

"Yes, it's Mia. How can I help you?" She thought it was Elizbeth from the library, but she wasn't quite sure.

"Mia, this is Elizabeth. I just wanted to confirm that you're still doing the library tea in two weeks."

Mia walked over to the calendar she'd hung on the kitchen wall to keep track of catering events. "I have you scheduled on the seventeenth at one. I'll be there to set up at twelve thirty. Why, is there a problem?"

Elizabeth exhaled. "No, I was just hoping you weren't going to shut down before the event."

"What do you mean? I'm not shutting down. I'm trying to build my business, not close it." A knot was forming in Mia's stomach. "Who told you I was shutting down?"

"I'm not sure now. We were standing around talking about the event and how amazing it's going to be, and someone asked who the new caterer was. Maybe it was

Sarah Baldwin. Or maybe Florence Meadows? Anyway, she'd been getting her hair done and heard it from someone at the beauty shop, who'd heard it from someone at church. I guess I can't tell you who's been telling people that you're leaving town."

Mia figured just because Elizabeth couldn't, didn't mean Mia couldn't, and she'd only need one guess. "Well, you can stop worrying about the catering for the event. That's all handled and you're going to love the meal, I promise."

"That's all I needed to know. And if anyone else comes up and tells me you're closing the business, I'll let them know they don't know what they're talking about. Thanks, Mia."

After she'd hung up the phone she scrubbed the kitchen, trying to get the mad out of her brain. It wasn't working. She went into her office and picked up the card John had left her. She dialed his cell number. When she got his voice mail, she let him have it. "You're messing with the wrong person here. I don't take well to intimidation. So just stop the games. I'm not selling the school, and even if I had to, I'd rather sell it for less than market price than to you. You can just crawl under a rock and die. That would make my life much easier."

After she'd hung up she thought of several other, better comebacks that would have worked, but she figured the less said the better. She didn't want to come off as crazy. Unless it would keep him away from her. Mia's luck was so bad that now that she'd told him she knew about his current sabotage, he'd probably see it as more of a challenge and keep coming at her.

She glanced around the office and decided she'd done enough for one day. She didn't have any pickup orders for today, so she turned the phones to voice mail and locked up the office and kitchen. Then she went upstairs to eat lunch with her grandmother. Maybe after lunch she'd spend some time reading or researching gardens so she got the right mix of herbs and vegetables.

Grans was on the phone when she came into the apartment. She went straight to the kitchen and put the enchiladas into the oven. Then she grabbed a soda out of the fridge. She picked up a new cookbook she'd just purchased and sat down to read it while she waited. When Grans finally came into the kitchen, Mia knew something was wrong.

"What's going on? Is everything okay?" Mia watched as her grandmother mirrored Mia's actions and grabbed a soda.

Opening the soda, she took a small sip, then set it down and took a place at the table. "That was Dorian's daughter, Cindy. She's coming into town next week to deal with an estate matter and wants to meet with me."

"About what? Dorian?" Mia put a piece of paper next to a recipe she might try this week. "Maybe he left you something in his will."

"We hadn't been together very long. I doubt he had time to change up his will for a woman he was just dating." Grans picked up a second recipe book Mia had left on the table. "I'm not sure, but she sounded frightened. Like she needed help."

"With?" Now Mia was curious.

"She didn't say." She pushed the book away. "Let's eat lunch, then I'm heading home. I need to work on some spells."

"Like the one for Mr. Darcy?" Mia went to the fridge, and the salad Grans had just made was sitting there waiting. "The enchiladas have a few more minutes in the oven, but by the time I get the table set, they should be ready."

"The enchilada dish is a strong seller. You should keep it in the rotation." Grans picked up the recipe books and put them on the bookshelf.

They chatted about nothing for a while, then ate lunch. Afterward, as they were cleaning up, Mia's grandmother grabbed her arm. Mia glanced down, and Mary Alice's face had gone white. "What is it? Are you okay? Do you need to sit down?"

Her eyes narrowed as she stared at Mia. "What? No, I'm okay. An idea just occurred to me. What if Cindy tried one of the spells in the grimoire and it backfired?"

"You should ask her." Mia put the leftover enchiladas in a plastic storage container. From her calculations, she had enough to make a dinner out of that as well.

"Oh, sure, I could just call her back to see if she's been playing with magic spells. She'd never talk to me again. And you'd probably get a visit from a lovely social worker from the Department on Aging, making sure I wasn't a danger to myself." She grabbed her purse. "I'm heading home. Call me if you need help cooking for this week's orders."

"You don't have to help all the time." Mia followed her to the front door. "I appreciate your help, but if you have something else to do —"

"What else would I do? Get a part-time job at the gas station?" She patted Mia's arm. "I enjoy working with you."

Mia walked downstairs with her under the pretense of checking to see if the office was locked up, even though she knew she had locked the doors earlier. After her grandmother left she wondered if Grans was lonely. She'd lost not only her best friend, but her new boyfriend in the last six months. No wonder she was hanging out more with Mia.

She grabbed the extra set of keys from the desk drawer in the foyer and went outside. She took pictures of the front, where she wanted the flower beds. And then stepped back to take pictures of the whole front. She needed to have a sign made for the business. Maybe the open hours listed. Or maybe that could be underneath, and she could change it out if necessary. She recorded a short note on her phone to remind her of the idea, then walked up the driveway into the small parking lot. She needed flower containers here too. Maybe those that would make the area look like a small European town. She'd find pictures tonight. When she hired a landscaper, that was going to cost her a fortune, but it would be worth it.

She walked around the area in the trees where they'd plotted out the garden. No paint on the ground. Hopefully they'd show up tomorrow morning. She really wanted to spend the weekend outside. It was supposed to be a lovely, mild spring weekend. No rain, just sun and a bit of wind to keep the temperatures down. Besides, having a project meant she wouldn't be stewing over the crap John Louis was pulling on her all the time. She'd told the man clearly and enough times she wasn't selling, it should have gotten into his thick skull by now.

Her fingers itched to grab the phone to call to yell at him again. Or maybe it was her magic wanting to be let out to play. Unfortunately, if that happened, the rule of three would make her pay for her lack of self-discipline. If she cursed his hair to fall out, hers would fall out and grow back pea green. If she cursed him with an inability to speak, she'd lose her voice and be rendered deaf at the same time. It might even affect her vision. Using magic for impure purposes was a mistake a young witch learned early and made only once. If she was smart, that was. No, Mia would stick with making potions and food magic that made people happy and healthy. That kept her karma clean, as well as helped out the townsfolk of Magic Springs.

She took a few more shots, then decided to take the pictures back to the apartment to make some new sketches. She could even finalize her planting list for the garden. So if the guy didn't get the plot cleared, she could still go shopping at the landscape center for plants and seeds. She paused at a spot under the weeping willow. Maybe she needed a fishpond and benches out here for people to take breaks when they were in class or waiting for a class to start.

She could see the rock fountain where the water would trickle down. She snapped a shot, then headed to the front door. She needed to get out of here before she thought of a thousand other new projects that just screamed to be done.

Upstairs, she worked on her designs until the light in the kitchen dimmed. She stood and turned on the overhead light, stretching the kinks out of her shoulders. Mr. Darcy wove himself through her legs. "It's probably dinnertime for you as well, isn't it, buddy?"

He meowed his response, probably too polite to tell her it was way past his dinnertime. The clock on the wall pointed that out.

She put her own dinner into the oven after feeding the cat and putting the papers she'd sketched into a folder and putting that onto her desk. Her grimoire was still out on the bookshelf and she remembered the promise she'd made her guardian; she took it to the bedroom and put it in her safe. No one but she knew where the safe was located. Well, she and the past school principal who'd had it put into the wall behind the bed. She didn't know what he'd had to keep safe, but she was glad he'd been a bit of a paranoid.

Mr. Darcy, who'd been sitting on the floor watching the door, meowed loudly, then focused his attention on Mia.

Mia shivered, the cat's unease flowing into her own senses. "I feel something too. Let's go check and make sure I relocked the front door. But no trying to sneak out."

When they'd finished their tour of the house, Mia took the stairs back to the apartment. All the doors were locked, even the inside one to the chemistry room with the secret entrance to the building that was hidden behind the teacher's desk. She might not be able to keep people from coming into the room, but that was as far as they would get. Unless they wanted to try to tear down a wall. And the walls were very sturdy. She double-checked the apartment door and then settled in for the night. The enchiladas were warm by the time she got back to the apartment. She turned on some music and, after dinner, spent time with a novel she'd been reading for a few days.

CHAPTER 4

The bell on the front door rang first thing Saturday morning. Mia checked the video feed, and Christina's smiling face filled the screen. "Hey, I didn't expect you until later today."

"I rode up from Boise with a friend rather than wait for Isaac to bring me home. I really need to buy a car." Christina's tone dropped. "Of course, when I suggested that as a gift for my birthday, Mom told me I should be grateful for the Bermuda trip. Which, of course, I am. But a car would have been cheaper and more practical."

"Your mom has strong opinions. Hold on, I'll be right down." Mia slipped on sandals and hurried downstairs, leaving the apartment door open. She was excited to have Christina back. And, even better, she didn't have to see her ex-boyfriend, Isaac, to do it. Yes, it was weird having your ex's sister as a roommate and employee, but Mia had left

Isaac, not broken her ties with his little sister. Besides, she knew their friendship bugged Isaac, so it was a total win for Mia. Not that she was vindictive or anything.

Mia opened the door and gasped. Christina had stepped close to the camera so Mia could only see her face. Now she could see the rest of her, and the natural blonde who'd turned into a redhead at a whim was now sporting goth black hair. Mia reached out and touched the straight locks that tumbled onto her multicolored dress. "Wow. This is new."

Christina spun and laughed. "Do you like it? I mean, everyone can come home from Bermuda with bright clothes, but I wanted my hair to make a statement too."

"Well, it certainly does that." Mia glanced out to the parking lot. A smaller-sized truck was in the lot. It had a company name on the door, and the logo for the underground utility call center on the back. "Looks like we'll be able to work in the garden today, as soon as he gets his job done."

"What garden?" Christina stared at the truck, then back at Mia.

She picked up one of Christina's suitcases. "Exactly."

Before they finished moving the suitcases inside the door, a man in a yellow emergency vest and a hard hat ran up to the porch. He was on the phone and his eyes were wide. "Hold on a minute. Lady, what's your name?"

"My name? Why do you need my name?" Mia glanced at Christina, who looked as confused as she felt. "Are you with the locating company for my garden?"

He nodded. "Look, the 9-1-1 operator wants to make sure she's sending the cops to the right place. You're Mia Malone, right?"

When Mia nodded, the guy focused back on the call. "It's in the backyard, but I'm staying out here in front. The homeowners are here too."

"Homeowner," Mia corrected. "This is Christina."

He nodded but didn't correct his misstatement. "Yeah, I'll stay on the line. I'm pretty sure I must be dreaming, so maybe having you on the line will help."

"Christina, run inside and get a bottle of water for . . ." Mia glanced at the name tag on the man's vest, "Jim. There's cold water in the downstairs kitchen."

"Thanks for the water, although I'd really like a beer." He looked at the steps. "Do you mind if I sit?"

"Not at all. What's back in the garden

51

area? A snake? Oh no, it's not a mountain lion, is it? I've heard they come down this far, but not usually in the spring. Maybe he's lost." Mia took the water Christina brought back and handed it to Jim, who was now sitting on her front steps. "Here you go. No beer in the house right now, sorry."

He took the water, opened it, and guzzled half of it down. "No worries. I was kind of joking about the beer."

"So a mountain lion, then?" Mia hadn't seen someone that scared for a while. It must have been huge. She pulled the front door closed so Mr. Darcy couldn't get out. Maybe she should send Christina to find him and shut him in the apartment. She'd left the door open. She turned to tell Christina just that when Jim spoke again.

"Lady, that was no mountain lion. You have a dead guy behind the house."

Christina looked up at the sound of the approaching sirens. "Tell Baldwin I just got back into town. This isn't my fault. I'm going upstairs with my suitcases."

"Make sure Mr. Darcy is in the apartment, please. I don't want him getting out." Mia started to say, "Because of the mountain lion," but there wasn't a big cat in her yard. She turned to Jim, who had finished his water and was methodically crunching the plastic bottle. "Who is it?"

He frowned at her question. "The dead guy?"

"Yeah, the dead guy."

Jim shrugged. "I don't know. I'm only here doing this area temporarily because the regular guy got fired. Are you missing someone from the house? You must have a lot of people living here, it's huge."

"Actually, only me and my assistant live here. It's a cooking school." She hesitated and wondered why she'd just told a stranger that two women were alone in the big school. She wondered if he'd even heard her statement as he watched two police cars and an ambulance pull up into her driveway, lights and sirens going. They turned off the sirens but left on the lights.

Jim spoke into his phone. "They're here." Then he disconnected the call. He stood and touched the brim of his hat. "I'm going to talk to them, then I'm out of here. Have a nice day."

Mia sat down and watched as Jim directed Mark Baldwin, the police detective in town, along with the other officers back to the area where he'd found the body. She didn't want to find out who it was. Her first thought was that it had to be some drifter.

She waited about thirty minutes and was

about to go inside when Baldwin came and sat next to her. She leaned against the porch rail. "I take it someone is really dead in my backyard."

"You're the unluckiest person in town. Yes, there's a dead guy in the yard. Worse news is who the dead guy is." Baldwin took off his hat, then pulled out a handkerchief and wiped his forehead.

Her eyes flew open. She should have been calling and checking on people. "Oh my God, Jim said it was a guy. It's not Trent. Or Levi, is it? Or maybe Kev?"

"No. None of those three. Sorry, I should have been clearer. I don't know the man in your backyard." He studied the sky, then nodded to the door. "Can we take this inside? The sun is getting warm."

Mia noticed when his eyes flicked toward the hearse that had just pulled up. He didn't want her to see the body. That was actually thoughtful. She guessed she and Baldwin were on a good path now. "Come on in. We can talk in my office. Do you want some water?"

"That would be nice." He glanced at the police cars in the parking lot. He caught someone's gaze, then pointed to the door. Which must have been code for *I'm going inside.*

She grabbed two bottles of water and led him into the office, which was still clean and put together. Mostly because she hadn't been busy enough to actually spend much time inside it for it to fall into disarray. She couldn't believe another dead body had been found on her property, but at least she didn't do the finding herself this time. "Go ahead, ask me if I killed this guy."

Instead, he focused on his notebook and asked, "How long have you known the utility locater?"

Baldwin's question threw her off. She'd been expecting questions like *Where were you at six o'clock this morning.* Not how well she knew the man who'd found the body. She shrugged, then looked at her watch. "Jim? About ten minutes now. We met when he came up to my door and told me there was a dead guy in my yard. Your dispatcher should have the exact time because he was on the phone with her."

"You didn't know him before today?"

Mia shook her head. "Nope."

"Then how do you know his name's Jim?" He leaned forward, watching her face.

"Because he has a name tag on his vest." She rubbed her face. This was not the way she'd planned on spending her day. "Christina had just come home from a family trip

55

and I was letting her inside when he came running up to the door. He'd already called 9-1-1 and was on the phone by the time he got to my door."

"Christina is back? Where did she go?" Baldwin started making notes again.

"Don't start messing with her. She went to Bermuda with her family last Sunday and came back today. She said a friend had given her a ride from Boise. She's upstairs. Do you want me to ask her to come down?" Mia narrowed her eyes, hoping she was giving Baldwin a hard stare. She'd never tried to do that before, so she didn't know what it would actually look like.

"Maybe after I finish with you." He went back a page in his notes. "So, Jim came up to you and asked to use your phone?"

She shook her head. "Nope. He had his cell. I guess the dispatcher asked him who owned the property."

"Why would you say that?" He narrowed his eyes.

Mia took a deep breath. "Because he *said* the dispatcher wanted to make sure who owned the building so she was sending people to the right house, so she asked him to find out who lived here. And I said I did."

"What about Christina? What did she say to Jim?"

"Honestly, I don't remember if she even talked to him. I told the dispatcher that I owned the place, not both of us, as Jim said he'd found the *homeowners,* lumping us together. When it was clear you and the rest of the police force were on the way, Christina went upstairs to put away her suitcase and to get ready for the day. We have cooking to do tomorrow for this week's orders. We deliver the takeout orders on Tuesday, and then we have an event next Saturday so we'll be in the kitchen all week." She rubbed her temples. At least she would be if John Louis stopped telling her customers that she was getting ready to leave town.

He stood. "Okay, then. I'll check back in with Christina later. I need to get going. I want to talk to the coroner about how this guy died."

"You said you don't know the victim?" Mia thought about possibilities. "Maybe he was hiking in the mountains and came down the wrong path. He could have had a heart attack."

Baldwin shook his head. "It's a good theory, except this guy was shot. You didn't hear anything last night, did you? The initial theory is that the guy was killed between midnight and four this morning."

"I'm a pretty heavy sleeper." She saw

Baldwin's grin and knew he was thinking about the night Adele Simpson had died and she'd been taking a walk because she couldn't sleep. "Well, I am, unless I'm worried about an event. No event this morning, so I was in bed by ten. I understand the previous occupant of the apartment soundproofed the walls. So unless someone came and rang the bell, I wouldn't know."

"Did anyone ring your bell?"

She shook her head. "I have a video doorbell now. If anyone walked near the front, I'd get an alarm."

He glanced around the room. "Did you set it up with that security company I sent over here?"

"Yes, and it's costing me an arm and a leg, but they assured me I'm getting a deep discount because of your referral. I hate to see what they charge their other clients."

He chuckled. "Their other clients can afford it. That's why Trey gives me a discount on my referrals. He's making his money off the Sun Valley set. You're getting the normal-person rate. Anyway, I'll call Trey to see if anything showed up on their outside cameras last night. So, unless you're going to confess to killing that guy in your backyard, I guess we're done here. I can see myself out."

"Thanks, Mark. I appreciate your coming out on a Saturday morning." She stood to walk out of the office as well. "I can't believe anyone would just shoot someone else. Especially here."

"No worries. You got me out of cleaning the garage. Things were getting a little calm around town. Sarah had started making a honey-do list." Baldwin paused before leaving the office. "This place was abandoned for too long. Maybe the killer didn't realize you'd bought it and were opening your business here. You might want to get a sign up to show people you're open."

"It's on my to-do list. See you later." Mia followed him out and put up the Closed sign in the window before locking the door. She went upstairs and collapsed onto the couch. Mr. Darcy hurried to her and jumped on her stomach. "It's okay, I'm all right."

"Good, because I was worried. Well, we were worried. Do you know who it was?" Christina smiled at Mr. Darcy as she brought out a bowl of tomato soup and a grilled cheese sandwich. "I wasn't sure you'd eaten this morning, so I thought you wouldn't mind an early lunch."

"No, not yet. Lunch was a good idea. I'm surprisingly hungry." She pointed to the other chair. "Come eat with me and tell me about your trip. Let's not talk about what happened just yet."

"Putting that on pause is a great idea." Christina held up a finger. "Let me get a tray set for me."

Mia dunked an edge of the sandwich into the soup. The soup Christina had gotten out of Mia's freezer stock, but the sandwich she'd made on her own. And it was good. Mia held it up when she returned from the kitchen with her own lunch. "This sandwich is terrific."

"Good. I hoped using provolone would work for grilled cheese. The recipe I looked up online used cheddar."

Mia nodded. "That's the standard, but this is yummy. And typically, you can use anything in the fridge. I appreciate your thoughtfulness."

Christina curled up in her chair and hugged a pillow around her waist. "You're the only one."

"What does that mean?" Mia knew Christina had a different outlook on life than her family, but she'd hoped the vacation would be a stress reliever and bring them together. Maybe she'd been too optimistic. "Uh-oh. What happened?"

"Mom just kept harping at me when I did

anything. Like said 'thank you' to the guy who brought my drink. She kept reminding me that we were paying for their services. They weren't doing it out of charity, so I shouldn't feel obligated to say thank you." Christina screamed into the pillow. "I made a special breakfast the morning we got there for everyone, thinking it would be a great way to show off some of my new ninja kitchen skills."

"That was sweet of you." Mia knew where this was going.

"You would have thought so. Instead, I get a lecture about how we pay people to do that kind of stuff, we don't do it ourselves. She and Dad both refused to eat what I made. Isaac's new girlfriend went with them to the restaurant."

"Oh, Christina, I'm so sorry." Mia saw the tears in her eyes that she was trying to hold back.

"Isaac ate breakfast with me and told me it was really good. Then he helped me clean up before they got back." Christina wiped at her face. "He said I should keep working with you because you're the best chef he's ever known."

Surprised at the compliment, Mia didn't know what to say at first. Finally, she nodded. "Isaac can be sweet at times. And he does know his food. You should feel good about his praise."

Christina smiled. "I know my brother can be a real jerk, especially after what he did to you, but what he said made me happy. He's my brother, after all."

And he'd acted like it for the first time in Mia's memory. She focused on her lunch. It had already been a crazy day and it wasn't even noon yet. "I'll give you today to get settled back in, but tomorrow we've got some cooking to do. I've doubled my delivery orders this week. And the class went really well. I talked to one of your friends, Bethanie."

Christina went still. "I'm not sure we're friends yet or anything, but she's cool to hang out with. She said she really wanted to take your class, but she was scared you'd hold that whole thing with her dad and brother against her."

"Water under the bridge. I was surprised that she was working for John Louis. I still don't think he should be out of prison yet."

Christina waved her sandwich at Mia. "That was such BS. He got this sweetheart deal because he knew someone, and he didn't actually 'hurt' you. He's a royal butt."

"It appears to be going around." Mia used the last of her sandwich to get the last bit of soup out of the bowl. "Thank you again for lunch. This was just what I needed. And I'm glad you're back."

"I'm glad to be back. I'm not sure time on a beautiful island is worth hanging out with my mom. I think I'll be busy in January, when she invites me to go again." Christina picked up the plates and bowls. "That is, if she ever talks to me again. Since I'm turning into such a common person."

"You can choose if you let her words hurt you," Mia reminded Christina.

"I definitely won't be wasting my time cooking for them again. I just kept making notes of what I'd do in my notebook because cooking there was out of the question. I have some recipe ideas I'd like to try out after we get done with the work part of the week."

"Sounds good."

Christina paused as she picked up the last plate. "Can I ask? Did you know the guy in the garden?"

Mia shook her head. "Baldwin didn't know him, so I don't think he's a local. Probably a hiker who ran into the wrong crowd on the trails."

"Levi told me not to go wandering off the trails if I hike alone. He says there are some growers out there who don't like people

63

finding their crops." Christina shivered. "Do you think it was them?"

"Most likely option. Anyway, make sure you keep the doors locked around here. I'd hate to have someone else wander off a trail and think the house is abandoned. Let's hope this is the last time we'll have to deal with a body in the backyard."

CHAPTER 5

Trent and Levi Majors sat in Mia's kitchen later that day. The two had arrived within minutes of each other and were both in foul moods. Their arrival had proven the Magic Springs rumor mill was active, if not truly accurate. Mia glanced at Christina, who shook her head — neither one of them had called the brothers to come "save" them. Mia held up a coffee cup. "Is it too late for coffee? Maybe some iced tea? I had some made just in case I got to work on my garden today. When do you think Baldwin will release the scene? I suppose I'm going to have to recall the utility guy too. I don't think he finished his job once he found the body."

"Mia, this isn't funny. Someone killed a man in your backyard," Trent reminded her. "Why didn't you call me? Or Levi? We should have known."

She set down the cup and went to the

fridge. "Iced tea it is, then."

"Mia . . ." Trent started again, but she whirled on him, narrowing her eyes.

"Do you really think I'm not freaked out about the implications of having a dead body show up at my house? I'm an adult. I remember to lock the doors at night. Especially living in this huge place." Mia pressed her lips together and finished pouring four glasses of tea. "And you and Levi might be important people in our lives, but neither one of you are the boss of me."

"I'm sorry. I overreacted, and I should have been more supportive." Trent took his tea and nodded at her. "Let me start again. Thank you for the drink. Can we calmly talk about what this means?"

Mia set down the last glass in front of her own spot and sat looking at the three of them. "I don't know, can we?"

Levi grinned and sipped his tea. "I'm not saying a word. It's like watching Mom and Dad fight. You know Mom always wins, dude."

Trent shot Levi a dirty look, then took a sip of his tea. "I think we should make a plan. Maybe gather the troops like we did this winter? Do you have room for your grandmother to stay here? One of us could sleep in the living room."

66

"I don't need either of you here, but Grans is another story. That's actually a good idea. I would feel better with her close by." Mia took a breath and let some of her anger release. "I'll give her a call to tell her that Christina and Levi are coming to get her, and to plan to stay here for a week. We'll adjust that when Baldwin finds out who was in my backyard. And if things escalate, we'll talk about adding the two of you to the party as well."

"Are we sure this is the right place to be?" Christina's gaze went to the window that looked out on the mountains. "Maybe we should hole up at Mary Alice's house. There haven't been any dead bodies found there."

"Valid point, but we have a business to run, and I can't just shut down because of something like this." Mia pulled out a notebook. "Okay, I'll admit that having someone killed in the backyard isn't a normal day, but maybe we can figure out why if we look at what happened first."

"We need to make a list of people who have been around the building for the last week or so." Levi took a notebook from the desk and started writing. "What's been going on here?"

"Give me a minute, I'll make the list." Mia punched the number, and her grandmother's phone rang several times before Grans picked up the call. "Hey, I hate to spring this on you, but Levi and Christina are on their way to get you. Pack up enough clothes and food for Muffy for a week. Something has happened, and I'd feel better with you close by."

"Dear, that's not going to be possible right now. I'm at the Lodge, having lunch with Cindy."

Now Mia could hear the background sounds of a crowded restaurant. "Who's Cindy?"

"She's Dorian's daughter. We talked about this. But I think you're right. I'll have Cindy check out of the hotel and we'll meet Christina and Levi at my house."

"Wait, why is Cindy checking out of the hotel?" Mia had a bad feeling she knew the answer. "Is she leaving already?"

"She can't stay alone here. Not with the bad mojo in town. The killer would find her in a heartbeat."

"How do you know there was a murder?" When there was no answer, Mia sighed and hung up, realizing her grandmother had already terminated the call. "Wait a bit and Grans will call you when she's ready to be picked up. And there will be an extra person with her."

"We can make a food run to Majors now and get some drinks and snacks." Levi glanced at Christina. "And you can tell me about all those rich playboys you snorkeled with last week."

"One rich playboy, or at least that's how he presented himself. I went out on this guy's boat, along with Isaac and Tanya." Christina grinned at Mia. "He was bragging about how big his boat was and all the diving he does. Come to find out, it's his dad's boat, and when we got back, he got in trouble for taking it out without permission. Man, was his face red. When I refused to talk to him the next day, he blamed his daddy for breaking us up."

"When really you weren't going to talk to him again anyway. Unless you wanted to use the boat. That's kind of diabolical." Mia glanced around the apartment, wondering what she needed to do to get ready for two overnight visitors. She grabbed her notebook and started making another list. "Christina, would you call Grans when you're at the store and find out what this Cindy wants to drink? I'll get the spare bedroom cleaned out and put clean sheets on the bed. Trent, would you help me move some boxes?"

"Sure." He went to the pantry and

grabbed the key to the third-floor storage room. "Did you ever find a key for the other third floor door?"

"No, and I think I'm just going to have it rekeyed. Maybe this week." She opened the fridge and inventoried the contents. "Good thing I just went to the store and got some extra stuff. I was planning on testing out some recipes. I guess the Goddess knew I'd be having company."

Gloria giggled, but Mia was pretty sure she was the only one who could hear her. But when she ran into Trent, standing in the middle of the room and looking around, she wondered. "What's going on? The boxes are in the spare room. Do you need me to show you?"

He shook his head. "No, I know where I'm going. I thought I heard a child laughing."

Mia's gaze darted to Gloria, but the doll didn't appear to be watching anymore. "You heard laughter?"

"Weird, right? Probably some ghost of a long-ago student. I'm kind of sensitive that way." He leaned down to kiss her. "Don't worry, we'll get this room set up in no time. Your grandmother sure knows how to adjust on a dime."

Mia nodded. "She's always been that way.

I'm just glad this apartment is big enough for all of us. I would hate to have to bunk up with Christina or sleep on the couch."

"That couch is comfortable." He grinned at Christina. "Not that sharing a room would be bad, but I hear you snore."

Christina threw a dish towel at Levi. "You tell your brother that's not true."

"So you did spend the night at his place?" Trent teased. "I'm going to tell Mom."

Levi came and put his arms around Christina. "Stop messing with her, big brother. And besides, Christina's already met Mom and Dad. They like her even though she snores."

"I do not snore." Christina tried to wrestle out of Levi's hug, but he held her tight. Until she stomped on his foot and he released her with a howl.

"Man, you're strong." Levi hopped on one foot while he held the other one.

Christina tried to push him over. "And you're playacting."

"Come on, children, let's get a plan ready and get this thing going." Trent put his arm around Mia. "They grow so fast. What are we going to do when they have their own lives?"

"Be able to talk to each other and eat a meal without a meltdown?" Mia grinned at him. "You know, real kids would be more of a hassle. I'm thinking I'm going to only have fur children when I get married."

"Monkeys?" Trent grinned. "I'll go for that."

"I was thinking cats and dogs, not monkeys. Besides, who said it would be with you?" she teased as she waved him away. "Go get the boxes out of there so I can get the room ready for Ms. Cindy."

Mr. Darcy meowed and jumped on the table. He pawed at Mia's arm.

She looked down at him. "No, I don't think we'll mention your current status, Dorian. Sometimes people just don't understand. And she's only had your grimoire for a few months."

He rubbed his face against her arm in agreement, then jumped down and ran down the hall.

"I guess Dorian's checking out the room?" Trent shook his head as he followed Mr. Darcy out into the hall. "It must be hard to be stuck in a cat."

Mia got together a list of supplies and gave it to Christina. When she tried to give her a credit card, Levi pushed it away. "Trent and I will cover this. Don't worry about it."

"Sounds good. Call me when you're close and I'll come unlock the door for you." Mia watched them walk out the door together. They made a good couple.

She shook off the notion and went to grab clean sheets. It was time to get Cindy's room ready.

An hour later, she got the call. She stood up from the table where she'd been talking to Trent about the incident that morning. "Time to play hostess."

"Sit down; I'll go down and let them in. You relax with your tea for a few minutes. I've never seen you so agitated about having one more person here. What's going on?"

Mia shook her head. "I guess it's all the hoopla about the dead guy. I just wish Baldwin would find out who he was and why he was killed in my yard."

Trent leaned over her and kissed the top of her head. "He will. Things will work out, just relax."

When they got into the apartment, Cindy stood by the door looking like she was ready to bolt. Mr. Darcy, or maybe Dorian, wove through her legs, trying to calm her. Mia held out a hand to introduce herself, but Cindy waved it away.

"Sorry, I don't touch people. No hand-shakes, no hugs, and definitely no kisses. I'm always freaked out about germs and who's going to give me something that might keep me from accepting a movie role." She smiled at Mia. "Thank you so much for opening your home, but I could have stayed at the hotel."

Grans stood by her and reached out, then dropped her hand before she touched Cindy. "Don't be silly. You're having some issues and this is the best place for us to figure out what's going on so you can go back to your normal life."

Mia flicked a look at her grandmother. The only way Cindy was going back to her normal life was for her to give up and renounce any power Dorian had left to her. She didn't know the woman, but she didn't look like the type to give up power easily. "Let's get you to your room. We'll have dinner around five, but I can make you something for lunch if you need it."

She shook her head. "Is there someplace I can put my meal shakes? I'm on a protein diet and all I need are my shakes and bottled water. I asked whoever called to grab me a supply of water at the store."

"You may change your mind. Mia's a professional chef. She caters for local events and has a take-home service with bake-your-own-dinner options." Christina held up the oversize package of bottled water. "I'll put your water in the fridge."

"No need. I like it room temperature." She nodded to Christina. "Just bring it to my room. That will be fine."

Mr. Darcy let out a cry. He stood in the kitchen doorway watching Cindy.

"Sorry about that. He's very talkative today." Mia nodded for Cindy to go on.

Cindy shrugged. "No worries. I'm not too much for any type of animal. Hopefully, he'll leave me alone if I leave him alone?"

"One could hope," Mia muttered. When Cindy looked at her strangely, she squared her shoulders and nodded toward the hallway. "Let me show you to your room."

Christina stepped in front of her. "I'll do that."

As they left the living room, Mia glanced at her grandmother. "She's so . . ."

"Warm and cuddly?" Trent offered.

Mia shook her head. "Are you sure she's Dorian's daughter? I only met the man once — well, when he was alive — but he was so engaged with people. She seems like she's all about herself."

Grans sank into a chair. "Believe me, if I didn't feel like I owed this to Dorian, I wouldn't be trying. She's cold, distant, and completely full of herself."

"And those are her good characteristics," Levi added.

Trent glanced at Mia. "It's your house."

"Grans is right. If we can help her figure out what she's going to do about the grimoire, we have to at least try. I know it's not going to be easy, but apparently I don't have another mouth to feed. Are the rest of you ready for dinner? I've got stew on and I baked rolls two nights ago when I couldn't sleep." Mia put on a smile she didn't feel and held out her hand to her grandmother. "Are you hungry?"

"I'm starving, but I need to put my suitcase in my room and set up food and water for Muffy." Grans reached down to stroke the small white dog that sat on her lap, leaning into her like he knew she was upset.

"I'll take your suitcase and Levi can set up Muffy's bowls." Trent handed the large grocery bag to his brother. "You just sit here and put your feet up. Can I get you a cup of tea?"

"That would be nice." Grans beamed at Trent. "You're such a sweet man."

Mia went into the kitchen to make the tea Trent had promised. When he came into the room a few minutes later, she nodded to the steaming cup on the tray. "There you go. You can take it to her."

"Why? I just offered it. You made the tea. You should take it in."

She shook her head. "No, I think she'll enjoy it more coming from you. I think she's missing Dorian tonight."

He kissed her forehead, then picked up the tray. "I'll have Levi sit and talk with her while I come in here and help you finish up dinner. Have you heard anything from Baldwin?"

"Nope. But I've got a bad feeling about Cindy." Mia glanced around to see if Mr. Darcy was around. It wouldn't be good for him to hear that Mia suspected his daughter of anything. "I know, she just got into town, but something's off."

"She's been in town for three days." Trent paused in the doorway. "I know the night clerk at the Lodge. Heidi says she checked in alone, but she hasn't been the only one in that room. She said the room service waitress said she had a gentleman caller. Does Cindy know someone here?"

"Good question." Mia wondered what Grans had gotten them into by inviting Dorian's daughter to stay with them.

CHAPTER 6

Mia hung up the phone and refilled her coffee cup. Mia had been waiting for it to be a reasonable time to call the police station. She and Grans had been sitting at the kitchen table since early that morning, talking about the day. "Baldwin still doesn't have a clue who the guy is. Shouldn't there be some sort of fingerprint database they can just access?"

"Do you want to submit your fingerprints to a general database? I don't think most people would comply with that type of an invasion of privacy." Grans sipped her coffee.

"It's only an invasion if you're planning on committing a crime or winding up dead with no identification on my property." Mia sighed, conceding the point. "You're right. I'm just anxious about getting this behind us."

She and Grans were still sitting at the

kitchen table when Cindy came out of her room. She dropped her bag on a free chair before scanning the room. Muffy and Mr. Darcy sat together on the window seat, watching her. Cindy grabbed a cup and poured coffee. She wore satin lounger pj's and a head turban.

The perfect image of an actress at home? Mia was surprised to see Cindy was significantly older than she'd appeared the day before. Maybe early forties? Mia wondered how to delicately bring up the question of who had been dining with her in her hotel room.

"I suppose you want to talk about that book my father left me." Cindy sat at the table and looked at the other two women. Then she looked down at Muffy and Mr. Darcy again. "Are real animals supposed to be that quiet? I thought they'd be fighting each other by now."

"They know better. Haven't you ever had a pet?" Mia stood up and took a pan of cinnamon rolls out of the oven and put them on the stove. "Do you want one? I know they aren't protein shakes."

"Heavens no, I'd gain five pounds with the first bite. Besides my trainer would find out and come to drag me home. He's already worried I won't get my workouts in while I'm here. Pets are so messy, and frankly, I'm never home." She pulled the book out of the bag. "According to the letter my father left me, I inherited his grimoire. But imagine my surprise about how that happened. This is my book of magic spells. I received it when I was eight. Before Father died, it had five spells in it."

"It looks like there are a lot more now," Mia commented on the size of the grimoire.

"I pulled it out of a box in the attic the day after the will reading. I guess I was being sentimental." Cindy stroked the cover. "My father tried to teach me magic, but I didn't have a talent for it, or the interest. The only spell that ever worked was the one for hiding candy from my brother. I stopped trying when I couldn't get a candle to light. I figured he was being rhetorical when he said I had magic in my blood. If I'd known he had so many spells, I might have been a better student."

"What do you mean?" Mia glanced at the gold-filigree cover on the book. It was a lovely grimoire, but it looked brand-new.

Cindy shrugged. "There are so many times in my life when a little extra push from the universe might have changed things. I could have had parts earlier in my career that would have set me up for life. You know the phone stops ringing for women on their fortieth birthday, right?"

"Magic doesn't work like that. You can't use it for your own benefit." Grans broke into the conversation. She glanced down at Mr. Darcy. "I'm sure Dorian explained that."

"My father was a successful businessman. You're telling me that these spells" — she put her hand down on the book — "didn't help him? I find that extremely hard to believe."

Mr. Darcy let out a loud cry. Everyone looked at him, but his gaze was focused on Cindy.

"What is wrong with that cat? Did you feed him?" She shivered a bit, then refocused on the book. "Anyway, in my father's letter, he said you could help me understand the spells. I've tried working a few but haven't had much luck. And now some Realtor is trying to lowball my brother, Mike, and me on the real estate sale. I don't have time for this mess. I need to get back to my real life, see what I can change for my career path."

"Cindy, I'll be glad to help teach you, but you need to understand the basic tenets of magic. The first is to do no harm." Grans spoke in a calm, even voice.

"Like the doctors?" Cindy burst out laughing. "Seriously?"

"Exactly like the doctors. Where do you think they got the idea? Many of the original healers in our country were witches. They brought modern medicine to where it is today. Anyway, there's also the rule of three." Grans tapped the table. "This is the most important one. Whatever you do to someone else will come back to you three times worse. It's a protection to keep witches from using their power to hurt or injure others."

"So, if I tried a spell to get rid of a certain Realtor, he might go away, but I'd have something three times worse happen to me?" Cindy shook her head. "What's three times worse even mean? All I wanted was for him to give us a fair value for the property."

Mia and Grans shared a look. Mia thought about the dead guy in her backyard. Was there a connection? "What did you do, Cindy? Did you try a spell on someone?"

She pursed her lips together as she thought about her response. Finally, she pushed the book toward Grans. "I'm not sure. Can you check the book to see if it uploaded?"

"Spells don't upload, dear. It's fairly simple; did you cast a spell or not?" Grans asked Mia's question again.

Cindy stood and picked up her coffee cup. "Sorry, I don't know, and I don't have time for twenty questions. I've got to check in with my agent. He's got some irons in the fire for me."

Grans waited for her to leave the room, then held her hands over the grimoire. "I can feel Dorian's presence here."

Mr. Darcy jumped on the table and rubbed Grans's arm with his head. Then he reached out a paw and patted the book.

"We know, Dorian. Your family's spells went into Cindy's book." Mia didn't feel comfortable touching the book. It seemed too personal — not just an invasion of Cindy's space, but also Dorian's. She sipped her coffee and focused on Grans. "What are we going to do?"

" 'Me,' not 'we.' This is my boyfriend's mess. I'm the one who should clean it up." Grans rubbed Mr. Darcy's head. "I'm taking the book into my room and reading up on what's in it. Maybe I can figure out what spell Cindy activated."

"She had to have set something in process. She's about as nervous as a cat on a hot tin roof." Mia watched as her grandmother stood.

Mr. Darcy growled at Mia.

Holding up her hands in surrender, she laughed. "You're right. I shouldn't use that phrase. I suppose it offends you."

Mr. Darcy winked at her, but no, Mia was sure it was Dorian doing the winking. The mix-up was confusing.

"Anyway, get off the table. You know cats don't belong on the table," Mia pointed out.

He meowed and jumped down, following Grans down the hall to her room. She called after him, "You two be good in there."

Mia heard Grans chuckle as she shut the door and went to work.

Christina came into the kitchen still dressed in pajamas. "Is there coffee?"

"Yes, and muffins. In thirty minutes we're going to start cooking, so get food, take a shower, and come downstairs by nine. I'd like to get everything done by five. Then tomorrow we'll do the deliveries."

"And Wednesday we'll start the catering job. It's always something with this business, isn't it?" She filled a cup with coffee and sipped, watching Mia. "I suppose you've been up for hours."

"Yes, I have." Mia grabbed her notebook and pens and headed down to her office. It was "time to make the doughnuts," as that old television commercial used to say. Although she'd planned the week so she could sleep in until seven. Christina didn't realize it was a luxury to sleep that late. "I'll see you downstairs. Don't make me come up or I'll give you all the bad jobs."

Christina snorted. "There's good jobs? When were you going to tell me?"

"Smart aleck." Mia unlocked the front door to the apartment and tucked her keys in her pocket. She'd leave it open today because there were so many people in the building. And she didn't want Grans to lock herself out. Humming, she made her way to her office and started planning the day.

She'd already started peeling potatoes when Christina came into the kitchen. She was only twenty minutes late. It was a full-on miracle. "Hey, why don't you grab those carrots and peel them?"

Christina held up the bunch by the tops. "All of these? What are you making? Carrot soup?"

"Not today, but that's a good idea." She glanced around the empty kitchen. "I like seeing people eat. And when it's food as fresh as this, it's a double blessing."

"You're a good person. Want to know what happened to Tanya at the beach this year?"

Christina didn't wait for Mia's answer. "She burned herself into lobster mode. I can't believe anyone could be that stupid."

"That must have hurt. So, what's going on with your brother that has you so upset? And don't tell me nothing, I can see it all over your face." Mia picked up another potato and quickly peeled it, putting it in the strainer to the side of the workstation.

"Mom said that Isaac was thinking about asking Tanya to marry him. I guess she's got family connections," Christina said in a low voice.

"Which probably means money in your mom's eyes. Don't worry about it; you get to choose how much time you spend with your brother and his soon-to-be new wife. You're not a kid anymore." Mia picked up the last potato.

"You're not mad?" Christina turned away from the sink and stared at Mia. "You were together for years. Why aren't you mad?"

"Because Isaac and I were never meant to be. I didn't realize that until after I left. Believe me, I'm not a fan of your brother. He was a jerk and he betrayed me by going outside our relationship before we broke up. But you and I talked about the power of forgiveness. If I hold on to the anger, that's only hurting me."

"I'll say it again: You're a good person. If I had your" — Christina paused and looked around to see if anyone was nearby before continuing — "special skills? I would have made him remember what he did to me every day of his life."

"Vengeance isn't a positive trait either." Mia smiled as she finished the potatoes. "But believe me, I thought about leaving Isaac with a going-away present. It just wasn't worth the karma rebound."

Christina was quiet for a few minutes while Mia put the potatoes on the stove to boil. She was making a potato salad for one of the delivery dishes. She was thinking about the recipe as she got several onions out to chop.

"Is that what Cindy did? Put a revenge spell on someone?" Christina blushed as Mia looked up at her. "Sorry, I heard the discussion from the hallway. I was going to come in, but then Cindy started talking and your grandmother was mad, so I thought I'd just hide in my bedroom. I'm afraid of your grandmother, just a bit. Look what she did to Dorian."

"That was an accident and he was already dead anyway." Mia thought about Christina's interest. The girl hung around kitchen witches and dated one of the local coven witches; she guessed the question wasn't too out there for her. "We don't know yet. I think Dorian's death made Cindy's spell book more powerful and she set something loose. We're just not sure what yet, and she isn't being very forthcoming."

"She's a little full of herself," Christina added. "Speaking of people who worship themselves, I'm having dinner with Bethanie tonight. She wants to hear about Bermuda."

"Just be careful there. I'd hate to see you get involved in one of her schemes." Bethanie might not be as bad as her father or half brother, but you never knew.

"She's okay. She just grew up rich. I could have totally been like her if you hadn't come into my life when you started dating my brother. Maybe that's why you were with Isaac — because I needed a good role model in my life. You know, the universe has a plan for everything." Christina finished peeling the last carrot and held it up like a trophy.

"Who's been talking about destiny and the universe's plans for us? Grans?" Mia nodded to the peppers. "Julienne those, please."

"Levi. He's trying to make a romantic proposal without the proposal part." Christina nodded and moved to the fridge. "I left my knives down here the last time I cooked. Should I keep them in my room?"

"Maybe in my office would be safer. It's locked up when we're not here. I take mine upstairs and leave them in the kitchen. You can do that too; there's room. So whatever you want." Mia studied Christina as she drew out her chopping knife and carefully sharpened it. Then she set up her cutting station. The girl was learning. She could make a living in the restaurant industry if she wanted, but she had other plans, which either were event planning or going into the management part of hospitality and, specifically, high-end hotels. She did aim high. "What's Levi's pitch? Does he want you to move in with him?"

Christina laughed. "Not even close. I think he's just talking about being exclusive. I told him I went out with that guy in Bermuda a few nights when I was down there. Just casual fun, not even anything physical, and he about flipped. I guess I didn't think we were at the exclusive stage yet."

"Just because he's there doesn't mean you have to be." Mia thought about her dates with Trent. Both of them were older, ready to settle into a relationship, if not *the*

89

relationship. But maybe . . . It felt right to be with Trent. So much different from when she dated, then lived with Isaac. This never felt like work. Being with Isaac, she'd felt like she'd had to prove herself over and over.

"I don't know; I really like him." Christina held up her knife. "He's just so . . ."

"So what, Ms. Adams? Who are you talking about while you wave that deadly knife?" Mark Baldwin walked into the kitchen and paused in the doorway. "Is there something I need to know?"

"No. And I don't have to talk to you. My mother said." Christina refocused on chopping the peppers.

"Well, I hate to disagree with anyone's mother, but that's not quite true, but I'm here to see Ms. Malone anyway." He pointed to her office. "Can we chat?"

Mia took off her apron, then went to the sink and washed her hands. "When you're done with that, check the prep list if I'm not back yet. I'm hoping this will be quick."

He smiled at them both as he waited. When Mia stepped past him and toward her office, he called back, "Been nice chatting with you, Ms. Adams."

"Stop messing with her. You'll make her cut herself." Mia unlocked the office and turned on the light. "How did you get in

90

the building anyway?"

"Your grandmother let me in and told me you'd be in here, cooking." Baldwin pulled out his notebook. "I found out more about the man we found in your backyard on Saturday. His name was Denny Blake. Did you know him?"

Mia shivered. "Not by name. Honestly, I didn't even see him. I kind of glanced over when the utility guy was on the line with 9-1-1, but I didn't want to see a dead body. Especially not someone who died so close to the school."

Baldwin took out a photo from an envelope and slid it across the desk. Mia was expecting one of those morgue photos, but instead, it was a prison shot. Or an arrest shot, whatever they called those. "Take a look; do you know him?"

Mia studied the picture. Dark hair, mean eyes, a nose that had been broken more than once, and a snarl to his lips. She pushed the picture back. "No, and I'm glad. That guy has a lot of anger in him. You can see it through the camera."

"You're right about that. He's a professional hit man. Not a very good one. He'd been caught and served time for the last job he tried to do. The guy lived and pointed him out of a lineup after the LAPD tracked him down using fingerprints he left on the scene. He may be mean, but God didn't give him any brains at all from what I can see in his rap sheet." Baldwin studied the picture too. "The problem is, I don't know why he was here or, specifically, on your property."

"You don't think he wanted to kill me, do you?" Mia laughed at the idea. "My background is squeaky clean except for maybe the time I lived with Christina's brother. I could have been arrested for thinking about all the ways I wanted to kill that guy. But thinking about and doing are two different things."

"True, but this guy didn't go anywhere without a contract. And he'd been living in Florida on the beach in a condo the last time he checked in with his parole officer. Why come to Magic Springs?"

That was the question, wasn't it?

CHAPTER 7

The smell of Italian seasonings and tomato sauce cooking met Mia on the stairs after she'd closed up the kitchen for the day. Tomorrow they'd pack the containers in the back of the van and she and Christina would complete the deliveries. Tonight her feet hurt and she was glad she didn't have to deal with what to serve for dinner. Grans must have started dinner preparations when Christina went up to get ready for her night out with Bethanie. She was glad Mia's Morsels was doing well already, but if the business expanded anymore, she'd need to hire a third person. She liked it just being her and Christina. At least for a while, she needed to get her feet beneath her so she could make the company successful. Which reminded her: she needed to set aside a few hours to do her monthly planning this week.

When she entered the kitchen, her grandmother looked up from the book she was reading. Or scanning. Mia couldn't tell which. "You look beat. Let me make you some tea."

"Just tea. No energy spell, or love spell, or confidence booster, okay? I just want some dinner; then I'm crashing in my room for a while. I haven't had a good romance movie-thon for a while." Mia sank into a chair, but then got up and got her planner.

"I thought you were tired." Grans shot the planner a dirty look as she stood to turn to heat the kettle.

"I am, but I need to set a time for next month's planning session so I don't forget. And I need to start training Christina in how to do these so she has some practical experience in project management." She scanned the week and boxed off a time next Monday. Then she grabbed a piece of paper and wrote the time, date, and the office under the heading Strategy Meeting. She glanced down the hall. "Is she still here?"

"You just missed her. She was so excited to go meet this girl. I hope she doesn't get hurt. I don't think Bethanie Miller has many friends. There's probably a reason for that." Grans glanced out toward the road, as if she could see Christina striding toward downtown and the restaurant. "What about oolong?"

"Perfect." Mia folded the note and stood. "I'm just going to put this on her dresser so she'll see it. I'll be right back."

Grans didn't respond.

Mia opened Christina's door and saw her travel bag lying open on the floor. Clothes were strung out, some in piles, which Mia assumed were loads of laundry. The worst part of coming home after a vacation was the laundry. She stepped around the piles and went to her dresser, where Christina had taped pictures of Levi and some of the group she hung around with. One was of Bethanie. The girl looked like she was smirking at Mia. Like she had a secret. She studied the arrangement of photos and smiled. Christina was finally fitting into Magic Springs, even if she was hanging out with coven witches. Mia set down the note on the top of a pile and turned to leave.

She was almost out of the room when she saw a picture of Isaac on the floor, sticking out from under one of the clothes piles. She picked it up from the floor and realized it was of him and Tanya, smiling at the camera. Really smiling. Had he ever looked that happy with Mia?

Tanya was hanging on his arm like she belonged there. And, Mia thought, she did. The two of them were both shallow and lacked character, but she had to admit they made a lovely-looking couple.

She walked out of the room and closed the door. That was her old life. Her new life was here. With Grans and Christina and, maybe, Trent. She liked this life better.

"Your tea is ready," Grans said. Then she jerked her head up and stared at Mia. "What just happened? You're stronger than you were five seconds ago."

"Am I?" Mia sat and picked up her cup. She sipped the tea that had been her childhood favorite. Especially when her folks had taken her out for Chinese food.

"You deal with issues in such an odd way." Her grandmother studied her closely. "It's like a switch was flipped inside that closed a door."

"Maybe it did." She glanced at the stove. "That sauce smells amazing. Are we having spaghetti?"

"Ravioli. But close enough." She glanced over at the part of the front door. "I'm hoping it will stay warm in case Cindy's hungry when she gets back."

"Cindy left? Where did she go?" Mia hadn't felt another presence when she came into the apartment, but she'd forgotten Cindy was even there.

"She had a meeting with one of her agents

at the Lodge. I guess they're working out the details on another contract for her. She's been pretty lucky lately," Grans said dryly.

"You think she's spelling for her good fortune? She has to realize it's going to backfire on her sooner or later. You can't use magic for personal gain." That had been one of the first lessons Grans had taught her, and still she'd tried to get away with doing a spell to finish her history report. The printer had just kept spitting out pages with one word on each until she'd hit her mandatory ten pages. Mia figured karma had an odd sense of humor.

"Dinner's ready. What did Mark want this morning?" Grans went to the cupboard and took out two pasta bowls.

"Just to make sure I didn't know the dead guy. He was some sort of contract hit man." Mia grabbed silverware and paper napkins and went to the pantry for a loaf of Italian bread she'd baked a few days before. She glanced at the table. "We should have a salad with this."

Grans set the bowls of steaming pasta on the table, then grabbed some grated Parmesan Mia kept in the upstairs fridge. "I won't tell if you don't."

Mia grinned. That had been Grans's standard answer when Mia had been feeling guilty about something and said she should do one thing or another. Grans had always called it "shoulding" on yourself. "I think this is just perfect."

They sat and ate and talked about little things, including a call Grans had received from Mia's mother. "They love the cruising life. I think they're trying to get on another one before they come home from Florida."

"I'm not sure I'd like being on such a big ship." Mia shivered at the thought. "What if one of those big waves came up? The ship would just go down and no one would know where to look."

"You watch too many disaster movies." Grans laughed.

A few minutes later Cindy came in the front door. She paused by the kitchen. "Well, I'm back."

"Thanks for letting me know," Grans said, even keeping a straight face. "Do you want some dinner?"

Cindy looked at the two of them as if they were eating poison. Or something exotic. Like carbs. "That's fine. I had a salad at the Lodge."

"Okay, but if you get hungry, there'll be leftovers in the fridge," Grans called after her. She waited until she heard the door shut in the hallway. "That girl needs to figure out what she really wants before she gets lost."

Mr. Darcy meowed in agreement.

Mia glanced over at the hallway. "I don't know. It looks like she has her life pretty much together. She has a job and a life in California. All she needs to do is put away her book of spells and leave it alone. Some people aren't meant to have power."

Grans stood and got the water pitcher out of the fridge, then filled both of their glasses. "Looks can be deceiving, dear. Besides, she wasn't meeting someone about a new opportunity. She met John Louis at the Lodge to talk about Dorian's land holdings. Mike is going to be upset when he hears that she's going behind his back on the estate distribution."

Mia stared at her grandmother, who now had put the water away and was resuming eating her dinner. "How on earth did you find that out? Did you put a tracking spell on her?"

"Heavens no. I have a friend who works at the Lodge who just so happened to call me when Cindy arrived. Harriet didn't hear the whole conversation while she filled the water glasses, but she heard enough. It's a good thing Cindy drinks a lot of water to keep her skin clear."

"What are you going to do? I don't want you getting involved in this, especially in a fight with John. We both know he fights dirty." Mia remembered her last run-in with the man when he'd tried to get his way.

"Don't worry about it. No one will know I'm even aware of the situation. Having Cindy here gives us more information and some control over her actions. At least in the realty situation. She's afraid of what she's done with the book and doesn't want to ruin her chances of fixing it with me." Grans smiled as she speared the last ravioli on her plate. "I might have told her some horror stories about other witches who got their power inheritance early and failed to follow the rules. She's willing to work with us and learn what she needs to do at least until she figures out that she's in control. I just hope Mike can get here before she signs off on her share of the holdings."

"I take it you've called him?" Mia picked up her plate and took it to the sink to rinse. She was beat. And listening to Grans's plans was draining her energy even more. "I really wanted a calm week. I've got back-to-back catering gigs the next two weekends. I'm not sure I can deal with one more project."

"Don't worry about it. I've got it all under control." Grans met her at the sink. "You go to bed. I'll clean this up. I've got some thinking to do and washing dishes always helps."

Mia would have argued, but even her fingers hurt. And she had to agree — washing dishes by hand in warm, soapy water was the best time to work out problems. At least she'd always thought so. She kissed her grandmother on the cheek. "Leave the apartment door unlocked. I have a feeling Christina might have taken off without her keys."

"I have a feeling she might be home early."

With that, Mia headed to the bedroom. She soaked in the claw-foot tub the last principal of the school had had the forethought to upgrade to, the steam wafting out of the water and making shapes around her. Mia needed to focus on food and the business. Not dead guys in the backyard and whatever this thing was with Cindy and Grans. She took a deep breath and gave up the investigation to Baldwin, Cindy's spell work to Grans, and her business to the Goddess. All she had to do now was do the work that was put in front of her.

A tiny laugh echoed in the back of her mind. Gloria, her familiar and kitchen witch doll, was chiming in her opinion. Which Mia knew basically was "Good luck with that." She sank down farther in the water.

The next morning Christina was at the breakfast table and ready to go when Mia entered the kitchen. A sweet smell of vanilla and blueberries came from the oven. She went over to the coffeepot and poured a cup. Sitting down at the table, she studied Christina's too-serious face. "You cooked? How long have you been up?"

"Since five, but I didn't come out to the kitchen until seven." She pushed the local paper across the table. "I got that from the front porch."

Mia glanced at the headlines that showed the parking lot of Mia's Morsels and the emergency vehicles parked there. This was the one time she was glad she didn't have a sign. "It could be worse. They could have taken a picture of the building."

"Yeah, I read the article. It was pretty vague about where the body was found and didn't mention you or Mia's Morsels at all." The oven timer went off and Christina stood to retrieve the muffins. "You know everyone in town already knows a body was found behind the school. I don't know why the newspaper even exists here. Gossip runs the news channels."

Mia watched as her apprentice took the treats out of the oven, turned it off, and left them on top to cool. "Okay, so it's not the article that has you in a bad mood. What happened with Bethanie last night? Did she stand you up for dinner?"

Christina threw the hot pads on the counter and refilled her coffee cup before returning to the table. When she did, she didn't raise her eyes to meet Mia's gaze. "I'm afraid you might have been right about Bethanie's motives."

"What do you mean?" Mia didn't want to be right about this, but she could see the pain in Christina's eyes.

"When I got to the bar and grill where we were going to meet up, Bethanie was already there. And so was Levi. They were playing darts and she was sitting on his lap." Christina pressed her lips together before she went on. "I know we haven't said we're exclusive or anything, but it kind of knocked the wind out of me, seeing them together like that."

"What did Levi say?" Mia knew the guy had been a playboy before Christina, but she'd thought he'd put those habits away.

"He pushed my concerns away. Said Bethanie was just like that. She'd been flirting with him since she'd arrived." Christina

103

finally looked up. "I'm not sure who I'm mad at — Bethanie for flirting with Levi or Levi for not shutting her down."

"I'd say a little of both." Mia stood and took the muffins out of the tin and put them on a cooling rack. Then she put four on a plate and took it back to the table. "Who picked the meeting place?"

"What?" Christina took one of the muffins and broke it open. The steam flowed out with all the good smells too. "Let me think. Bethanie. She set up our dinner."

"Is this a place where Levi hangs out?"

Christina took a bite, nodded. "Yeah, he and the EMT guys go there after a shift. It's where they unwind. Wait, you're saying Bethanie knew that?"

"She's lived here longer than you." Mia let that soak in as she grabbed one of the muffins. They were fluffy and just the right mix of bread to blueberry. Christina had done an excellent job. "Maybe she was just trying to see how you'd react? Some women like the games. It's kind of a power-play move."

"And Levi just got in the middle." Christina took a bite of the muffin. "These are really good. A lot better than the last batch I made."

"They are good. Practice makes perfect."

Mia nodded. "I'm not saying Levi couldn't have shut it down, but maybe he was just seeing Bethanie be Bethanie. The girl has a bit of a wild side. Talk to him about how the situation made you feel, not what he did to you. I think he'll understand."

"Man, this love thing is filled with pot-holes. Maybe just staying single is a better path." She reached down to pet Mr. Darcy. "What do you think, kitty?"

He bit her hand.

"Ouch. I guess I'm talking to Dorian, right?" Christina rubbed her finger. "Sorry for the confusion."

"He needs to get used to it." Mia directed the comment to the cat. "It *is* Mr. Darcy's body."

Dorian — or Mr. Darcy, Mia couldn't tell which — blinked his eyes at her, then jumped on the window seat, where he settled into a spot of sunshine, apparently done with the conversation.

"I wish Grans would find the spell so Mr. Darcy could have his body back. I'm tired of not knowing who I'm talking to." Mia glanced at Christina's finger. "Is it bad?"

"No, he just nipped at me. Maybe he was telling me to give Levi a break." Christina looked hopeful. She glanced at her phone. "I'm going to call him." She finished her muffin, then threw away the paper wrapper. "Thanks for the chat."

"Anytime." Mia settled in and read the rest of the paper, hoping that the news wouldn't affect her business. She finished a muffin and grabbed a second one as Grans came in the kitchen with Muffy. She looked tired. Mia started to stand, but Grans waved her back down.

"I can pour my own coffee." She glanced at the muffins. "I take it you couldn't sleep?"

"Actually, Christina made these. I'm afraid my ways of dealing with stress might have worn off on her. Can I at least take Muffy out for you?" Mia rubbed the little dog's head as she spoke.

"That would be nice. I was planning on asking Christina, but I guess she's not here." Grans sat down at the table and sipped her coffee. "I love staying with you, but it's hard on Muffy. He's used to having his own backyard and doggy door."

"Not sure I can fix the doggy-door problem, but I can put up a little yard for him so we could let him out on his own. Maybe off the downstairs kitchen." Mia refilled her cup. "Hold that thought. Maybe Trent has some ideas. Is his leash downstairs by the door?"

"In the basket."

Mia and Muffy made their way downstairs, and she clicked a leash on his collar. When she opened the door, a man stood there, ready to knock.

He jerked back as she opened the door, and Muffy ran toward him, barking.

"Oh, I didn't see you," he stammered.

Mia closed the door behind her and studied him. "Can I help you?"

"Maybe. I'm here to talk to Mia Malone?" His eyes were dark and almost lost in his pudgy face.

"That's me; what can I help you with?" She let Muffy's leash out a little so the little dog could reach the grass in front of the building. "Sorry, he needs some room."

"Cute dog. Anyway, I just wanted to tell you that you need to be careful." He glanced around the building. "This isn't a very safe place to live."

"I'm sorry, what?" Mia had stepped around him so Muffy could explore more of the grass and do her business.

"You're in danger. I can't tell you how I know, but I don't want anyone else to get hurt." He turned around as Trent's truck pulled into the driveway. "I have to go. Just consider leaving for a while. Maybe selling. Selling would be good too."

She watched as he hurried away. Trent was

107

standing outside his truck, watching the man almost run away down the street. She called after him, "Who are you? Why are you threatening me?"

"It's not me that you have to worry about, Mia Malone. Just listen to my warning and leave this place. Before it's too late."

CHAPTER 8

Trent hurried over to her side. "Are you okay? What did Dick Hodges want?"

"That was Dick Hodges? The man who runs the hardware store?" Mia bit her bottom lip, thinking. "Well, he wanted to tell me that it wasn't safe here. That I should sell. He probably recognized the house from today's newspaper article and decided he'd had a vision or something. There's nothing to worry about."

At this, Muffy barked and ran in circles. Then the dog stopped, barked again, and sat.

Mia smiled and leaned down to pet him. "I guess he agrees with my assessment."

"I don't know." Trent looked down the road at the disappearing figure. "Something's been bothering me. Did you ever find out who was taking your cooking utensils, then giving them back as gifts?"

Mia rubbed her temples and glanced

inside, where she'd left her coffee. Right after she'd moved here, someone had stolen her chef's knife and a corkscrew. Each had shown up later, wrapped up as gifts. "No, I didn't. I assumed it had to have been John. He's the one who wants me out of here. But now? I don't know. Anyway, come on in and have some coffee. Christina made muffins, but she might still be mad at Levi, so if she's grumpy, I'm sorry."

"What did my brother do now?" Trent held open the door for Mia and the little dog.

Mia let Muffy off the leash once the door was closed, and the dog ran upstairs, disappearing into the apartment. She dropped the leash into the basket. "That's between her and Levi. I'm not breaking her confidence, but let's just say he was thoughtless last night."

"Sounds like him." Trent pulled her into his arms and looked at her. "Are you sure you don't want to call Baldwin on Hodges?"

She shook her head. "No. If he comes back, I promise, I'll call then. I just think he's someone who wants attention. Besides, what did he say? I'm in danger. He didn't say he was going to hurt me himself."

"Sure, of course. It's not like you didn't have a dead man in your backyard a few days ago." Trent followed her up the stairs. "I'm not trying to tell you how to run your life, but . . ."

"Then don't. I'm not stupid. I'm not going to put myself in danger, but if he'd wanted to hurt me, he had time to do it before you arrived. He didn't. He wanted to warn me. And there was something in his words, I believe." Mia paused at the doorway. "If you don't mind, please drop the subject. I'd rather Grans didn't know about this. With Cindy here, she's a little on edge."

"You all are a bunch of nerves around here." Trent nodded. "I'll keep it between us, only if you'll promise you'll tell me if you see the guy again. Even if it's in the police station or at church. I want to know if he's hanging around."

She put her hands under her chin and batted her eyes. "Such a strong, protective reaction. It's good to have someone worried about me."

That made him smile. "Don't forget it. But I get the point. I'll tone down the alpha-male routine."

After breakfast Trent went off to work at the store. Cindy still hadn't come out of her bedroom. Mia and Christina went down to the kitchen to load up the deliveries for the day. Mia left Christina filling the carts and

111

went to the office to print off the delivery route. She glanced at the blinking light on her office phone. As she booted up the computer, she let the messages run, hoping for a few more orders for the week. Instead, she listened to message after message asking if she was okay, and if the delivery would still be made. The grapevine had been busy. She finished printing the delivery schedule and decided she'd have Christina drive so she could call each of the stops on her list to make sure they'd be expecting them. Maybe a short conversation would limit the amount of time it took to complete the delivery, because everyone would want the gossip.

They got the van loaded and headed to the first stop. Mia had the next three people called before they arrived at the Danvers estate. She glanced at Christina. "In and out. That's our plan. If they start asking, we don't know anything more than what was in the paper. And yes, it was horrible."

"That's a script I can follow. I know nothing, but I'm as shocked about it as you are." She put a hand to her forehead. "I almost fainted when I heard."

"Okay, don't go all high-school drama queen on me." Mia grinned at her. "Let's get this day started."

As she'd expected, Mrs. Danvers had heard about the body found behind the school. As had everyone else.

By the time they were finished with the deliveries, they had multiple orders for next week because they had to wait for the form to be filled out, which gave the curious customer a reason to hold them for one or two more questions. True to her word, Christina had been a trooper. She showed shock and dismay at the poor man who'd lost his life, while keeping the details to a minimum. She even got them moving when the discussion ran long and Mia hadn't been able to extract them.

After the last delivery Mia took over the driving, but before she backed out of the last driveway, she leaned back and closed her eyes. "I can't believe how draining that was. Seriously, we don't know anything about this guy, but everyone needed the same story. Maybe I should have put out an announcement to all our customers this weekend, telling them what we knew."

"Man, I need a massage." Christina rolled her shoulders and stretched out her neck. "Besides, it wouldn't have changed anything. A murder is a big deal here in Magic Springs. I know they've had people die, but this guy was a complete stranger. And a contract assassin. Some of them may be worried he got whacked at the wrong house and he was really after someone else."

"That's what I'm thinking," Mia admitted. She pointed out the McMansion in front of her. "I guess it's not far off to think they might be too. The problem with that story is, he'd have to be a complete moron to mistake our old schoolhouse for a place like that."

"I guess he didn't have a subscription to *House Beautiful.*" Christina hid a yawn as she picked up her phone and started texting.

"Do you have plans tonight?" Mia pulled the van out of the driveway and thought about dinner. She had an extra chicken marsala downstairs, and since she and Grans had just had pasta, she could make a spaghetti squash for the noodle portion. Which might ease Cindy's mind over the carbs.

"I did. I just told Levi we'd have to reschedule." Christina tucked her phone into her purse. "I'm beat. Can I help you with dinner since I'm going to be staying in?"

"Sure, but it's going to be pretty easy. Maybe you can make a salad." Mia went over her plan for the meal as they drove home. As she parked, she grabbed her tote, into which she'd put next week's orders, and locked the van.

Christina glanced at the vehicle. "Are you sure you don't want to bring in the racks?"

"We can do that tomorrow, before we start prepping for the party on Saturday. Tonight the only other thing I'm doing is dumping this tote in the office and grabbing the chicken." She shut the door and locked it after them. If Cindy or Grans were out, they could buzz the apartment. She shivered a bit as she thought about the guy this morning. "Let's keep this door locked up for a few days, okay?"

Christina nodded as she moved toward the kitchen. "I'll get dinner, you handle the office."

"Dinner's in the first fridge, where we store the deliveries," Mia called after her. She dumped her tote on her desk, then glanced at the phone again. The blinking light was back. She ignored it. She'd been foolish to think it was new orders last time. Tonight she was done with work. It was time to relax.

She locked the office door, and when Christina appeared with the aluminum pan with their dinner, she locked the kitchen too. It had a double-keyed lock, so if somehow, someone got in the back door at the kitchen, they wouldn't be able to access the rest of the building. It made Mia feel a little more secure in this really big house. No, building. She paused and looked around the yellow lobby area. No, house. The apartment was home, but the building was no longer a school; it was a house. Her house.

Grans and Cindy were at the kitchen table when they came in. Muffy barked to announce their arrival. Christina glanced at Grans. "Can I take him out?"

"He probably needs to go. We've been at this for a while." Grans smiled at Christina. "I'd appreciate that."

Christina set the pan on the stove, then glanced at Mia. "I'll be right back and start that salad."

"Don't hurry, I've got to get the squash in first." Mia went to the credenza, where she had bowls for the fresh fruit and other produce that didn't need to be kept in the refrigerator. She grabbed two spaghetti squashes and took them to the sink to wash. She glanced over to the table, where Cindy and Grans were still huddled over Cindy's spell book. "Did you find the spell?"

Grans sighed. "Not yet. We thought we had, but it hadn't been cast for more than two years, so Dorian must have been the last one to use it."

116

"You can tell when a spell was cast?" Mia cut open the squash and carved out the seeds. Then she sprinkled the cut side with salt and olive oil and put them into the oven to bake. "Can I see what you're looking at?"

Grans shook her head. "I'll have to show you the next time we find one that Cindy recognizes. I don't want to accidently activate something just to show you a trick I've learned over the years."

Mia turned to Cindy. "I get that. Dinner's going to be ready around seven. Are you staying?"

Cindy shrugged. "I guess. What are you eating? More pasta?"

Mia told her the menu and saw a small look of surprise on Cindy's face. "Although I could do something else for you if that doesn't work."

"Oh, that would be great. I'm just surprised you even attempted to make it less heavy." Cindy sighed. "I'm sorry, I sound like a food snob. But when I was at the Lodge, everything was either fried or covered with sauce or came with pasta. It's all so heavy. My only slightly healthy meal was a chef salad with processed meats."

"We like food here." Mia took a sparkling water from the fridge. "But I get it, you have a different diet. I'll try to be thoughtful during your stay."

"I'll try to be more grateful." A look passed between Cindy and Grans. Apparently, they'd been talking about more than just the grimoire today. "I *am* very thankful you took me in after they found that man."

Mia paused at the doorway. She'd been about to say that the dead guy probably didn't have anything to do with Cindy's visit, but what if it had? She skirted the issue. "We're glad to have you with us this week."

She left the kitchen and headed to her room to shower and relax for a while. Except all she could think of was why a two-bit contract hitter would have been found dead in her backyard. Cindy's visit was just coincidental to this killer thing, right? She'd never ask about her visitor at the Lodge. Mia shook the idea away. Now she was questioning everyone's motives and alibis just because they were strangers. Besides, all her investigative paths of thought went back to John and his offers on the school. Did he think that if she died, Grans would let him buy the building?

She decided it was time for her to get involved in this investigation. Baldwin wasn't going to like it, but she had a stake in the outcome. And if someone — okay, ten to one it was John — was targeting her, she deserved to know. She took a notebook from her desk and opened her laptop. What did she need to know that she didn't yet?

As she wandered around the Internet, looking for hints, she focused on John Louis. Most of the hits were from last year, when he was on trial and went to jail. A few about his development company. Some complaints about shoddy work or bad deals, but really nothing she could plop down on Baldwin's desk with a here's-your-killer announcement.

"Of course it couldn't be that easy." Mia leaned back on her pillow and considered the situation. What had been going on in the Magic Springs area last week? She opened the Chamber of Commerce website and scrolled through the activities. Maybe someone had posted pictures. She didn't know if Baldwin had found out where this Denny Blake had been staying. She opened a new window and searched under his name.

She hit a few bad links, then found a Facebook page. Did professional hit men even have Facebook pages? She opened it and found the man from the picture Baldwin had shown her yesterday. Well, that answered that question.

It didn't look like he'd put up any privacy blocks, so she was able to see a lot of his posts. Christmas in a Florida bar with a well-endowed girl in an elf costume sitting on his lap. The post only said Kaelynn, Santa's little helper. The next post showed Denny on a deep-sea fishing boat pulling in a marlin. She glanced at his information. He'd listed his employment as an independent contractor. And he liked chicken wings. He looked like your average everyday Joe. Not much to go on.

A lightbulb went off and her mind went back to the list of activities Magic Springs had posted on their website. There it was. The winery had held a Karaoke and Wings Night last Tuesday. Maybe Denny had been in town then. And if so, maybe someone had talked to him at the winery. Or seen him talking to someone else. Like John. Now, that was something she could take to Baldwin.

She glanced at her watch. It was five thirty. If she accepted Christina's offer to be in charge of dinner, she could zip out to the winery, then be back in time to toss the spaghetti squash and dish up the plates. She slipped her shoes back on and took a screen-shot of Denny's Facebook page with her phone. Maybe she'd get lucky.

She knocked on Christina's door, announced her plans, then grabbed her keys and purse from the kitchen.

"Where are you going?" Grans called after her.

Mia didn't stop, but called back, "I've got to run an errand really quick. I'll be back to dish up dinner."

She didn't wait for a response, just shut the apartment door behind her so she couldn't hear Grans's rebuttal. It was fine, though; she was an adult. She could go anywhere she wanted. Mia knew that her grandmother worried about her, but she needed to do this. If she had a target on her back, she needed to know, so she could bob and weave. Not hide in fear.

It just took a few minutes to get to the winery. It wasn't busy, which was probably why Priscilla Powers, the winery owner and Dorian's ex, had started the monthly karaoke night. Mia knew that Priscilla thought the winery was too classy for something like that, so someone else had to have convinced her it was good for the bottom line.

She locked the van, just in case, and headed to the door. The doorman nodded toward the van, which was taking up two, maybe more, slots.

"Nice parking job. Please tell me you're in

and out so I don't have to have your piece of junk towed." The bouncer towered over her.

"Good evening. I am in and out, but it's kind of up to you. Did you see this man last Tuesday?" She held up her phone.

Frowning, he took the phone from her and blew up the picture. "I think so. Not sure, but if it's the same guy, he came for the singing thing, then left just before last call. I tried to call him a cab, but he said he was walking back to his hotel. I watch out for guys who've had too much. Ms. Powers counts on me to help protect the winery."

"Did you see him again?" Mia felt a slight stab of hope. There were only two hotels close enough to walk to. One was the Lodge, the other an older motel that had seen better days.

The bouncer handed her phone back. "Nope. I don't work Wednesday or Thursday, but I didn't see him Friday at all. That's usually date night for most of our customers, so a single guy, he would have stood out."

"Thank you. You've been really helpful." Mia moved through the open door and made a beeline to the bar. The dining room was off-limits. She didn't think Priscilla would take kindly to her walking from table to table showing a picture of a dead guy. She nodded to the bartender.

"What will you have?" The woman studied her as she climbed onto a stool.

Mia almost said nothing, but she needed some time to mingle. "Sparkling water with lime."

The woman nodded, then brought over her drink. "Five even."

Mia blanched at the price but pulled out a ten. The bartender made her change and set it by the drink. Mia glanced at her name tag.

"You get free refills, so don't worry about the cost." The bartender glanced around the room but didn't move.

"Can I ask you something? It's Alicia, right?" When Mia got a nod, she pulled out her phone. She showed Denny's picture to her. "Alicia, did you see this guy on Tuesday?"

The bartender's face lit up. "Of course. That's Denny Something. He didn't use a credit card, cash only. Good tipper. He drank domestic beer in the bottle. The guy was clearly on some business trip."

"Why do you say that? Did he keep his receipts?" Mia tried to sound casual but interested.

"No. He didn't. Which, now that I think

about it, if he was here on business, he needed them." She shook her head. "I could have been wrong. But the guy was talking to any available woman in the bar. Or perceived available. One guy came back from the head and found Denny at his table and in his seat, chatting up his girl. There was almost an issue, but Denny smoothed it over. Said the girl looked like his sister and picked up the couple's tab for the night."

"Still in cash."

Alicia nodded. "He had probably a couple thousand in his wallet. If we'd been in Boise, I would have warned him not to carry so much, but we're a small town. No one's going to jack you for the money in your wallet."

CHAPTER 9

No one else in the bar had been there for karaoke night, so Mia gave Alicia her card and asked her to give it to anyone who had talked to Denny.

She stared at it for a moment. "You're a caterer."

"Yeah, and we give cooking classes. I bought the old schoolhouse. I'm doing home delivery for easy weeknight dinners as well. You should check out our website." Mia put on her best sales voice. Upbeat and preppy.

"So why are you asking about this guy? You're not a private investigator or a cop. Why do you care?" Alicia studied her carefully, still holding the card by the edges, as if it could bite her.

Mia wondered what the best answer would be, then decided to go with the truth. "He was killed behind the school. I want to find out why before someone starts to blame me."

Alicia didn't say anything for a while, just turned the card over and back a few times. Then she met Mia's gaze. "I've been suspected of something I didn't do too. I get what you're doing, but you need to be careful. If Denny was murdered, someone might not like you running around asking questions. Even in an upscale place like this."

Mia thought about Alicia's warning and decided she'd let Baldwin know about what she'd found out. Then she could just focus on the catering job she had this weekend.

Her event was a baby gender reveal party, and the wife had planned it to a tee. She'd hired a DJ and a bartender. And servers. All Mia had to do was show up with the food, then come and tear the service down. She wondered if she should start offering servers too, as part of her service. She could have a group of people who wanted on-call, part-time work and put them in Mia Morsel's uniforms. It would expand the brand and maybe get her more catering gigs. Most of the parties she'd done so far had hired staff from the Lodge. She knew James was making a killing on the temporary fees, and the waitstaff was just making overtime on their normal paychecks. She could pay them more and still make a profit.

But then again, it was a risk to move quickly. She couldn't make decisions based solely on feelings. She'd have to look at the actual numbers next week, once this job was done.

Mia pulled into the parking lot to find a police cruiser at the house, colored lights flashing on the building. She turned off the engine and ran toward the house. "What now?"

A police officer stopped her at the door. "I'm sorry, who are you?"

"Mia Malone, the homeowner? What's going on?"

He used his walkie-talkie to announce her, then nodded to the office. "Detective Baldwin is in the office on the main floor. He asks that you meet him there."

She hurried into her office and found Baldwin sitting at her desk, on her phone. He motioned her to the visitor's chair. Aggravation made her want to remind the man whose office it was, but she held her tongue. It was more important to find out what was going on than have a fight over standing. She'd learned that lesson early on in the kitchen.

When he finished, he made a note, then leaned back in the chair. "Sometimes it surprises me when you're so in the middle of these murders. Other times, I just wait and expect your name to come up."

"What are you talking about? Where did my name come up? Are Grans and Christina all right?" She studied him. He didn't look anxious, like he'd just witnessed a violent murder. Or the aftereffects. "What's going on?"

"Your grandmother and that girl are fine. And so, by the way, is your houseguest. You didn't ask about her. Anyway, she's the reason we're here tonight. Guess whose phone number was on Denny's cell phone? Not once, or twice, but more than a dozen times?"

"Cindy's?" Mia leaned back, shocked.

"And on the first try. We're taking her in for questioning. Your grandmother isn't happy about it, but I've got a female officer upstairs going through her things. It's our first good lead." He pinched his nose. "I'm beat. And whatever you have cooking up there smells amazing. I'm going to get her settled in one of our lovely cells, then head home to eat with Sarah. I'll question her after I eat. Maybe I won't be so grumpy."

"Has Cindy eaten?" Mia didn't know why she was offering the murder suspect food, but it felt right.

"Your grandmother is making her up a plate. We'll let her eat at the station before she goes into the cell." He stood. "Where were you tonight?"

"I ran over to the winery." Mia decided to tell the truth as far as he asked.

Baldwin studied her. "Did you run out of wine?"

"I wanted to see if Denny had gone to the winery last Tuesday," she admitted.

He leaned back in the chair, surprise showing on his face. "Wow, that's random. Do you want to tell me why?"

She explained how she'd looked him up on Facebook and he'd mentioned he loved wings, and how the winery had that event last week.

When she stopped talking, he rolled his finger. "Go on. Now you're going to tell me you found someone who remembered him."

"Two someones. The bartender, Alicia, and the bouncer. I didn't get his name, but they both remember talking to Denny that night." Mia leaned forward, happy Baldwin was finally taking her seriously on this.

"You are freaking intuitive on this investigation thing." He stood and headed out of the office. "But I'm only going to say this once. Stay out of my investigation. If I think you're messing around with the case, I can charge you with obstruction of justice."

Mia took in a breath. "I was just talking to people."

"Mia, it's dangerous. You need to stop doing this." Baldwin walked out of the office without saying another word to her.

She followed him upstairs, and by the time she got to the apartment, the female officer was walking Cindy out the door. "Do you need me to call someone? A lawyer? Your agent?"

Cindy shook her head. "I already did. They're flying in and meeting me at the station. Maybe when I get out, I should just stay at the Lodge. I mean, until we figure out the other thing."

"You will not. Mark will find out that your involvement in this is innocent, and then you will come back here and we'll get your life back on track." Grans looked at Mia for support. "It should only take a few more days, if we get time to really work with the book."

"What are you doing, genealogy?" Baldwin asked Grans. "Or are you helping her with Dorian's estate?"

"Something like that." Mia let Baldwin think what he wanted. It was better than bringing up magic. As long as the man had lived in Magic Springs, you would have thought he'd be wise to the undercurrents in the town. Though Baldwin might know about the coven and treat it like it was a Masons meeting, or the Knights of Columbus group. "Cindy, let us know if there's anything you need, and we'll see you soon."

Baldwin shook his head. "I would have thought you'd be happy we found out who killed that dude. Instead, you sound like she's going into the hospital for some cosmetic surgery. You realize there's damning evidence against her?"

"I didn't kill anyone." Cindy glanced at Grans, and even Mia could see the other question in her eyes. *Had she killed someone by accident?*

"Of course not, dear." Grans gave Baldwin a Tupperware container with Cindy's dinner. "Make sure she eats before you throw her into the slammer."

Baldwin took the container. "I will, but she's only being held for questioning, not sent up the river to the state penitentiary."

"And yet you're not just inviting her into the station for a quick chat," Grans shot back. She watched as Cindy and the officer moved down the stairs to the front door. "Be careful with her. Cindy's fragile still around the death of her father."

"I'm not a monster, Mrs. Carpenter. I just

want to solve this murder case." He nodded at Mia as he moved out of the apartment. "Thank you for your time. And the tip."

Mia followed them downstairs to make sure the door locked behind them. She watched out the window as the two police cars left her parking lot. Living in Magic Springs was never easy, but she didn't think she deserved to have a murder happen right where she wanted to plant her herb garden. Now she was going to have to sage the area to get rid of any lingering bad vibes. She glanced around the house and smiled. At least it hadn't been inside. She didn't want to worry about angry spirits in her home.

She checked the kitchen and office doors again, then turned off the lights and went upstairs to eat and update Grans and Christina on what she'd found out. They may be able to add something to the list of things she wanted to look into. Baldwin may be the actual investigator, but he wasn't looking at the whole picture. Mostly because he didn't know magic was involved. It didn't feel like Cindy had killed Denny by accident. But she clearly had had some dealings with him. And Mia needed to find out what they were.

When she got upstairs, she found Grans and Christina in the kitchen, getting food on the table.

"Good, you're back. I don't want to rush dinner, but I need to get back to working with Cindy's grimoire. Maybe I can figure out why she called this Denny before his death." Grans set the chicken marsala on the table.

"You don't think she actually killed the guy, then." Mia grabbed a soda out of the fridge and sat down at the table.

"No, dear, I don't believe that. There's no black mark in Cindy's soul. If she had killed him, even remotely, I'd see it on her. I have a bit of a gift." Grans took Mia and Christina's hands and sent up a quick word of thanks for the food to the Goddess. "Sometimes it's a hard one to deal with. So many people are damaged, but at times like this, it helps me know who to trust."

"And you trust Cindy." Mia took a bite of the chicken and smiled. It had reheated perfectly. No toughness of the chicken. No aftertaste. Just good food. She needed to get working on the next bunch of recipes so she'd have a list to take with next week's deliveries.

"Of course." Grans glanced at Christina. "This turned out really well. Are you happy with your work?"

"Yes, ma'am. I enjoy cooking with Mia.

I'm learning a lot, and with school, I actually have things to talk about when we're doing case studies. I can't believe having a real job is actually fun." Christina went on to tell them all about the classes she was going to take next school term. She was enjoying her life immensely. However, the one thing she didn't talk about was her relationship with Levi. Maybe having some distance wasn't a bad idea.

Mia hoped for Levi's sake that Christina hadn't decided his reputation as the town's bad boy was too much to deal with. Either way, though, it wasn't Mia's business.

Grans hadn't told her any more about what being a Bishop descendant meant, but they had been busy. And now they had one more thing on their list: get Cindy out of jail. Mia glanced over at Mr. Darcy, who was on the window seat, staring out the window. Dorian must be worried. One more reason spirits should go on after death. They couldn't do anything but worry about the ones they loved.

She excused herself after dinner and went downstairs to her office. She needed to work on the record keeping for the business. And post next week's orders into the system. Most of the work she was doing now was manageable, but if things picked up, she needed to see a pattern before expanding too soon.

Mia sipped the cup of tea she'd brought down as she waited for the program to load. The joy of owning your own business — there was always something to do. In her last job, the accounting department would send her reports on what she was doing. Her budget was set by Isaac, which really meant she did it for him. As long as she kept the costs reasonable, and made the hotel money and him look good, he didn't care.

After she'd finished what had to be done she opened her Internet search program and keyed in Denny's name again. Nothing popped out at her except a link to one of his jail stays. She opened it, wondering if it would tell her anything, but no, you got inmate name, stay dates, and charges listed. All things she knew about Denny.

As she was shutting down the site, she noticed an alert for visits. She clicked on the link and was taken to a page with a few phone numbers. And this message: ***Don't waste your time visiting the wrong facility. Prisoners are housed in multiple locations, including out-of-state facilities. Call the prisoner visitation line listed below for current updates.***

Space issues. She'd read articles about the

overcrowding at prisons. Had Denny spent his time in a Florida facility or somewhere else? Did it even matter?

Glancing at the clock, she groaned. It was already almost midnight. And she had a big cooking day ahead of her to get ready for the next catering job. Time to put this hobby, as Baldwin would call it, away and get ready for her own life.

Still, something bothered her about Denny, and now Cindy. The pieces didn't fit together as they should. Cindy was a piece of work, but killing just seemed a little too much effort for the woman.

At least Mia hoped so, because if not, she'd brought a killer into her house. With Grans right here. She was some sort of amazing protector, wasn't she?

She turned off all the lights and locked the doors. She checked the lock on the front door before she went upstairs. No use giving someone easy access to a place that used to be abandoned, a known teen hookup site. She patted the wall. "It's okay, now you're under my watch. Things will be better."

The house groaned in response. Mia got a positive feeling from the response. Hopefully, she could keep her promise.

CHAPTER 10

"What's on the schedule today?" Christina sipped at her coffee. She pulled her jet-black hair away from her eyes. It didn't matter what color her hair was, she looked beautiful.

"I need to make a quick run to the hardware store, then we need to do prep for tomorrow's cooking. Shopping, making sure we have what we need, maybe making a test dessert to make sure it's going to be what I wanted." Mia sat with Mr. Darcy on her lap. Her cup of coffee had been sitting on the table for the last thirty minutes and the coffee inside it was still piping hot. Dorian was playing with his magic. Letting her know he was still around. "What are your plans? Having you with me will cut my work time in half, but you usually take Wednesdays off."

"No plans," Christina said quickly. A little too quickly, and Mia glanced at her from the end of the table.

"Are you sure? I bet Levi missed seeing you while you were in Bermuda. Maybe you should invite him out for a hike and a picnic. It's going to be a lovely day." Mia wished she was outside today, but it was her business. She was responsible for making sure the Roths' baby gender reveal party was a success. When — or if, she corrected herself — she had a baby, she wasn't going to find out the gender until the baby was born. That way she'd be surprised too. Of course, the sonogram might reveal the gender accidentally, but still, she definitely wasn't going to hold a party and watch some pink or blue smoke come out of the cake when it was cut open.

"I'd rather work with you. If we get done early, I've got a book I've been dying to finish. I'll take it out to the park and read the lazy afternoon away. At least until Baldwin kicks me out for being a bad influence on the kids in the playground." She peeled a banana.

"You shouldn't let him get to you. He teases you because you react. Didn't Isaac do that when you were growing up?" Mia sipped her coffee and wondered how Cindy was doing.

"No, he was in high school when I was

five, so he just kind of ignored me. Like the rest of the family." Christina finished her coffee and took the cup to the sink. "Let me know when you're ready. I want to check in with some guys from school to see when they're coming back to Twin. I'll probably take a day then to go see everyone."

"I'm going to wait for Grans for breakfast, then I'll run my errand." Mia hated that Christina wasn't close to her family. However, on the other hand, Mia knew what a pain the Adams family could be. At least she'd dodged that bullet.

Christina paused. "She's already gone. One of her friends came to pick her up this morning. They were going to visit the jail to see Cindy. I think they were stopping for doughnuts from Majors to take with them."

"She always has to be taking care of people." Mia sighed and glanced at the clock. "Okay, then, I'm going down at nine. I'll see you then."

"Perfect." Christina disappeared down the hallway.

Mia glanced at Mr. Darcy. "That grand-mother of mine can get into trouble in a blink of an eye."

Mr. Darcy — or had it been Dorian? — snorted in reply, then jumped over to the window box, laid his head on the sill, and fell asleep.

Mia grabbed her purse and headed out to talk to Dick Hodges. He owed her an explanation. Her instincts said John was behind it. If she could prove it, maybe Baldwin would take her seriously and look into John for the murder as well.

Dick Hodges had just brought a snow-blower out to the sidewalk to entice walk-ins. He turned to greet her, but his sales-man's smile fell off his face when he saw who it was. "I can't talk to you."

Mia followed him into the store and back to the storage room. "Look, you either talk to me or I'm calling Mark Baldwin right now and telling him to charge you with trespassing, and maybe even participating in murdering that guy in my backyard."

"I didn't kill anyone. And I didn't trespass. I knocked on the door." He focused on a box of screws that looked like it had many different sizes dumped in. "Just leave before he sees you."

"You're talking about John, aren't you?" Mia leaned over to get into Dick's line of sight. "What does he have on you that you're willing to be his messenger boy?"

Now Dick sighed and lifted his head. "I was behind on my bank payments for the business. He offered to buy me out. When I said no, he told me he'd put in a good word for me at the bank to get me more time. All I had to do was deliver a message to you."

"So you told me to leave town."

He nodded. "I still think it's a good idea. When John Louis has it in for you, you're probably leaving sooner or later. I went to school with the guy and he still scares the crap out of me. I can't prove it, but I'm pretty sure he beat up Jimmy Marks freshman year because the guy wouldn't write a term paper for him. Jimmy was in the hospital for a month. John Louis is bad news."

"So that's all that happened? You didn't kill Denny?" Mia believed his story. Dick looked nervous even now, telling the old story from high school.

He held up his hands. "I don't know a Denny and I would never have hurt another soul. I'm a Methodist."

Mia wasn't quite sure what his religious affiliation had to do with the topic at hand, but she could see that Dick was being honest. "Please tell John Louis if he wants to talk to me, he can call, and I'll give him the name and number of my attorney."

Walking back home, she thought of the encounter. She was still shaking, but not from confronting Dick. No, her anger was at John Louis and his ability to get everyone to do his bidding. The guy was a bully. Plain and simple.

Mia was late getting back to the work kitchen. Christina sat on the bench outside the kitchen, reading a book. "I didn't hear you leaving. I hope you didn't have to wait long."

"I headed out about an hour ago. Trent called and told me one of the books he'd ordered for me had come in, so I went down and got it." She held up the cookbook. It was written by a late travel writer, about different foods in the world. "It's really interesting. One of my professors last semester studied him for her final paper."

Mia had never felt comfortable cooking with unusual proteins. She'd even shied away from sweetbreads and other organ meats.

She grinned as she thought about the typical witch potion lore. Eye of newt, blood of a snake caught under a full moon. Luckily, real witches didn't use those things in their potions. Herbs and tonics were more her style. "I like that he opened up other culture's foods to the US market, but honestly, I'm not sure I could eat or work with the recipes."

"So you don't have to cook everything?"

Christina eyed her warily.

Mia unlocked the door and opened the kitchen, her gaze still focused on Christina. "Not when you're out of school. You can choose what area you're going to focus on. And if a customer wants something you don't want to do, well, it's out of your expertise. They can go elsewhere."

Mia stopped in the middle of the room. What looked like every pot, pan, dish, and utensil was out on the floor. The pantry had suffered the same fate. She heard Christina, next to her, whistle.

"Man, someone went to town on your stuff."

Mia stepped out of the room and closed the door. She pulled out her cell phone and called Baldwin. "You need to come see this."

"Mia, I'm a little busy. Are you hurt?" Baldwin's exasperated tone told her he wasn't open to helping, but she pushed on.

"Just come. I need you to tell me if this is a crime. Oh, and don't let me forget to tell you about my talk with Dick Hodges." She hung up, hoping her lack of specifics would bring him to the school sooner rather than later. She focused on Christina. "No one was here or near the kitchen when you came down or went out to the store?"

"I haven't seen anyone. Who in the world

would do something like this?" Christina glanced around the empty lobby. "You don't think they're still in the building, do you?"

Mia glanced at the door and lock. "No, I locked the door from this side to double protect the rest of the building from the back door in the kitchen. That way, if we ever have a time where we rent out the kitchen, I don't have to worry about people wandering the other floors if I'm not here."

"Smart idea." Christina stared at the kitchen door. "But I don't get why someone would break in."

"Could have been kids. This was a hang-out when the place was empty. Maybe they wanted one last party?" Mia sank into one of the chairs. "All I know is I need to get a better lock on that back door, and maybe a camera system on it too. Although that's going to take a big bite out of this month's budget."

"I'm still getting paid, right? Mom's been kind of iffy about the living allowance since I'm taking classes in Twin instead of going to BSU or U of I. I guess I should be glad she's paying my tuition. Of course, she's paying it out of my trust fund from my grandmother, so it's not like she's hurting for the money." Christina let her shoulders sink. "It's never going to be easy with her unless I follow the life plan she made for me, is it?"

"Yes, I'll pay you for the hours. But life with your mom probably isn't going to be easy. The thing is, life isn't meant to be easy. If you're enjoying what you're doing and moving forward, learning new things, that's all you can ask for. Besides, you have people here who care about you." Mia gave Christina an encouraging smile. "Right?"

"I thought I had a few more." Christina waved away the look on Mia's face. "Don't worry about it. I'm handling the drama."

Mia wanted to ask her about Levi and what was happening, but she decided Christina was right. If she could handle the drama, Mia needed to stay out of it. Besides, before long, Grans would figure out what was going on and try to insert herself into their relationship to fix things. There didn't need to be two meddlers in one family. "Sounds good. Baldwin should be here soon. Hopefully, we can get back to work by noon. I really want to make sure this party goes off without a hitch."

"Since this is just the gender reveal party, do you think we'll get the baby shower as well?"

Mia nodded. "That's my hope."

A knock sounded at the front door. Mia

hurried over and found Baldwin on the porch.

"This better be good," he snarled. "You realize you could have called 9-1-1 if this was an emergency."

Mia smiled sweetly, or at least she hoped that was what it looked like. "I wanted the best. I don't think this will take long. Besides, you always get snippy if I don't tell you things. So I called you."

"Fine, where is it?" Baldwin came inside and looked around the lobby. "Everything looks fine here."

"Christina, open the kitchen door for our guest." Mia nodded in that direction. "I'm assuming they got in from the back door."

Baldwin went through the doorway and whistled. "Man, someone hates you." He picked up his cell. When someone answered, he said, "Get an evidence team over to the old school. There's been a break-in."

Mia sank into the sofa and watched her plans for the day get delayed. Luckily, she'd built in two prep days for the event. She waited for him to come out of the kitchen. "How bad is it?"

"Someone jimmied your back lock. You need to call Dick over at the hardware store and he should be able to get it fixed. Or you could call Trey and get a camera system for the back too. This building is too big just to have the one at the front door."

"Dick and I have been having issues. I'll call Trey. It's on my list for today. When will I be allowed back in the kitchen? I have an event this weekend." Mia held her breath for the answer. She didn't want to try to find a kitchen and repurchase all the food. That would really hurt this month's bottom line.

Baldwin glanced back toward the kitchen doorway. "I'll get everything done before nightfall, but you really need to have that lock replaced as soon as I release the scene."

"I'll call Trent to see if he can come over tonight." Mia hated calling in favors, but Trent had construction experience. And besides, she'd feed him his favorite meal and throw in some treats to take home with him. The man loved her cooking. "Look, this might not be a big issue, but Dick Hodges came over the other day and said I was in danger. He said I should sell."

"Dick has had his own run-ins with John Louis. Maybe he was just sharing some neighborly advice." Baldwin watched her reaction.

"Yeah, he told me about that today. Maybe he came to destroy my kitchen so I would leave." Mia swept out her hand in an inclusive gesture. "Like this."

"Nothing's really destroyed. Except the lock. It looks like someone was looking for something."

"What? A can opener?" Mia couldn't keep the sarcasm from her voice.

"I get it. I'll talk to Dick. But I know you're barking up the wrong tree there. The guy's just getting a little old. He gets ideas in his head and can't get them out." He tapped his temple. "His wife needs to keep a closer eye on him. He's got the dementia disease."

"Oh. I didn't realize."

"We go to the same church. You learn a lot about the community when you attend a house of worship." He studied her. "Are you connected with a good church?"

"No, and I'm fine. Thank you."

"Okay. Now that we have that settled, I need to interview everyone who was in the house last night after we picked up Miss Alexander. Can I use your office for interviews?" Baldwin grinned at Christina. "You can be first, Miss Adams. I'd love to hear about your Bermuda trip. And I hear there was an incident this week down at one of the bars? Someone messing with what you think of as yours?"

"Totally off topic." Mia stood and opened

148

the office door. "Christina, don't answer anything except where you were today and last night. Baldwin can get his gossip from the rumor mill."

It was almost four before Baldwin released the kitchen. Trent waited with her downstairs while the evidence techs collected their samples and packed their bags. Mia followed the last one out of the building and locked the door after them. Grans and Christina were upstairs. Mia leaned against the wall, studying the kitchen door.

"Maybe I bit off more than I wanted here." She glanced at Trent. "I need you to tell me the truth. Do you think I should sell the school?"

He pulled her into his arms. "No way. This will pass. We're ninety percent sure of who's behind this, and once he realizes you aren't going away, he'll give up and start annoying someone else to sell him their property. He's responding to pride right now. You won the bid on the sale. Then you got him arrested."

"For trying to force me to sell." Mia stepped back.

Trent patted down the air in front of him. "Calm down, slugger, we all know why John Louis was arrested and convicted. Except for maybe one man — John Louis. That man has such an ego on him, it's pathetic."

"I just hate to put Grans and Christina in danger." Mia glanced up at the apartment. "If it was just me, I'd ride it out to the end."

"You're not alone in this situation. You have friends who care about what's happening to you. I swear, everyone in town is buying your home-cooked meals. My grocery receipts have decreased each week, and I'm assuming your orders are increasing." He studied her, watching for the tell.

She shrugged. "Okay, so yeah, business is picking up. Sorry it's affecting your sales."

He laughed and picked up the bag that had the new lock and a small toolbox he'd gotten from the back of his Blazer. "It will even out, eventually. If not, I'll just have to raise my prices. Then they'll appreciate what a service Majors is to the community."

Mia worried about that as she followed him through the kitchen. Or at least as she walked through the door. Then, looking at the mess, the only thing she was worried about was getting the kitchen in order so they could cook tomorrow. She frowned at the mess. "I don't think this is random."

"The break-in?" Trent looked around. "Or the mess?"

She turned in a small circle and walked over to the bookcase, where she'd stored a lifetime of cookbooks. "The mess. It looks like they were looking for something. See how my cookbooks are all stacked neatly in a pile? Then everything else is just thrown out of cupboards, like they were looking for something specific."

"Didn't your ex try to steal your catering cookbooks once? Maybe this was him too?" Trent picked up a book and dusted it off, setting it up on one of the shelves.

"He was just in Bermuda with Christina and the family. Besides, I told him he wasn't getting those recipes." Mia grabbed a towel from a drawer. "Why would he come up here now? He has to know I keep the recipes locked up. And that Christina wasn't going to help him."

"Maybe she said something by accident about you and the catering recipes. He could have thought he knew exactly where you would put something. He lived with you for several years; he can probably figure out what you'd do." Trent helped her pick up the books as they talked, wiping each one to get rid of the fingerprint dust the police had used.

"He would have had to have been actually paying attention. You've heard Christina talk about the two of us together. He was checked out of our relationship long before it was officially over." Mia adjusted the last book and glanced at the doorway. "You'd better get that door fixed or I might have to reshelve these books again tomorrow after tonight's break-in."

"There's not going to be a break-in tonight. At least not through this door. You're keeping the rest of the building locked up tight, right?" He moved to the doorway and examined the frame.

"No, I've been leaving doors open with a Welcome sign that points out where all the gold is hidden. What do you think?" She studied him as his gaze moved from the door frame to her. He hadn't known she was kidding until he'd seen the smile on her face. Man, the boy was wound up tight today. Maybe she'd just go upstairs and see what Grans was up to. "Well, if you don't need me . . ."

He watched her trail off, then nodded to the pots and pans all over the floor. "I'll help with the washing if you want to get this all together tonight so you can cook tomorrow. I know the reveal party is this weekend. I'm sure you'll need to bake tomorrow."

Mia studied him. "Are you sure? I mean, I can drag Christina down here early tomorrow and we can clean before we cook."

"You have me here without even one drag,

you should use me. Besides, I love it when you talk dirty to me." He pulled a screwdriver out of his bag and checked it against the head of the screw.

"We're talking about cleaning." She bit back a smile.

"If we're talking about cleaning, then there's something dirty in the picture." He went for a second screwdriver. "Your choice, but if I were you, I'd pick me over Christina."

"You're so modest."

He chuckled as he started unscrewing the lock mechanisms. "Maybe not modest, but I know I can outwork her with one arm behind my back. Face it, the girl doesn't know hard work."

"She was raised differently. This is the first time she's ever done anything remotely like actual work. For money. She's trying. That's all I can ask of her." Mia walked over to the next pile and moved things from the floor to the large metal table.

"She's your project, not mine. Besides, I know you love working with me more anyway." He popped out the bent-up lock and tossed it onto a nearby table. "I want to talk to you about Levi and Christina. What in the world is going on?"

"What do you mean?" Mia was trying to

stay out of it, but everyone wanted to know the facts behind their very public fight.

"She's been MIA the last few days. Before she left on her trip, she was tied to my brother's hip. Now he's grumpy and won't talk about it. And she's not around, anywhere. Did he mess up this thing?" He paused in his work to watch Mia answer.

"I don't really know anything." She hedged her answer, not meeting Trent's gaze.

When he didn't respond, she turned toward him, hands on hips. "You ask your brother, don't ask me. I really don't know what she's doing, but I see the same things as you do. I'm sure they'll figure it out."

Trent put the final screw in the lock, then stood, testing it. "Now, see, that's where we disagree. I love my brother, but sometimes he's an idiot. Bethanie's been hanging around the house, trying to get his attention. She even came out to the farm to see if he was there. Mom about had a coronary. I'm supposed to fix that too. Mom likes Christina."

Mia started a load in the dishwasher and went to the next area to clean. "I'm glad to hear that. Christina is good for him."

"I agree, but we have to do something before he drifts too far." Trent closed his toolbox. "So, what else can I do to help?"

"One, stop thinking you can change Levi's life. He and Christina need to figure this out themselves. And if Bethanie gets in the way — well, then, Levi's loss." She met his gaze. "You can't fix everything."

He held up his toolbox. "I beg to differ."

"If only a hammer and a screwdriver worked on a broken heart."

With Trent's help, she was able to get the kitchen back in order by the end of day. He offered to take her to the diner for dinner, but she asked for a rain check. With only one day of prep available for the party Saturday, she needed to reset her plan for the next day. There was a note on the kitchen table when she got to the apartment. Grans had gone to bed early and Christina was out for a few hours.

Mia wondered if she was out with Levi or just a friend. The note didn't say, so she threw some good wishes on the event and made herself some leftovers while she opened her notebook to reschedule prep. In all her years as a caterer, she'd learned one thing: A solid plan always got you through even the worst event. She had a solid plan for two days, but just one was going to call for some creativity and a lot of hard work.

Hours later, she was finally finished with

the plan. Maybe not totally happy, but it would have to do. Baldwin could deal with whoever broke into her kitchen, and the new security system that was being installed on Saturday while she was out at the party would deter future attempts to disrupt her process.

That was why she knew it was John Louis. Not that he would have done anything himself, but Mia figured he could hire people. And with some time in jail, maybe he knew even more of the darker element who would like to take a job tearing up a kitchen. But one thing still bothered her. Someone was looking for something specific. And John only wanted the house. Or at least that was what he said. This attack felt personal to her. She brushed off the bad mojo and smiled at Mr. Darcy. "Ready for bed?"

He jumped off the window seat where he'd been watching her work and headed down the hallway. Mia glanced at the video feed of the front door. No Christina yet. She had her keys; no use staying up for her. Yawning, Mia headed for bed. Tomorrow's alarm was going to go off early. She hoped Christina would be ready. She needed her help.

Late in the night Mia heard the apartment

front door open and close. Then footsteps to Christina's room. Mia rolled over and smiled. When had she become den mother?

CHAPTER 11

The next morning Christina was already at the table, eating yogurt and a banana and reading the paper when Mia came into the kitchen.

"Good morning. I figured I'd have to drag you out of bed this morning," Mia said as she made her way to the coffeepot.

"I knew we had a job and that you needed my help. So I'm here." Christina looked over the paper at her. "Is that a crime?"

"No, I just didn't think you'd be up so early." Mia grabbed one of the croissants she'd made early in the week. She pushed the notebook toward Christina. "I have a plan. And, hopefully, nothing else will happen to keep us from the kitchen."

"Rumor is that Baldwin paid a visit to John Louis yesterday." Christina didn't look up from studying the notebook. "Bethanie said they were in the office together for over two hours, and John Louis left for the day after Baldwin exited. Don't you think that's odd?"

"Actually, no. John was my first bet too. The guy wants to bulldoze the school and build a fancy strip mall. He'd probably make a fortune in rents." Mia sipped her coffee. "Are you sure of your source?"

"Do you mean I trust Bethanie to have my best interests at heart? Are you crazy? She's going after Levi. I have my own rumor sources." She tapped on the paper. "This is good. We should be ready for the party early tomorrow morning."

"That's my plan. That way I can worry for a couple of hours before we start. I'd hate to break a tradition." She smiled at Christina, who had turned back to the paper and was starting on the crosswords.

"It's okay. I don't really have any traditions anymore. It would be nice to see that one break. You need to have confidence in your ability to put on amazing events. You were always being written up in newspapers in town. I heard Isaac say their bookings have gone down by over thirty percent." Christina grinned. "And you didn't even curse him and his business to fail. It's just happening without any bad karma."

"Got it; no magic on your brother, his life sucks anyway." Mia picked at her breakfast.

"Trent was here yesterday. I'm supposed to ask you about Levi."

"I guess I had that coming by bringing up Isaac." Christina ran a hand over her jet-black hair. "Look, I don't want to be someone's girlfriend just when I'm in front of them. I want him to remember me when I'm away, and not put himself in compromising positions."

"So, you want to be exclusive." Mia didn't look at her. "Like maybe not going out on a guy's boat just because you're out of town."

"That wasn't the same thing." Christina paused. "Okay, maybe it was the same thing. I know what you mean by exclusive. So what about you and Trent? Are you exclusive yet?"

"We aren't talking about me and Trent." Mia glanced at the clock and then put her cup in the sink. "We need to get busy if we're going to be ready for tomorrow's gig. I'll meet you downstairs."

Christina shoved the notebook into Mia's hands before she could escape. "You'll need this. And besides, I'm going to be down there with you. There will be lots of time to talk."

"Not about that," Mia muttered as she hurried out of the apartment and downstairs. It wasn't that she didn't like Trent; she did. But she'd just gotten out of a long-term relationship. Why would she want to jump back into the fire? If it was right, Trent would be there in a year or two, when Mia was ready to try again. Right now, she just felt the burns from her relationship with Isaac way too intensively. She couldn't bring Trent into her broken life.

When Christina came down, Mia was focused on the cake batter. She didn't look up, just pointed to the fridge. "Why don't you start chopping the vegetables? I have a list of what I need. We need to be ready to cook by noon so everything has time to cool. I have to get these cakes into the oven before we do anything else."

"Many hands make light work." Christina pulled on an apron. "Your grandmother told me to tell you that she's going down to get Cindy today. I guess Baldwin verified her alibi."

Mia wasn't sure bringing Cindy back to the house was a good idea. She might not have killed Denny Blake, but she brought enough bad karma into the house. Mia might have to sage it after the woman left, just to keep the energy flowing. "I wonder if Baldwin found out anything."

"Not from John, or at least that's what

161

Bethanie says. Of course, you can't trust her to tell you the truth if her lips are moving." Christina checked the list and then got everything from the fridge. She set up her chopping block, got a clean towel, opened her knife set, and then got out bowls for the chopped vegetables. "You know, we could have asked Majors if they could special order this."

"Not the same. Besides, I'm trying to build repeat clients. If I wasn't worried about it, I'd just stay home tomorrow and let you drop off and pick up. But no, I'll play the social butterfly for the event."

"I'm sure you could get clients without networking. You would think everyone would be here ordering a meal to take home to their family, your food is that good." Christina started chopping.

They worked beside each other for a few hours; then Mia's phone rang. "Mia's Morsels. Can I help you?"

"You can help by not sending your guard dog over every time something happens at your shop. It's not my fault you chose to live in a ghetto. People used to hang out there doing drugs and whatever, and now you're questioning your neighborhood?"

John Louis had returned her call.

"I don't think it's the neighborhood I need

to watch out for. And I didn't send Baldwin over to talk to you. Your actions made you look like the best suspect, not my dislike for you." Mia put the call on Speaker so Christina could hear what he said. Better to be safe than sorry.

"And unfortunately for you, I have an ironclad alibi. Carol dragged me to one of her inane dinner parties. I have ten people who can vouch for my whereabouts. I just want to let you know you were barking up the wrong tree." The phone clicked, and Mia saw he'd hung up.

"The break-in happened sometime during the night. I don't know any dinner parties that go through nine the next morning," Christina commented on the call and John's alibi.

"You're right. And of course Baldwin knows that. So what game is John Louis playing now?" Mia glanced at the clock. "We've worked through lunch. Let's make something fun to eat."

"No sandwiches?"

Mia shook her head. "We're ahead of where we needed to be for prep. What about fajitas? I can show you how to make home-made tortillas."

By the time they finished prep work, they were both beat. Walking up the stairs, Christina looked back at her. "No offense, but I don't want to cook for a while. And I mean, like years."

"We don't have to cook anything tomorrow, just bake some appetizers and get the plates ready. Shelly hired waitstaff from the Lodge, so we don't have to serve either. We'll set up the cake and then we can leave, so you can rest up for Monday's kitchen session. We have tons of new orders."

"Great," Christina said without emotion. "Tell me we don't have an event next weekend."

"I could, but I'd be lying. It's the library tea, remember?" Mia paused at the top of the stairs and looked at the locked door down the hall. "I need to get a locksmith out here next week. Remind me to put it in my planner to call someone."

"Sure. Well, at least I have a few months before I have to go back to school. With the speed you're expanding, fall is going to be brutal." Christina held the door open for Mia. The apartment smelled wonderful. "Someone's been cooking up here too."

"It does seem that way. If school and work get to be too much, I'll hire someone else." Mia closed the door behind her, locking it more from habit than anything else.

"Let me know when you're planning on

hiring. Several of the guys in my classes have been asking me if there's a job with you. They live in the area too." Christina grinned. "And I can tell you who the slackers are."

"Much appreciated." Mia stopped in the kitchen doorway. Grans was sitting at the table and Cindy was standing at the stove, stirring what appeared to be a stir-fry. "What's going on here?"

"We're making dinner. I figured after cooking all day the last thing you'd want to do is cook again, so after I picked up Cindy from the station, we stopped at Majors and got supplies." Grans looked up from the grimoire. "And we've made some progress on the spell Cindy cast that started this problem."

Mia sat down at the table. "Cindy, why were you calling an on-call hit man?"

Cindy turned around, her cheeks pink. "Well, about that. I knew he was a hit man, or at least claimed to be one. I have an upcoming part where I'm a female assassin, and I wanted to learn more about the character."

"You were researching a part?" Christina set a bottle of water in front of Mia and sat down at the table with her own. "Cool. How many people had he killed?"

"More than I want to think about, now that I realize he was being honest with me." Cindy shuddered as she sat down at the table. "Look, I didn't know he was coming here. He told me during our last call that he was going west for an assignment and he'd call when he got back home. He joked that he hoped he didn't run into me while he was working. I thought he was all hat, no cattle."

"What?" Christina looked around the table.

"It means a big talker," Mia explained. She studied Cindy, who looked like she'd been telling the truth, but actors and all? "So, how did you convince Baldwin?"

"Easy, I had a real alibi for the time of death. Mike and I were FaceTiming about what we're doing with Father's property. He has the transcripts. Let's just say my brother doesn't quite trust me. And they didn't find any missing money or transfers from my account, so he believed me." Cindy pointed to the book. "Your grandmother thinks I did a prosperity spell without the proper grounding."

"No, I said you had wrong intentions." Grans sighed, like it wasn't the first time she'd explained the difference.

"So, to get this straight, you didn't kill

Denny." Mia rephrased the conclusion so there would be no wiggle room. "Was he the man who ate room service in your Lodge room?"

"Freaking small towns. Yes, I had dinner with him a couple of times. But I've never killed anyone. Why would I start by killing someone who was an excellent subject matter expert for me?" Cindy pointed to the spell book. "Now, all we have to do is correct the spell and I'll be out of your house and your cute little town."

The way she described Magic Springs indicated that she didn't think it was cute at all. Mia sighed and stood. "I'm heading to my room to shower some of these kinks out of me. I may also take a bath before I go to bed just to make sure they're gone. I need to be fresh and sunny tomorrow at this event."

Cindy nodded. "I understand preparing for an event. I have to have someone come and do a full body massage the day before any premieres or release parties. Too much stress ages your face."

Mia wasn't sure if Cindy was just making a comment or if Mia's face had accidentally shown the true level of her stress. If so, she must look over one hundred.

Grans called after her, "I'll send Christina

to get you when dinner's ready. But if you're asleep, we're not waking you. You look tired."

"Thanks," Mia called back. *Thanks for telling me I look like crap.* She'd wanted to relax, but if she was this stressed when they were at less than half booked, she would hate to see it when she was fully booked and working off a waitlist. Maybe then she'd be used to the volume. Or maybe not.

She opened her door and fell face-first onto her bed. Then she promptly fell asleep.

The light was coming from the windows, but she wasn't in bed. She glanced around and realized she was in the house. She could see the flagpole in the parking lot, an old and tattered St. Catherine's Prep flag flapping in the wind. But the flag was torn and stained, the words faded. She had to be on the third floor from the view she could see from the window, but she'd never been here before. Unless this was her apartment, just years before she'd bought the place. And before the last principal had remodeled the place she now lived in.

A woman in a cloak sat on a wooden chair, watching her. Her hood was down, her copper hair braided tight on each side of her head. She held a staff. "Have you found what you need yet?"

She woke from the dream abruptly, and she sat upright in bed. Mr. Darcy was at the end of the bed watching her. He meowed quietly.

"Sorry, big guy. A bad dream." Mia patted the bed next to her and stroked his coat. "Too many things going on, and none of it makes any sense. Especially why I'm part of this and every murder that happens in Magic Springs."

He started to purr, which always put her to sleep. But she had a thought stuck in her head. Maybe Baldwin was right and she had terrible luck. Maybe she'd always be knee-deep in investigations.

CHAPTER 12

The next morning Mia woke starving. She hadn't heard Grans try to wake her for dinner. And with the weird dream, she wondered if she could have been pulled out of the visit anyway. She shivered as she crawled out of bed. The apparition that called itself her guardian had been clear this time: find whatever resource she didn't have or die. That was pretty cut-and-dried. And the missing something had to be in this house. She'd seen the flagpole. She'd known where she was, in her apartment looking out the window. There were things that didn't make sense. But she'd known where she'd been in the dream.

Or had it been a message? Either way, Mia was going to have to find these things before the lack of them killed her. She'd talk to Grans this morning.

Cindy was alone in the kitchen when Mia arrived. She was ready for the event today.

Then she could work on guardian business, maybe after she figured out who had broken into her kitchen. Although she thought she knew who it was — John Louis. "Hey, Cindy, where's my grandmother?"

"She's not up yet." Cindy looked up from the notebook she'd been writing in. "Look, Mia, can we talk?"

"Aren't we talking now?" Mia poured herself a cup of coffee. She wouldn't eat until after the event. She didn't trust her stomach on big days like this. Isaac used to kid her about how seriously she took her catering jobs. She should have realized then that they were on two different wavelengths.

"I mean, I need to thank you for taking me in. I know I haven't been the easiest person to have here, and I guess I think a little too much of myself sometimes. I've always just had myself to worry about. And people took care of me. Mostly Father, then my agent handled most of my decisions. Now, with him gone, I think I'd better figure out how to take care of myself before I get myself in trouble again." She studied the table as she talked. "I didn't like being in jail. It gave me a lot of time to think about what's important."

"Everyone has times in their lives when they have to take stock of what's happening. You're just hitting that spot. I hope you find yourself soon." Mia could relate to what Cindy was saying. She'd never been too focused on herself, but she had lost herself in her last relationship. Now, she was finding herself again. And she liked who she'd become. "You'll be fine."

"Because you and your grandmother were there when I needed someone. I know, I messed up with the spell. Father always said not to spell for yourself. That the power was a gift I'd been given and not to waste it. I thought he was being metaphorical. At least until last week. Did I tell you my agent's hair fell out? I was mad because Merry didn't get me a job I wanted, and her hair fell out the next day. I don't think it was a coincidence. Of course, I didn't tell her that I might have been responsible." She rubbed her forehead. "Okay, so I know it wasn't random. I knew the book had power. I touched the cover and said that Merry should pay. And then I heard she wasn't seeing anyone because of a health issue. Her secretary told me the truth."

Mia didn't want to ask, but she needed to. "Did you wish harm on Denny?"

Cindy shook her head. "No way. I still needed him. This part is going to be killer, and he was helping me walk in the character's shoes."

"The book is telling the same story. Well, it is now that we figured out why it wasn't talking," Grans said as she walked into the kitchen. She patted Mia's shoulder. "Cindy didn't kill that man. She has a nonmagical alibi that satisfied Mark Baldwin as well. She's off the hook for that, at least. Now we have to fix the damage she did to her agent."

"And find out who did kill Denny Blake." Mia stood and went to the cabinet to grab a banana. There was no way she could get through the event without something in her stomach. "I've got to wake up Christina and get the van packed. We need to be at the venue in less than an hour."

"You go get ready and I'll wake up Christina. The girl listens when I call her name. I think she's afraid of me." Grans smiled.

Mia knew that Christina did, in fact, fear Grans, but she wasn't going to confirm her statement. Christina needed to deal with that on her own. "Sounds like a plan."

She filled a travel mug with coffee and went downstairs to get ready. She had parked the van near the kitchen's back door. She opened it and started loading the van with the boxes and tubs she'd packed last night. The cake would go in last so nothing would happen to it.

173

As she carried out a tub, a man's hands grabbed it from her and took it to the van. "Let me help."

Mia looked up into the bluest eyes she'd ever seen. Levi Majors might be just a little more handsome than his older brother, Trent, but he didn't have wisdom in his sparkling eyes. Not yet. "Thanks, Levi. What are you doing here?"

He grinned as he set the tub in the van. "I believe you know. Where's Christina? We need to talk."

"She doesn't have time right now. We have an event. And if you take off with my sous chef, you're going to have to deal with me."

"No, I don't want to run off with her. Well, I do, but right now I'd settle for five minutes." He followed Mia into the kitchen. "And I can help you load so you won't lose any time that I might hold you up."

"That's nice of you." Mia glanced toward the door.

Christina was coming into the kitchen. She stopped short when she saw Levi. Then she crossed the kitchen, grabbed a tote, and stepped around him. "I don't have time for this."

"Christina, I'm sorry. I didn't know she'd be there, and I didn't expect her to sit on my lap. If you're going to blame anyone,

174

blame Bethanie. She timed that stunt just so you'd see it." Levi picked up another tote and followed her.

Mia decided she'd start in the fridge so Levi and Christina could have some privacy. With Levi here, as long as they worked while they talked, they'd be ready in no time. When she was done with the food, she glanced out the doorway. Christina and Levi stood by the van. Mia watched as he nodded and left to get into his car.

Christina came inside and picked up the last tub.

"Everything all right?" Mia asked, focusing on the cake.

Christina didn't answer as she turned to walk out to the van.

"Christina?" Mia asked again.

She paused, not turning to look at Mia. "I'm not sure yet. I have a bad feeling about this. I know he wants to be with me, but I'm not sure yet."

Mia let the comment hang because she didn't have time for relationship drama right then either. Hopefully, Christina could keep her head in the game long enough to get through this party. They could sit and talk after that. Maybe an answer would come then.

Christina came back into the kitchen. "So,

tell me how we're going to get the cake to the event."

Mia was setting up the decorations around the cake in the ballroom when she heard men talking in an alcove. At first she tried to drown them out, focusing on getting the cake positioned just perfect so that when the prospective parents cut into the cake, the colored section inside would show to the gathering.

"You shouldn't have brought him to town. Now, we've got the police looking into his death, which is going to stall our deal. We need this to go through. You know how much money this will bring into town."

Mia froze. Who was talking? She focused and moved toward the sound. She didn't want to be seen, but on the other hand, she needed to know who was talking.

". . . not my fault. He was supposed to . . ." a male voice responded, but Mia realized they were walking away from the ballroom.

Were they attending the party? Did they work at the convention center? She glanced around the corner of the alcove and found the area empty. A door at the end of the hallway was swinging shut. She ran to it, but the parking lot was empty. She stepped outside after making sure the door wouldn't lock behind her and heard a car take off.

"What are you doing?" Christina asked behind her.

Mia whirled around.

Christina held up her hands. "Hold off, what's wrong? You look like you saw a ghost."

Mia let out her breath and went inside the building. "Nothing. I heard someone talking. I thought they said something about hiring Denny."

"What? Here? Someone was talking about that? Who was it?" Christina peppered her with questions.

Mia paused in the alcove where she'd heard the men talking. Nothing was around. No lost piece of paper with John Louis's name and address on it with a written to-do list starting with "hire a hit man." She blew out an exasperated breath and went into the ballroom. She had put a small stork on the front of the cake so she could make sure it showed correctly when it was cut. And she'd cut out an arrow for the couple and taped it to the table, to make sure the reveal would be perfect. Now the execution was in their hands.

"How are the appetizers?" She turned to Christina, who'd followed her back from outside, still waiting for her answers.

"Fine. I mean, everything's ready. All we need are the servers and the guests and then we'll be done with another successful catering job." Christina smiled at the cake. "This is lovely and such a great idea. Someday I'm going to do this for my baby reveal."

"Are you saying you worked it out with Levi?" Mia turned and studied her helper. Christina looked hopeful, at least in Mia's view.

Then she shrugged and the hopeful look disappeared. "Maybe. I've just got a lot of thinking to do. Levi has quite the reputation for being a bad boy. I don't want to cramp his style with what I need, but then again, it's what I need."

"Exactly." Mia smiled and put her arm around Christina. "I'm proud of you for standing up for what you want in a relationship. Now, let's get this all set up so we can leave as soon as we train the servers."

"Sounds good to me. I didn't sleep well last night. I could use a nap." Christina moved with her into the kitchen.

And with that one statement, Mia knew Christina's heart was in catering. They were just alike. Neither one of them could sleep before a big day. Except Mia had worked herself into sleep yesterday. Well, sleep and a vision or a dream, whatever you wanted to call it. All she knew was, her guardian had reached out to her again. As soon as today was over, even if Grans was still working with Cindy, they needed to have a talk. It was clear Grans was holding something back. She wasn't sure what it was yet, but she'd find out. She always did.

Back at the house, Grans and Cindy were walking out as they pulled up in the van. Mia stuck her head out of the window. "Where are you two going?"

"Cindy wants to see Dorian's old house. The Realtor has a buyer, and Cindy wanted to make sure there wasn't anything in the house that she needed to move out before selling," Grans called from the driver's side of her car. "We'll bring home dinner from the Lodge. Go upstairs and relax. I know you've had a busy week."

Great, Mia thought as the car drove off. So much for her getting to the bottom of the guardian stuff. She grabbed her tote bag with her notebook and tablet and swung it over her shoulder. "Let's go fix some sandwiches for lunch. Then I'm crashing for a few hours."

"Sounds good to me." Christina yawned. "What time are we going back?"

"Four. Then when we get back, it will take about an hour to clean everything and put it away before dinner." Mia set an alarm on her watch. "I'd hate to sleep through the night again."

"You were out yesterday." Christina bounded up the stairs. "It was almost like someone had drugged you. You missed a great meal."

"I guess I was tired." Mia was almost to the apartment when she heard the locks click. "What the heck? No one is supposed to be in there."

As she watched, Mr. Darcy ran out of the apartment and down the stairs. She turned to follow him, but then she decided not to fight it. She called after him. "Remember to be back in the apartment by eight. I'm not sure I can stay up much longer."

Christina was staring at her. "How did he do that?"

"Do what exactly?" Mia strode into the apartment and was greeted by Grans's dog, Muffy. He'd stayed inside, but he was watching the open door, waiting for someone to come inside.

Christina leaned down and rubbed Muffy's head. "Mr. Darcy has Dorian. Do you think it was the cat or the spirit who ran out of here so fast? Maybe he was looking for Cindy. Is she in danger?" she asked Muffy. The dog turned around on the carpet and laid in the middle of the rug. He was ignoring her question.

Mia watched the interaction with amusement. Christina seemed to be taking the magic stuff surrounding Mia and her grandmother in stride. She seemed more curious than concerned.

"You think Dorian's trying to follow Cindy?" The idea hadn't occurred to Mia, but it was a good one. She dialed Grans's cell. It was answered after one ring.

"I can't talk, I'm driving, and Baldwin gets miffed if he sees me holding my phone," Grans explained.

"I'll be quick. Keep an eye out for Mr. Darcy. We're not sure if he took off following you two."

She heard Grans's hesitation. "Well, cats do like to chase cars. I'll be careful, but I think we're too far away now for him to catch us. Anyway, Cindy's holding the phone, so I've got to hang up now."

Mia heard the undercurrent. Grans hadn't told Cindy yet that her father's spirit was stuck in Mr. Darcy. Which was probably for the best. Cindy seemed to have a bit of a temper and could be a loose cannon, especially concerning Dorian's family's grimoire. New witches didn't have to do much to get a spell book to work. It was as if it anticipated your every move. Not unlike a boyfriend, but without the need to watch hours of sports a week. She realized Grans was still on the line. "Okay, bye now."

"We'll have dinner there right at six." Grans knew Mia would have to go back to the event.

"Sounds perfect." Mia ended the call, then looked around the apartment. It looked presentable. Besides, Cindy wasn't really a guest. She glanced at Christina. "We'll just need to watch out for him. I'm sure he didn't take off after Grans. At least I hope not."

"I can go search the downstairs for him," Christina offered.

Mia knew the cat had a lot of hiding places in the building. "No. Let's just eat. I need to make some phone calls and make some notes about the catering job. Mr. Darcy will come back when he's ready."

"Okay, then." Christina opened the fridge and started grabbing lunch meat and fixings for a sandwich. "Tell me what you want."

"Surprise me." Mia grinned as she handed Christina the bread. "I'm hungry, so don't go all tea party on the sandwiches. I want some substance."

"I can do that." Christina disappeared into the kitchen.

Mia curled up on the couch and pulled out her tablet to make notes about the catering. Using the Lodge's servers, they would need to do more training next time because they didn't understand her instructions. She called out to Christina in the kitchen, "I think James hires every homeless man in the area for these events. Then we have to train them."

"It's a good quality in a man to take care of those less fortunate," Christina reminded her as she brought in a pastrami and swiss sandwich with some potato chips on the side and set it in front of Mia. She got her own plate from the kitchen and sat down on the couch. "You never told me what you saw at the convention center. Do you think they might have been ghosts? Or maybe soldiers?"

"I didn't see anything. That was one of the problems. If I'd seen something, I could actually enjoy my time teasing you. However, you're right about James's bent toward charity. But we do have to plan time to train the servers at the next event, even if we aren't the ones paying their wages." Mia wrote down all this about costs and setting up the party into the file. This could be a popular event.

She'd just finished her lunch and was curled up in the recliner when the business phone rang. "Mia's Morsels, how may I help you?"

"You can keep your nose out of my affairs. And your grandmother too. I don't want to give her a heart attack when she sees what I'm up to," the male voice reminded her. "You'll get instructions on what I need."

When she hung up, she looked at Christina's worried face. "I think we just got a blackmail or kidnapping threat. I couldn't tell what he was going to do."

"Call Baldwin. But I'm going into the bedroom. I'll come out after he leaves." Christina picked up her plate and headed to her room. "Let me know when he's gone. I'm going to see what John Louis is doing today via his computer passwords that Bethanie sent me yesterday."

"Don't get caught." Mia figured that was the only piece of advice she'd hadn't broken when she was a young adult.

CHAPTER 13

By the time they'd gotten back from the conference center, Trent's car was in the lot and he was sitting on the porch, playing with his phone. Mia opened the back door of the van and nodded to him. "You were off on your timing. Now you have to help us get all this in the kitchen and put away."

"My timing was just fine. Besides, my mom taught me to work. I don't mind." He smiled at her and picked up two of the tubs.

"Man, he's strong. Are you sure you still need me?" Christina grabbed a single tote and followed him inside.

"Of course I do. Do me a favor and unpack those dishes straight into the dishwasher before coming out for a second load. If we can keep the dishwasher going, we might be done with this sooner rather than later."

Christina nodded. "Just don't keep me too long. I'm meeting Bethanie for a drink after dinner."

"You two seem to be okay, then?" Mia followed her into the kitchen, where she noticed Trent staring at the back door. "What's up?"

"I'm not sure; it feels like someone tried your locks and failed. Did you get the security cameras installed yet?" He unpacked one of the totes, then used a soapy rag to wash it out at the sink.

"Not yet. They said they'd be back on Monday and set it all up." Mia threw him a towel. "Come help me get out the rest of the bins. I think there's some leftover cake you can take home if you want."

"Now that sounds like a plan." He dried the tote, then set it and its cover over by the storage closet and followed Mia out.

"So, why are you here besides to help me unpack the van?" Mia grabbed a tote from the back and hauled it to the porch. "Did Baldwin tell you about my cryptic phone call?"

"No, but you might as well tell me now." Again, he grabbed two bins and followed her inside. "I'm here to try to break into your mystery room. I figure I can see if I can pop the lock before you hire someone else. I'm sure you weren't budgeted to do a new camera in the back."

"That's the truth." She set down the bin by the dishwasher and pointed Trent toward the worktable. "Put those over there. They have the food in them."

"How can you tell?" He glanced at the different totes around the room.

Christina laughed. "She color codes everything. Blue is dishes and flatware and utensils. Pink is food. And white, those are linens."

"Which can go over by the washer and dryer," Mia pointed out. "I don't think we'll get all the laundry done, but we can at least make a dent in it. I want tomorrow to be as restful as possible."

"Good, so you can go out to dinner with me tomorrow. I was going to ask you later, but this will work." He opened the tote and, after peeking inside, grinned. "Cake."

They spent the next hour cleaning up the supplies and the bins. Mia told him about the phone call. She put the last load of linens into the washer and glanced around the kitchen. Christina was showing Trent where to stack the now-clean totes in the side closet. "A place for everything and everything in its place," she repeated her tidy kitchen mantra.

A face framed by two dirty hands peered inside the window insert in the door. Mia heard the doorknob click and hit the lock. She picked up her phone and opened the camera app. She walked over to the door and started snapping pictures. The man started backward and stepped away from the door, which gave Mia an even better picture. She kept taking shots as she called for Christina and Trent. "Christina, call 9-1-1. Tell them we have someone trying to break in. Trent, go around the front and see if you can detain him."

"Detain who?" Trent asked as he walked back into the kitchen. Mia heard him swear when he saw the guy in the backyard. "I'll go around to the parking lot and cut him off. Christina, call Baldwin."

"Already on it." Christina stepped closer to Mia. "Hello? There's someone trying to break into the kitchen at 4242 Harrison in Magic Springs."

Mia heard someone on the other end of the line announce they were sending a car. She stopped taking pictures and watched as Trent came around the side of the yard. The guy didn't see him, and when Trent approached, he turned and started talking to him. "What the heck?"

"What's going on?" Christina asked, trying to peer around Mia. "Is Trent okay?"

"He's fine. The guy is just talking to him.

Hopefully, he doesn't have a gun or any-thing."

The dispatcher on the other end of the phone asked loudly, "Who has a gun?"

Christina put it on Speaker. "Sorry, no one that we know of. We were just talking. Trent Majors is out back talking to the guy."

"Why in the world is Trent there?" the female dispatcher asked. "Wait, is this the building that houses Mia's Morsels?"

"Yep. We had a break-in a few days ago too. Maybe it's the same guy." Christina looked at Mia. "He looks homeless."

"Yes, he does." Mia stepped closer to the doorway. She almost opened the door but heard the sirens out front. "Christina, stay here. I'll go meet the police."

The officers were just getting out of the car when she opened the front door.

"You're having a bad week over here." One of the officers waved at her. Mia recognized him from when he was part of the team that found Denny's body. "Where's the action?"

"Yes, I am." Mia pointed to the back. "He's behind the building, talking to Trent. I might have overreacted, but . . ."

The officer nodded to his partner, who took off running. "No worries. We weren't busy anyway. I'd say it's been slow this week, except I've been out here several times."

"Don't remind me." Mia rubbed her arms. She wasn't cold, but for some reason she had a chill. She looked up to the third floor. A shape stood in the window. Grans and Cindy must be back already.

She started to step toward the officer when she saw Grans's car pull up. Cindy was sitting in the front with her. Mia looked back up at the window. There was no shadow. And she realized the apartment didn't look over the front. It looked over the backyard. That window was in the storage area without a key. No one should be up there.

Mia froze for a second. No one was up there that could have caused a shadow that Mia would have seen. She decided she was going to get into the storage room sooner rather than later.

The police officers, Trent, and the man who'd been peering into her kitchen all came out from the back of the house. The man was in cuffs, but he didn't seem to be fighting the officers.

The one who'd talked to her earlier nodded to the car and the other one took the man by the arm and tried to lead him away. The man leaned into him and stared at Mia.

"The man said you had money hidden in the kitchen. Money I could have if I found it. It was a game."

Trent stopped and stood beside her. "Like hide-and-seek."

"Yeah, yeah, like that. Grocery man gets it." The homeless man narrowed his eyes at Mia. "But you were supposed to be gone. The man said you'd packed up. Left town. Left the money in the kitchen. He said it could be mine."

"What man?" Mia asked.

The guy shook his head. "The man. You know. He lives on Drury Lane."

"Come on, dude, let's get you buckled in for the ride." The officer who'd been in charge of him pulled him away from the group and into the car. He secured his seat belt, then closed the door.

Waving a hand in front of his face, the officer grimaced. "I guess it's five o'clock somewhere."

"Almost five here. If he'd waited a few more minutes, we'd be off shift. Sorry he bothered you, but he's all but confessed to breaking into your kitchen earlier this week." The officer pulled out his card. "I'll call you when the chief decides what he's going to do with him, but at least he'll be able to dry out in jail. Maybe he'll make more sense then."

"Bob, Rich, thank you for coming so quickly." Trent held out a hand and shook both officers' hands.

"No problem, Trent." Bob, the one who'd been chatting all this time eyed Mia for a second. "You all have a good day."

By this time Grans and Cindy were out of the car with bags in their hands. Grans came up and watched the police cruiser leave. "I take it that's our vandal?"

"It would appear that way. Otherwise Magic Springs has a man in custody whose only crime is peeking inside houses," Trent said as his gaze followed the cruiser disappearing into the tree-lined street.

"Well, let's go inside and get dinner set up. Mia, is the kitchen downstairs cleaned?" Grans started taking charge of things. Something she'd learned early in her life, according to Grans. You did what you needed to do to get by. And that usually involved a lot of cooking and meals. Which was all right with Mia.

"Cleaned, but I'm going to have to finish a few loads of laundry." Mia sighed. "If it had been just the two of us, we still would be cleaning. But Trent lent a hand."

"Oh, really? You should eat dinner with us so we can pay you back." Grans moved toward the door. "I'd love to sit and talk, but I'm thinking my dog needs to go out."

Christina bounded over and took Grans's packages. "I'll take him out. I love having a dog around. Someday, when I get settled, I'm getting one. I just have to figure out what breed I want."

Mia glanced around as she watched the three disappear into the house. "Well, I guess it's just you and me. Grans is right, you should come to dinner. You did a lot today."

"I would, but I have a business meeting with the folks. They like to look over the books once a month to make sure I'm not stealing them blind." He nodded to the door. "I could come in and help you finish, though."

Mia waved her hand at him. "Don't bother. Like I said, all I have is laundry left. If the washer and dryer have finished, I can transfer a load and put the last one in the washer. Easy peasy."

He leaned down and kissed her. "I'm glad the event went well today. Magic Springs needs someone like you and your business."

"Well, just keep sending them my way. I've got room for more catering. Although I think I'm going to schedule a cooking class weekly, so people can try out the food before they decide to shower me with orders." She patted his chest. "Thanks for the rescue today."

"I think the cops were there before he even had a chance to wish me harm." He shook his head. "I never get to have any fun."

"I guess it depends on what you think of as fun." She leaned up and kissed him again. "Seriously, thanks for the assist today. I think we make a really good team."

"You're not including Christina in that, right? Because she made me do all the hard stuff just cuz I'm a guy." He glanced up at the door. "Just don't tell her I said that."

"What? Are you afraid of her?"

He held up his hand and measured out less than an inch for her. "A little."

"Well, get out of here then." Mia waved him off the porch. "I'll see you tomorrow for dinner. What time?"

"Be ready at six. Maybe we'll take a drive before." He lifted a hand before getting into his truck. "Tell Christina I was sorry I had to leave."

"Whatever." Mia laughed as she went inside. As soon as she closed the door, she realized they'd forgotten to open the third-floor locked door. She glanced out the window, but Trent was already gone. It had been a pretty crazy day. She'd talk to him about coming over next weekend. And she'd forgotten about the call. Anyway, Grans and Cindy were safe here. It had probably been a prank call, or one of John's friends being funny. But that couldn't be right, because Mia was quite sure that John Louis couldn't have any friends.

She went into the kitchen, switched out the laundry, and folded the clean linens. Then she made double sure the door to the backyard was locked and turned off the lights before locking the door to the rest of the building.

The good thing about buying an old, abandoned schoolhouse? It had a lot of room. The bad thing? It had a lot of rooms and ways to access the building. Mia decided she'd work on the sign design tonight and see if there was anyone local who could do it for her. Trent might know someone. She'd ask him tomorrow.

She stopped in her office to grab her current planning notebook. She went through those things like they were paper towels. She bought the spiral notebooks when they were on sale at back-to-school time, or when they found their way to the clearance rack. This one was a plain red spiral, but she loved writing out her schedules and making future plans on the pages. That way, if something changed — say, for example, the person you were catering a birthday party for wound up dead — you could just rip out that page and make a new plan.

She walked upstairs to the apartment, thinking she might be going through a lot of pages tonight before she settled on a design for the sign.

At her apartment door she paused and glanced right to the locked door. *It must have been a shadow.* She took a step toward the now-open door. Maybe Trent had unlocked it already and, in the chaos, had forgotten to tell her.

She set the notebook and pens on the floor in the hallway and pulled out her phone, setting it on Camera. Slowly, she stepped into the room. Large windows on the front side of the house let in light, but it was filtered through dirty panes. Dust mites danced in the dim sunlight that did break through. The room seemed to be L-shaped. She walked through the narrow hall, glancing at the years of school pictures in old frames on the walls. As the years increased, so did the number of students and teachers in the photos. Then the opposite happened, and by the time the hallway stopped, the number of people in the pictures had dwindled. The last picture showed only twenty people. More adults than kids. Kind of mirroring the first picture.

Welcome to the age of expanding free public schools, Mia thought. For a while, a lot of kids came to St. Catherine's because it was the only school in Magic Springs. When they opened an elementary school in Ketchum, rather than bussing all the kids down to Twin Falls, St. Catherine's probably lost a bunch of the local kids. She turned the corner and ran right into someone who was large. Big chest, tall, massive shoulders. She closed her eyes and screamed.

CHAPTER 14

Mia stopped screaming and took a breath. No arms surrounded her. The man was just standing there. She realized her fingers were touching fur. Was he wearing a fur coat? In this heat? And in a part of the school with no air conditioning?

She opened her eyes and met the glassy-eyed gaze of a large grizzly bear. He was stuffed to look real, even down to his teeth, which sparkled in the dim sunlight. "The better to eat you with, my dear," Mia quipped. What on earth was a stuffed bear doing in here?

She gingerly stepped away from the bear and glanced around at the space. It was filled with mementos from the old school. Old student desks, larger wooden ones for the teachers. All kinds of chairs. Bookcases filled with textbooks and, she found out when she reached out to pull one from the shelf, a lot of what she'd call chapter books and other books. It looked like this was the library when the school was open. Now, it had turned into a storage room.

She glanced out the window and looked down on her front lawn and the edge of the parking lot nearby. The room would make an amazing den. Leave the bookcases and probably a lot of the books, add some leather furniture, a stereo system, and a television. Add a desk to write or work at and this would be heaven.

She decided she'd talk to Grans about the stored furniture. She'd bought the building, but did all the stuff also belong to her?

As she turned to leave, she saw footprints in the dust by the window. Prints she hadn't made. She measured her foot against a print. It was much larger. So maybe she'd seen an actual person up here, not a possible ghost. And if so, who? Everyone who should be in the house had been downstairs with her.

She snapped a picture of the footprint and then set down her water bottle next to it to show the actual size ratio. Someone had been in her house. And it hadn't been the homeless man. If she'd been a betting type, she would have said John Louis. That answer shouldn't even give her odds.

She took a few more pictures, then, after

making sure the door wouldn't just relock, pulled it shut and grabbed her notebook. Now she had even more to think about and plan. Including getting a new lock put on the soon-to-be library door.

Mia was met outside by Christina. She'd poked her head out of the apartment and was looking around. When she caught sight of Mia coming from the other side of the hallway, she relaxed and opened the door wider. "There you are."

Walking inside the apartment, Mia glanced at her assistant. "What's going on?"

Blushing, Christina shrugged. "I thought I heard a scream, but I wasn't sure. I was in my room reading, and Grans and Cindy didn't hear anything, so I was just wondering where you were."

"I was in the storage room, or I guess I should call it the library. The space is amazing. It's got floor-to-ceiling bookshelves. Hold on, let me show you." She set the notebook on the couch and opened her phone to show Christina the pictures.

She scrolled through the snaps, then looked toward the wall where the storeroom met the kitchen. "This is what was behind the locked door? There's a lot of crap stuffed in there. Is that a bear?"

"Yep. A stuffed grizzly. That was the cause

of the scream. I ran straight into him. I'm wondering if we should move him down-stairs to the lobby."

Christina shivered. "I'd move him out the door and down the street. Maybe the Lodge would want it."

"You don't like bears?"

"Not at all. And is that a picture of one of the students near the bookshelves?"

Mia frowned. She hadn't seen any pictures other than the ones in the hallway, and she hadn't taken pictures of those, had she? "Let me see."

Christina handed her the phone, and standing between the bookshelves and the old desk was a young girl dressed in old-fashioned clothes. She hadn't looked into the camera, but even from the poor quality of the pictures, Mia knew. She was a ghost.

"I don't think that's a picture." Mia glanced up at Christina, wondering how much she really wanted to know. "I believe she's a spirit."

"Seriously? Maybe you should have built a business kitchen in town and rented a normal house to live in." Christina glanced at her watch. "I'm running out for a while."

"Spending some time with Levi?"

Christina shook her head. "No, just drinks with Bethanie. Levi and I — well, I think we're on a break."

"Is that what you want?" Mia could see the tears forming in Christina's eyes.

She grabbed her jacket and a tote. "I don't know what I want. Except a beer right now. I won't be out late, so don't finish cleaning the kitchen without me. I'll be there first thing in the morning to work."

"Everyone deserves some time off," Mia reminded her.

Christina stopped at the door and turned toward her. "Exactly my point. You work too hard."

"Go have fun."

Mia grabbed her notebook and the phone and took them to the kitchen. Grans and Cindy were working with their heads down, studying the grimoire. "I guess you still haven't found a reversal spell?"

"We haven't found the spell she activated yet. We thought we had, but when we tried to replicate it, it had a different focus." Grans looked over at Cindy.

Mia covered the laugh that came out with a cough. Cindy's hair was a light pink. "Oh, I see."

"Don't laugh. It was deep purple a few hours ago. We've got it toned down a bit since then." Cindy reached up and touched a lock. "I have to say, though, it feels softer.

Maybe pink is my color."

"I just don't know if the spell will let you color it, so unless all your future acting parts are okay with pink hair, we might want to totally disperse the spell." Grans pointed to the oven. "There's a meatloaf and scalloped potatoes staying warm in the oven. Christina said she'd reheat some when she got back, so can we push back dinner to seven?"

"That works. I need to talk to you, though. Do you think we could carve out some time tomorrow?" Mia knew her grandmother. If she tried to talk now, Grans would never hear her. And she needed some answers: about the new library's stored items, and a deeper talk about what her grandmother was keeping from her.

"Sure. Cindy's a late sleeper" — Grans smiled at the woman so she would know it didn't really bother her — "so we can chat during breakfast. I probably should head back home to check on things tomorrow for a few hours too. Maybe I have some books that will help us."

"Oh, that would be awesome." Cindy sighed. "It's all so overwhelming. You would have thought that Father would have at least tried to train me in all this."

Mr. Darcy let out a yowl that made Mia and the other women at the table jump. He took off from his spot on the window seat and ran to the back of the apartment. Mr. Darcy was having a bad day, but at least he'd returned and Mia didn't have to worry about him.

"Oh my, I guess he had somewhere to be," Cindy said, watching the hallway.

More likely he was objecting because he had tried to train you. Mia exchanged a look with Grans, who nodded. She'd been thinking the same thing. "Anyway, I've got some work to do, so I'm going to head to my room."

"I'll knock on your door if you're not back out before dinner," Grans said, then she turned back to the spell book.

Mia wondered as she wandered back to her room to do some sketching if Grans felt closer to Dorian as she paged through his spell book. It must be hard to grieve when the guy was sleeping on the window seat next to you all day.

Relationships were hard, as both Grans and Christina were finding out this week. On the other hand, Mia had a date with Trent to look forward to. A smile curved her lips. Trent was easy to be with. Funny and smart. Easy to talk to. She could do a lot worse — and had.

Mia stepped into her room and settled on

the bed. It was time to plan. An hour later she had a reasonably clear sign that she liked. And a few alternatives in case her first option was too expensive to build. She wanted the sign in white, with the open hours on a removeable section on the top, if possible. She'd have to ask Trent about it. Then she wanted spotlights installed that would light up the sign at night. That would probably be expensive, but she thought it would look good. Classy. Like a Southern teahouse. She turned the page and started to draw out her new library, but the homeless man's words kept circling in her head. The man, the man who lived on Drury Lane. Why did that sound familiar?

She pulled out the tablet she kept in her room for reading and watching TV shows and did an Internet search for the words. No Drury Lane in Magic Springs. Or in Sun Valley. She tried Boise too, but no luck. She was about to put away the tablet and go back to the library planning when she glanced farther down on the list and noticed a children's rhyme.

She opened the link and nodded. That was why it had seemed familiar. It was a kid's song about the muffin man. Did the guy who told him about the free money look like a baker? Or have a stomach that looked like a muffin? Or maybe smelled like muffins? Or — Mia froze — had he brought the guy muffins to pay for his time?

Mia nodded; that was probably it. Whoever had told him about the imaginary money being hidden in the kitchen had brought him muffins.

She texted Baldwin about her muffin man theory and the song, and then went back to thinking about her new library. The footprints had bothered her. Maybe Trent had gone into the room and that was why she'd seen the footprints. It had been a crazy afternoon. He could have forgotten to tell her.

She put away the thought for tomorrow when he picked her up. She'd call him, but he was at his folks' for dinner. She didn't want to bother him. Not for this.

She drew a floor plan of the library, using the pictures she'd taken. It would be a lovely addition to the apartment. And, if she was right, she could install a door between the back kitchen wall into the room. Maybe someday, when the business was stronger financially, she could expand the kitchen into the area as well. Just not now, not with her bank account. She was doing good keeping the lights and heating bill paid with the catering jobs she snagged. Soon the business would be busier. It took time. And the takeout portion was booming already. She might have to hire someone just for that sooner rather than later. At least someone to do the deliveries. As it was, she was stretched doing deliveries once a week.

She turned the page and started thinking about what she could make if she expanded that section of the business. She was knee-deep in calculations when a knock sounded at her door. She finished this one last note, then called, "Come in."

"Dinner's ready, dear." Her grandmother crossed over to the bed, where she glanced at Mia's notebook. "As quiet as it was in here, I assumed you'd fallen asleep."

"No, I'm just daydreaming." She turned the pages back to her sign drawing. "What do you think?"

"I love it. Lighting it at night would be amazing so if we did evening events here, people could see where we are." Grans pointed to the top of the sign. "It would look more Southern if you added some flourishes on top and on the side."

"Yeah, you're right." Mia added some curls at the sides. "But I want to put a changeable Hours Open sign on top, where people can see it."

"It could hang underneath if you moved

the sign up a little," Grans pointed out.

Mia stood and left the notebook sitting on the bed. "I know, but I really wanted it at the top. I have to find someone to build it; maybe they can tell me if it's possible. Oh, and we might have a ghost issue in the new library."

"I can't believe this place is so attractive to the other side. Why do you think there's a ghost in the library?" Grans sank onto Mia's bed as she gave her the phone, queued up to the picture of the library.

Mia watched as her grandmother studied the picture, then handed the phone back to her. "Well?"

"It's possible. We need to get in there to see if we can call up anything. I don't like dealing with spirits I don't know. Let's go eat, and Cindy can fill you in on what we found." Grans left the bedroom and Mia followed.

The table was already set and the food had been served family style. Mia slipped into her seat and sent a big thank you to the Goddess for the meal. She turned to Cindy. "Grans said you had a breakthrough. What's going on?"

"We think we found the spell. I'm going to try to break it tomorrow, and then I can finally go home. Magic Springs's nice and all, but I'm missing my own bed."

"Did you deal with the estate and property issues?" Mia dished up scalloped potatoes, one of her favorite dishes. She made a recipe just like this, but hers had a touch of sriracha for a little spice.

"I stopped by the real estate office of that low life Louis and told him to stop harassing me or any of mine or I'd sue him. We'll see where that takes us. At least he knows now he can't lowball us and get away with it. I'm not stupid. I shouldn't have agreed to meet with him without Mike. Now he thinks we're partners in crime or something." Cindy took a bite of the meatloaf. "I'm really going to have to watch what I eat when I get home. I bet I'm up five pounds."

"Stress will do that to you. You should go get a massage when you get home and wash away the emotions for a while." Mia was long past what she considered her tune-up. She should schedule herself, Christina, and Grans for a spa day for the girls. It could be fun. Maybe next week.

"Earth to Mia. Did you hear my question?" Grans was staring at her. She'd only tuned out for a few minutes, but apparently that had been long enough to be caught.

She shook her head. "Sorry, no."

"What are you going to do with that area? Maybe it would be better if you just kept it locked up." Grans didn't meet Mia's gaze and she could tell she was hiding from something.

"Are you kidding?" Mia looked incredulously at her grandmother. "Even if we don't use the space, we need to deal with the spirit. Whoever lived or died there is stuck between worlds. We need to help them."

"Maybe someone's tried before and they can't get out? Isn't trying again just cruel?" Her grandmother glanced at Cindy, who seemed to be on her phone. She shook her head, asking for Mia to let it go.

Mia let the subject drop and they finished dinner listening to Cindy's boring stories about the ins and outs of a television actress. Stories that, apparently, she'd told before, because Grans corrected her when she went off the script from the version she had told her already. Mia wondered if Grans had blocked Cindy's awareness of the ghost conversation.

When the dishes were done, Cindy disappeared into her bedroom. Grans nodded at Muffy and told the dog that she'd take him for a short walk.

"I'll come with you." Mia followed them out of the apartment, tucking her keys into her jeans.

"Oh, if you want to take him . . ." Grans started, but Mia pointed to the stairs.

"I've been trying to talk to you for days now. We have some time; you can tell me why the library is freaking you out. You want me to be protected, right? How can I be if I don't have all the information?"

Grans didn't talk as she made her way down the stairs. When she reached the bottom, she clipped the leash onto Muffy's collar and handed the lead to Mia. "You walk him, I'll talk."

They left the building and wound their way down the driveway to the county road. One way led into town, the other out to the riverbank. Mia let Grans lead. She took the river walk.

"I need to tell you a story about the house. First of all, I don't think this has anything to do with the dead guy or the break-in." Grans looked around the empty sidewalk as if she expected to see someone following them.

"Denny Blake. The dead guy's name was Denny," Mia corrected her. She needed to call Baldwin to see if he'd identified the homeless man who'd broken into her house. Names had power, and she needed all the information she could get in this situation.

211

"You're right. Denny Blake, sorry." Grans tucked her hands into the jacket she'd grabbed when they'd reached the front door. "This goes back before my time at the school. There was a death."

"The girl who left through the tunnel?" Mia had heard that story before.

Grans shook her head. "No, long before that. I don't think it was ever solved, and officially, no one ever talked about it. Which meant, of course, that everyone at school did. The girl was found in the library. She'd been choked. She was only fourteen. And she was a scholarship kid."

"What, did that mean she wasn't important?" Mia didn't like where this was going.

Grans shook her head. "No, it was supposed to mean she wasn't from a magical family. Most of the kids who attended the academy were from families who were in the coven. Daisy was just a normal girl. At least, that's what people thought."

"She had power?"

Grans nodded. "Enough to curse her killer. It's said that the killer's family would be stricken from magic forever. Now, there were several kids each year who didn't pass the magical part of the exams. But that always happened. Even before Daisy's curse. Now the story and the curse have been all but forgotten."

"So why are we talking about this?" Mia was lost. She didn't know why her guardian would want her to know this story. Maybe Grans had gotten it wrong.

"When Dorian and I started dating he brought up the curse and Daisy's death. He'd done some genealogy, and he thought our family was tangentially related to Daisy. She was a great-great-great-aunt, according to Dorian." Grans nodded to the bench where the river trail started. "Can we sit?"

"Of course, but Grans, what does this have to do with anything?"

Grans put her hand on Mia's arm. "Because Dorian thought there was a faction of the coven that was trying to break the curse."

"Okay, so how is the curse broken?" Mia figured she knew but needed to hear it from her grandmother.

"A descendant from Daisy's line has to die. Dorian thought the coven might be going after you."

CHAPTER 15

Mia sat on the bench watching Muffy sniff the grass while the river gently bubbled around rocks and waterfalls in front of them. She thought about what her grandmother was saying, but she couldn't believe it. "Grans, there's no way anyone thinks that killing someone will end a curse from years ago. If they even believed in the curse."

"There are powers at work that we can't control, Mia. I made a mistake bringing you here. After Dorian died I read his journal. He's been studying our family for years. He wondered why we only dealt with the softer, home-based magic."

"Why we call ourselves kitchen witches," Mia supplied.

Grans sighed. "Exactly. What I'd been told by my grandmother was we were different for a reason. That we had turned our back on the darker magic that can eat at a practitioner. That our family was here to help the world stay in the light. To never be tempted by the larger spells that came with my grimoire. We have the spells and the power to do anything, Mia. We choose not to go there."

"I just can't see anyone holding a grudge that long." Mia shook her head. "It doesn't make sense."

"It does if their power had been taken away. If one of us paid the price for the curse, it would mean the descendants of the killer would be unbound. That they could cast again." Grans took a book out of her coat pocket. "This is Dorian's journal. You need to read it before you try to talk to that ghost in the library. I don't know if it's Daisy or the witch who killed her, hanging around because of her guilt. But you need to be armed. And Dorian had a lot of information."

"Do you think that's why he started courting you?"

Grans laughed. "For the inside information? No, dear. Dorian could have gotten that just by asking. He and I had a strong bond. That's one of the reasons he's being stubborn about leaving poor Mr. Darcy."

"He opened the door with magic a few days ago," Mia told her.

Muffy came and sat at Grans's feet, done

with her wandering. Grans reached down absently and scratched behind the dog's ears. "I was afraid that would start to happen. Dorian was too strong not to have a little magic left."

The frogs began to sing from the riverbank, and Mia realized that dusk was settling in on them. "Maybe we should head back; it gets dark quickly."

Grans stood and took Mia's arm. "Now don't you worry. Dorian felt like the chances anyone would come after you were slight, he just thought it was prudent for us to talk about it." Grans paused for a minute before they crossed the street to follow the sidewalk back to the schoolhouse. She studied Mia's face in the gathering darkness. "You're a strong practitioner. I feel the magic in all you do, not just your discussions with the Goddess about food and community."

"Is that a good or bad thing?" Mia asked her grandmother.

Before she could answer, Muffy started barking, and Mia realized there was a dark form walking toward them. And they would meet before the turn off for the driveway. Mia knew she could sprint to the house, but Grans? No way. She reached down to touch the can of pepper spray she kept on her keychain. It was a one-time-use type, but it would do the trick if someone meant them harm. As long as it hadn't dried out or been damaged when she'd got it. Isaac had bought it for her because she'd worked long hours catering. It had been an easy way to seem like he was protective without doing something that would disturb his sleep. Like picking her up or even waiting up for her on those nights.

Pushing down the negative thought, she took a deep breath. Stating that you forgave someone and living it were two totally different things. Besides, she had an urgent issue before her. Was it just a random person, strolling down the street for their evening walk, or was it something more sinister? With the week she'd had, she wouldn't be surprised if a cartoon character from one of her favorite Saturday morning shows greeted her in a few seconds.

The barking continued until the dark figure knelt and called out, "Muffy, come see me. Come here, sweet boy."

Muffy ran out to the end of his leash, and Mia realized that the figure was Christina. She blew out a shaky breath that turned into a short laugh. "Christina, you're home early."

She stood up and walked over to take Muffy's leash from Grans. "I told you it was just a couple of drinks. Bethanie wanted to gripe about her boss. She's tired of being treated like an assistant. He sends her on personal errands all the time. She has to pick up his dry cleaning and take it to his wife at the house. And she's doing the grocery shopping, because Carol is busy with some society thing. And it's not just going to Majors. She has to go to the bakery, the fruit stand, and the meat market as well."

"Sounds like she's acting like an assistant," Grans said.

"Yeah, but Bethanie thought she'd be helping with real estate stuff. She wants to get her license and work in Sun Valley with all the big dogs. I told her she needed to learn the ropes first. I mean, that would be like me just opening up my own breakfast bar and expecting to know how to cook eggs." Christina chatted all the way up the driveway. "She's just impatient."

"And I bet working for John Louis isn't the most pleasant environment," Mia added as she opened the front door.

"Ha, that's an understatement. She says he's really moody. He yelled at someone on the phone a few days ago. Something about not following through on a contract. Bethanie said he was hot." Christina gave Mia a quick hug after letting Muffy off the leash.

"What was that for?" Mia smiled as she locked the front door and set the alarm.

Christina paused in the middle of the first flight of stairs. "For being easy to work with. Bethanie's job reminds me of what my life could be if I had to work with Isaac. You saved me from my crazy family."

Mia watched as the young woman bounded up the stairs to the apartment, Muffy on her heels.

Grans put a hand on Mia's arm as they walked slowly up the stairs. "The girl's not wrong, you know. You did take one good thing out of that relationship. And she's already upstairs reheating her dinner."

"Christina isn't Isaac," Mia said, but her thoughts were on curses and family dynamics. She'd start reading Dorian's journal tonight. Maybe that would help her figure out what was going on in her house.

Mia hadn't found out anything by the time she found herself yawning in her bed a few hours later. Dorian was painstakingly detailed about every part of his life. Which meant she'd gone through pages and pages about his import business and his traveling. Being detailed didn't mean it wasn't interesting and — she smiled as she set the book on the table — he had been funny and intelligent. It was hard to believe all that was left of him was currently stuck in her cat. And, worse, was watching her read as he sat on the bed.

She reached over and rubbed Mr. Darcy's head before turning off her reading light. "Good night, Mr. Darcy. Good night, Dorian. Sleep well."

The next morning she stayed in bed longer than usual. She had no plans today except finishing laundry and planning next week's schedule. She thought about reading more of Dorian's journal, but she really wanted some coffee. If she could get in and out of the kitchen without anyone noticing, she'd come back to bed to read. If not, it was a sign she should get up. The Goddess liked sending signs. Or at least that was the way her life felt to Mia. She was always looking for the next sign to know what to do. Coffee first, plan the day next.

She almost got out of the kitchen without running into anyone. A sleepy Christina had Muffy in her arms and was heading to the front door when she ran into her in the hallway. "Good morning."

"Yeah, whatever. Muffy has decided that waking up your grandmother to go outside is rude and because I'm young, he's picked me as his personal assistant," Christina groused. She smelled Mia's coffee. "Can I snatch that and take it down with me? Please?"

"Sure, I can make another one. It's black, though." Mia handed over her coffee.

"That will work. I'm trying to cut down on the sugar. Bethanie says it messes with your chi. Of course, she's always buying herself crap at the bakery when she runs errands." Christina opened the apartment door. "She's one of those listen-to-what-I-say-not-what-I-do kind of people."

"Thanks for taking Muffy out," Mia called after her.

She went back to the kitchen and made a second cup of coffee. This time, no one met her there or in the hallway, and she got back to her room with her coffee intact. Curling back up in bed, she opened the journal and continued reading.

A knock on the door brought her out of the book. "Come in."

Christina came in, dressed in jeans and a tank. "Hey. I just wanted to let you know I was going downstairs to get that last load of laundry done. Then you can relax today."

"Thanks. I could have done it." Mia glanced at her empty cup. She'd been reading for a while.

"Not a biggie. I've got a lot of energy today. Levi's coming by later and we're going for a hike." Christina came inside Mia's bedroom and plopped down on the bed. Fingering the quilt, she sighed.

"Are you worried about the date?"

Christina shrugged. "Maybe. I just don't want to get in too deep and then find out he's not the one, you know, like you and Isaac."

"Isaac was never the one. I should have known that early in the relationship, but I kept excusing away all the things that bothered me. You know who you are and I've never known you to do the easy thing. Even with your parents and your future. You could be in some swank college sorority right now, getting ready for the spring formal, not worried about working for another two or more years." Mia knew Christina was strong. Christina just needed to know that.

"That's true. I would have had salon appointments today to be pampered before going out with some doofus my mom would love because of the family name and money." Christina glanced at her nails, which were sans polish but clean. "Bethanie would have loved being friends with that girl."

"Bethanie *is* that girl. Levi isn't a doofus, though sometimes, like all men, he's a little dense. Don't give up on him so quickly. You two hit it off really fast. Maybe it's time to step back and get to know each other, so you can trust each other too." Mia stretched her arms, the journal upside down on her lap.

"You're a fountain of wisdom today, Mia." Christina bounced up off the bed and headed for the door. "If you want my opinion on what you're wearing for your date tonight, let me know before eleven. That's when Levi's picking me up. I'm not sure I'll be back before six. I might score a free dinner out of this hike as well."

Mia glanced at the bedside table. It was already nine and way past time for her to get going. With Christina handling the laundry and her talk with Grans dealt with last night, she already had two things off her to-do list. Now to finish the journal, plan next week, and figure out what she needed to do about the library. Oh, and figure out who was trying to wreck her business.

After grabbing a muffin and another cup of coffee, she headed downstairs to deal with next week's orders and planning. She turned on the answering machine to listen to the missed calls. She had two more events that needed to be scheduled if she was staying in business. Odd way to put it, but Mia took down the information and called the numbers back to confirm. Both were businesses, so they'd be closed until Monday, but she'd get her acceptance in their hands as soon as someone listened to the message.

She marked off the days on the calendar and then worked with the calendar to set up classes. She'd been adding names bit by bit and sale by sale to her contact list for the newsletter she'd been planning. Now she needed to reach out and actually give them the newsletter that had been promised for a few months.

She wrote about what was going on at the schoolhouse and Mia's Morsels. Leaving out the break-ins and the dead guy in the back, of course. She thought that wouldn't sell food very well.

She sent the newsletter to Grans and Christina, asking them to proofread the thing. Once she got that done, she'd read it again and hit Send. What could it hurt? She glanced at her calendar and set up a recurring Newsletter Reminder to pop up once a month. She'd question the frequency later. If it wasn't being sent on an effective schedule, it didn't keep people invested.

She was just finishing up the week's shopping list when she realized it was already close to five. Where had the day gone? She locked up the office and glanced at the kitchen door. Just to reassure herself, she unlocked the door and did a walk-through. No one was in there. Christina had finished the last of the laundry, as she'd said she was going to do, and everything was in order.

Mia let out a breath and was just about to check the back door when she saw someone in the backyard. Over by where she was planning on putting in the herb garden. Or had been before they'd found Denny there. She couldn't see the person's face, so she double-checked the locks and then went out the other door. Quickly locking it too, she put her cell in one pocket of her jacket and her keys in the other and went out the front door.

She ran around the house to the back and right up to the tree that indicated the start of the garden border. No one was there. No figure. No person. Nothing.

Glancing around the yard, she didn't see anyone at all. How could someone have disappeared so quickly?

She heard a noise coming from the front of the building and ran back around. Trent was just getting out of his truck. He saw her and waved, but must have seen something on her face because he hurried over to her side. "What's wrong?"

She glanced around the parking lot that held her beat-up van, Trent's pickup, and her grandmother's car. Other than those three items, the lot was empty. There was no one out here.

She felt Trent's hand on her shoulder.

"Mia? What's wrong?" he asked a second time.

She looked up at him and shook her head. "I was in the kitchen right now and I swore I saw someone in the backyard. But when I came around, they were gone. How could they have just disappeared?"

He looked at her and then pointed to the house. "Go inside and check out the chemistry lab. I'll go check out the tunnel. Be careful; he might be in the house."

CHAPTER 16

No one was in the house. The room where the secret passage entered the house still had the double locks sealed. Mia unlocked the one from the room to the rest of the house. Then she moved stealthily toward the second barrier, the door and lock to the actual passage. It was undamaged. When she tested the doorknob, the lock was still engaged. She listened to see if she could hear any sounds and jumped when her phone rang. "Hello?"

"I'm in the tunnel at the bottom of the stairs. I can see the door, but no one's here." His voice crackled on the speaker. "What do you see?"

"Nothing. The locks were still engaged. I checked the barrier door, and it's solid." She sighed. "Maybe I imagined seeing someone?"

"No, I believe you saw someone. I'm sure you scared them away, however." He paused, then continued. "I'm getting out of here. I'll meet you at the front door."

She jiggled the doorknob one more time, just to be sure, then glanced around the classroom. They'd taken most of the chairs out of here, so only the desk and the chemistry lab stands remained. No one was here. She walked out of the room and relocked it. If anyone was somehow hiding in here, she had them boxed in now. She hurried downstairs to meet Trent.

He stood there on the porch, dust and spiderwebs all over his hair and clothes. "I'm a mess. And it feels like I've got cobwebs all over me."

"That's because you do." She opened the door wider to let him inside. "Maybe we should cancel tonight."

"Are you kidding? Just because someone's playing games with you? You're stronger than that." He shook his head and used his hands to brush off any loose cobwebs or dirt on his clothes before he came inside. "I'll take out a broom and clean off your porch before we leave."

"Okay, but I'm fine with rescheduling if we need to."

He leaned in and kissed her. "We don't need to. It might have been someone from the trails. And you do have a habit of seeing the local spirits. Are you sure it wasn't one of those?"

Mia thought. She'd only gotten a glance at the figure. "It looked like a normal person."

"Man, woman?" Trent pressed.

Mia shook her head. "I was trying to get a better look, but I wanted to surprise them too. So I just took off running to see if I could catch them."

He shrugged. "I'd give you a hug, but I feel gross right now. Go get ready for dinner and I'll get cleaned up. Are there towels in the bathroom down here?"

"Yes, the gym bathrooms have walk-in showers and towels." She felt her face heat. "I was hoping to put an indoor swimming pool in the gym area, or at least a hot tub. But I've got to get the business settled first."

He grinned at her. "Sounds like fun. I'll give you some pool contractor names to get you an estimate. And if you do it off season because it's indoors, I bet they'll cut the cost so it might just be affordable this year."

"You're assuming I'm going to stay in business. If someone doesn't stop telling people I'm closing, I won't have any business." She tapped her finger on her lips. "I should call Elizabeth back. Maybe she'd remembered where she heard the rumor."

He took her arm and moved her toward the stairs. "Go get ready. You're doing Elizabeth's library thing next week. You can grill her then. And a lot of residents are attending, so you could just make an announcement when she calls you up to thank you for catering the event."

"You know, sometimes you have really great ideas." She kissed him lightly on the lips, not wanting to get too close to the dirt and grime. "I'll see you in fifteen."

"Perfect. I'll wait down here if I get done first." He nodded to the couch set Mia had bought for the lobby area. "I've got a few things I can handle on my phone if you need more time."

"I'm probably faster at getting ready than you are." She took in his clothes. "Casual, but not beachwear. I think I know exactly what to wear."

"Will I like it?" His dark eyes danced with humor.

It was her turn to shrug. "I don't know. I guess we'll both be surprised."

She took off up the stairs, leaving him at the bottom, watching her. And he was watching. She could feel his gaze burning through her clothes. Yes, life with Trent was never boring. Mia knew things didn't always stay that way, but for right now, she was happy. At least in her love life. The rest of her life was teetering on the edge, and she was watching with bated breath for what shoe or boot was going to fall next.

She'd been right; she was the first one down in the lobby waiting. Of course, she had the advantage of being in her own apartment. Trent was having to make do with a large, well-stocked, gym-type bathroom. The area was divided into girls and boys, but Mia had only updated one so far. Before the classes got too busy, she needed to get the second bathroom set up a little better. Right now, it was functional, but not remodeled.

Both bathrooms did have the old-fashioned weight scale you'd find in a doctor's office. That was a cool remembrance from the past and the school's history.

She scrolled through her phone and realized she'd missed a call. She hit the Recall button and waited.

A woman answered the phone, her tone upbeat. "Good evening, Magic Springs Winery. Do you wish to make a reservation?"

Mia hung up the phone. Why had someone from the winery called her just a few minutes before the man disappeared in her backyard? Priscilla Powers was the owner/ manager and a coven member. Had she been trying to distract Mia while someone broke in? And if so, why? Mia didn't want to be friends with Priscilla, but she drank wine from the winery, and she used it in her cooking. She even named the wine type when she put it in a recipe or paired it with a meal.

Or had the caller been someone other than Priscilla? That made even less sense, but Mia had the feeling she didn't know all the players in this game. She looked up and Trent stood next to the couch.

"Are you ready?" he asked as if this was a normal, everyday occurrence.

She decided to play along and put the troubles of the last week behind her. There was plenty of time to worry and think, though the one thing she did before standing up was to make a note in her journal about calling Priscilla on Monday. Maybe she could fake a friendly tone for at least a few minutes. Priscilla didn't make small talk easily. Mia tucked her phone and her journal into her tote bag and followed Trent out to the truck.

It was date time.

Except the first thing he did as they drove was apologize. "Look, I know this is date night, but I think you need to hear this."

"Hear what?" Mia assumed it was about the building. Or the feud. Or the guy who broke into her house. Then she stopped. She couldn't assume anything anymore. She smiled at Trent, who'd been watching her. "Sorry, it's been a weird few days."

"I think it's going to get weirder. My mom wants to talk to you."

"What?" The word came out more as a little scream than a question. She hadn't met Trent's parents yet, and with the problems she'd had with her last set of potential in-laws, she'd hoped to keep away from them for a long while.

"Don't freak out. It's not about us. She says she knows something about the building. And the locked room." He turned off the main road and headed out of town. "It will only take a few minutes; then we'll be on our way to dinner and you can order whatever you want because I'll owe you."

"Okay, let's talk about something else so I don't freak out about meeting your mother. Why didn't you tell me you got the storage room door unlocked yesterday?" Mia smoothed down the skirt of her cute, date-appropriate sundress. But maybe the neckline was too low for meet-the-parents night? Too late to worry about that now. The good news was, she'd brought a sweater in case the air in the restaurant was up too high. They always did that. And she always froze. She'd just slip that on before they went in. She realized Trent was watching her again. "What? You don't like my dress?"

"Your dress is fine, but Mia, I didn't open that door. I was going to, but then the guy was at the window and things got a little crazy. Are you saying it's open now? Like all by itself?" He stared at the road again. "That's not good. Mom needs to know this. She told me not to unlock the door. That there were things in there that were locked up for a reason."

A pit gnawed at her stomach. "Christina saw a ghost in one of the pictures. I was trying to ignore it, but I think she was right. Do you think they're in danger at the school? Should we go back?"

"Let's talk to Mom first. She was pretty vague about the 'danger.' I'd hate to scare everyone just because she had a bad feeling." Trent slowed for a turn off the highway and they drove onto a gravel road that ran along a fence line. "Welcome to Majors Ranch. The property runs from this spot on the road all the way back to the Salmon River. There's a great fishing hole back there if you want to fish. Chinook, trout, steelhead, I've caught them all."

"I've never been fishing." Mia pushed away her concern about the library and instead thought about the fish she'd prepared for events. "Maybe I should go see what the product looks like in the wild."

"You mean outside your freezer?" He squeezed her hand.

"Heaven forbid. I never use frozen salmon. Or any other kind of frozen fish. I try not to use anything that can't be sourced regionally. I think food should be fresh when you cook it." She pointed to the mansion coming up in front of them. "Wow. That's some house you grew up in. Just a little ranch, huh?"

"That's not the house I grew up in. Mom and Dad built that a few years ago, after all the kids had left. Which is stupid, because they have enough bedrooms to run a small orphanage." He pulled his truck up on the driveway. "I think Dad's trying to talk Mom into letting him do weekend hunting and fishing retreats. But she likes her quiet."

"You could do that here, no problem." Mia wondered if they'd like to rent it out for events. You could do a wedding here easy. But maybe they just wanted to treat it like a home. If she lived here, that's what she'd do. She wondered, not for the first time, if her pool idea was worth giving up the space for large events. She'd already hosted the reunion for the old school there. Maybe she should just nix the pool idea and upgrade the gym into a ballroom. Then she could do weddings without getting the Lodge involved. It could be a one-stop shop. But would people want to have their wedding in a remodeled gym?

So many decisions and questions to get clarity on before she made a final decision.

"Are you ready? This will be quick. I told my mom we had plans, but we'd stop by for a minute so she could update you on what she thinks she needs to tell you. Listening to her, you would think she'd had a vision from God Himself, giving her a directive." He opened his door and came around to the passenger side to help her out. "Just think of them as normal people. Mostly, that's what they are. It's just that sometimes they let this whole coven thing take over the thinking part of their brains. You'll be fine."

"I think you're trying harder to convince you than me." Mia squeezed his arm. "As long as they don't ask me when I'm going to make an honest man of you, we'll be fine."

"Do we need to have that conversation?"

Trent looked down at her, humor in his eyes.

"I don't know, do we?" Mia smiled back, enjoying the banter. Meeting Trent's parents would be fine. That was nothing to worry about; it was just more history about the school. Which she needed, because the people in her life were being less than up-front. Well, until last night. "Grans and I had a conversation last night about the school too. She thinks the problems stem from a girl who was killed because she wasn't magical."

Trent paused as he opened the front door. "That's almost the story Mom told me last night."

Mia shook her head, wondering what was going on. "At least they aren't contradictory versions."

Trent paused and called out a greeting. "Hey, Mom? We're here."

"In the kitchen, dear," a woman's voice echoed through the hallway.

The house was decorated in high-end Western cabin, if that was even a theme. Mia noticed the statue of a bull rider on a foyer table and, in the living room, a large rock fireplace with leather couches. As they walked through the room, they passed a floor-to-ceiling bookcase filled with a variety of books. Not just up there for show; some of the books looked well loved.

But she fell in love with the house when she reached the oversize kitchen. It had a lovely breakfast nook that was bigger than either of her entire kitchens, in the apartment and in the Boise house she'd owned with Isaac. There were two sets of ovens that bookended the working part of the kitchen. A woman stood by the large island, which was complete with a small sink, peeling potatoes. Mia could see the resemblance right away. She had Trent's hair and smile. Or, actually, he had his mother's hair and smile. Levi must look like his father.

The woman put down the potato and the peeler and wiped her hands on her apron. "Oh my, Mia Malone. I'm so honored to have you in my kitchen."

"Mrs. Majors, I'm happy to be here. Your kitchen is lovely and I'm totally jealous." Mia reached out a hand to shake, but Trent's mom ignored it.

"Put that hand down. We're huggers in the Majors family. And call me Abigail. Trent has told us so much about you. And, of course, Levi says good things as well. It's about time I got to meet the woman who has made such an impression on my boys." Abigail pulled Mia into a hug.

The feeling of hugging Abigail reminded Mia of what it must be like to hug Mrs. Claus. It wasn't that Abigail was soft and fluffy, as Mia expected Mrs. Claus would be; it was more than that. When she hugged you, you felt like everything was going to be okay. No worries. No pain. Just happiness. It must have been amazing, growing up with a mother this loving.

Mia blinked away the tears that wanted to sneak out. What was wrong with her? She cleared her throat. "Trent said you knew something about the old school building I bought?"

"Something? Of course. I attended school there until I went away to college. Oh, there were rumors all the time. We had the normal high-school rumor mill, of course; then there were the rumors that I guess I would say bordered on the supernatural, or maybe you would call it paranormal. I'm not good with the labels." Abigail waved them to the stools. "Please sit. I need to get these potatoes on the stove or dinner will be late. Levi's eating with us tonight."

Mia wondered if that was an invitation to talk about Levi and Christina, but she dodged the jab. "I hate to just drop in on you like this, but Trent said you needed to talk to me?"

"Trent takes care of his responsibilities well." Abigail smiled over at her son.

Mia wasn't quite sure what had just happened between Trent and Abigail, but there had been something. An unspoken agreement. It might have been a casual conversation, but Mia had no doubt she was being watched and judged. She let the silence settle.

Finally, Abigail spoke. "Like I said, I went to the school, probably at the same time as your mother. Theresa Carpenter, right?"

"Yes, she was, I mean *is* my mom."

Abigail shook her head. "Don't worry about it. Once someone gives up the power, it's like they're existing on another plane. That's all your slip meant. So, anyway, when we attended, a girl disappeared. And while she was gone, this story cropped up about a feud between a magical and a nonmagical student. It was said the nonmagical one lost and was sent home to her parents. Disgraced."

"Grans said she was killed," Mia interrupted.

Abigail paused for a second, and Mia could see the years running past in her brain to when she was in school. "Nope, sorry. The girl went home. And it's understood that she was a powerful witch in her own right. Apparently, her heritage hadn't been acknowledged when she came to the school. But she studied the softer spells and turned into what you now call a kitchen witch. Of course, I don't know that she's related to you or your grandmother, but there's been a strange hum in the valley since you've arrived here. I think you've woken something in the house. Something that may be dangerous."

"May be or is?" Mia pressed for an answer. She didn't want to tell her about the discussion she'd had with her grandmother.

"Now that's the question, isn't it? I may just be hearing the clicks of an old clock that stared working again since you're here. Or it could be something more sinister. I just want to make sure you know to be careful. And don't do anything foolish." She rinsed the last potato and put it into the pot. Turning away from them, she put the pot on the stove and turned on the heat underneath. "I'm afraid something will happen around the school. Something that won't be expected and will cause permanent damage to you and your family."

CHAPTER 17

After dinner they were still at the trendy steak house when Trent handed her a dessert menu. "Coffee and what?"

"Something. Maybe two somethings. I can't believe what a week I've had." She studied the menu. "Your mom seems nice."

"She is nice. She's a cloud of sugar and spice. She was always there for us. She did the books for the store for years, but when we came home, it was all about us. What our day was like. Who had practice, music lessons, or Scouts? We were always on the go and she made it all happen. We had treats in the car if we got hungry. Sodas in a cooler in the back. And pizza rolls or something hot if we were all just home doing homework. Kind of a perfect way to grow up." He pointed to a cheesecake. "I want that one. That way I get huckleberry and chocolate. Do you think they bake them that way?"

"No, I'm pretty sure they bake them separate." She laid the menu on the table. "That works for me. If you want to share."

"You get that and I'll get the apple pie à la mode. That way we get three desserts."

Mia rubbed her stomach. "I'm not sure how much I'll be able to eat. I'm stuffed from dinner."

"They have doggy bags here," Trent reminded her. "And we've been so busy lately with stuff, we haven't gone out for a while."

"You were just over at my place, helping unpack," Mia reminded him, even though she thought the three desserts was a perfect way to end the evening. And if you deconstructed it, it was four desserts, because one came with ice cream.

"That wasn't a date. That was work." He smiled at her. "I'm pretty sure the look on your face is because of the idea of desserts and not me, but don't ruin my fantasy."

She put her hand on top of his. "Thank you for this distraction. I needed to get out of the apartment. With Cindy and Grans there, it's a little over the top in the estrogen department."

"Has Cindy realized that Dorian's in Mr. Darcy?" Trent asked after he'd put in their order for coffee and dessert.

"No. She knows he's different for a cat,

but she has no idea her father's in there. Thank the Goddess." Mia rubbed the top of Trent's hand. "I'm going over to the winery tomorrow to talk to Priscilla. Someone called me from their phone. I'm wondering why."

"Maybe they want you to cater an event. Isn't that what you do?" Trent eyed her suspiciously.

"It was right before I saw someone behind my house. Maybe it was the homeless guy. Did you ever find out his name? I hate calling him 'that man.' "

"He'll just say it's Ronnie. No last name. No ID on his person or in his stuff. Baldwin finally got him sober yesterday, but the story is still the same, if just a little less wobbly. Some guy told him you had money hidden in your kitchen. Sober Ronnie knows it's silly, but drunk Ronnie thought he'd hit the jackpot."

"Ronnie, that fits." Mia sipped the coffee the waitress had just set in front of her. She'd probably regret the caffeine later, when she was trying to sleep, but it wasn't every night she got dessert after dinner. "Did he kill Denny?"

Trent shook his head. "No, and he actually has an alibi. He was at the soup kitchen in Boise for the week, helping out. It seems he does that off and on. He gets sober, goes back to his real life, and works with the homeless. Then, the next thing his friends know, he's homeless himself. Except for the fact that he owns a house in Boise just waiting for him to go there."

"Sad." Mia picked up a spoon and took a bite of the chocolate cheesecake as soon as the waitress turned her back after delivering it. "I guess my first suspect is still the best one. When is Baldwin going to arrest John Louis?"

"I guess when he can prove he did something. It's kind of the law." Trent took a bite of the huckleberry cheesecake. "This is heaven."

"I know. I'm really going to have to up my game if I cater desserts around here. These bakers are top-notch." Mia hid a yawn behind her napkin.

"Hey, none of that. Let's get these to-go and I'll get Cinderella back home before she turns into a pumpkin." He waved to the waitress. "Can we get a to-go box and the check?"

"Of course," she murmured and smiled at them. "You two are such a cute couple."

"Thanks," Mia responded, a little shocked. They were just dating; did that make them a couple?

"Stop overanalyzing and enjoy the compliment." Trent tapped the table. "Grab one last bite before she comes back, because you aren't eating in my truck."

"Stop reading my mind." Mia sipped her coffee, hoping it would keep her awake until she got home. She didn't want to fall asleep on his shoulder. Even though that sounded really, really good right now. "You baby that truck like it's a child, not a hunk of metal."

"It is my child." He signed the bill and picked up the dessert takeout box. "Thank you for a lovely evening."

"Oh, you're most welcome. I love visiting new restaurants. It keeps me on my toes when I can't figure out what to do next in my deliveries." Mia had responded automatically, her mind on the school and who killed Denny.

Christina was already in the kitchen when Mia got up on Monday morning. She poured herself a cup of coffee, sat down, and watched her apprentice as she read a cookbook. "Anything good in there?"

"Everything sounds good in here. It's from one of the New Orleans restaurants that have been in business for years. They have an older recipe they've been cooking for years, then they give you a modern version of it. We're supposed to learn to do that in one of my classes this year. I talked to this guy who took it last year, and he said it was the best class he'd had on campus. I hope he's right."

"Sounds like fun." She sipped her coffee as she reviewed her planner. "Looks like we've got a busy cook day. I was wondering if I could tempt you with a lunch at the winery, though."

"Tempt away. You know I love having someone else do my cooking." She closed the book and studied Mia. "So, why do you want to go to the winery on a workday? Typically, you won't even let me run upstairs for a soda. You keep me locked in the kitchen until we're done."

"That's not true. At least not the soda part. And I only locked you in the kitchen once by accident," Mia explained, but she looked up and saw Christina grinning. "Oh, I get it, it's mess-with-the-boss day. Maybe your paycheck will be lost by accident this week."

"You direct deposit into my bank. And I'm pretty sure you're paying me more than what we agreed on, so one lost check isn't going to strap me." Christina rolled her shoulders. "I'm going to go shower and get ready for the day. I'm looking forward to working with this menu. It sounds yummy."

"You're not the only one who saw it that way from the number of orders we got last week. I'd like you to take a shot at next week's drop-off menu. I'll need it first thing in the morning, before we do the drop-offs, so I can add it to the staples packet." Mia stood and grabbed a bowl. Time for some oatmeal. That should keep her from being hungry as they cooked.

"Wait, you want me to come up with a meal? In less than a day?" Christina squeaked. "And still cook today?"

"You have to be able to think on your feet. And the life of a chef is always changing. Of course, if you don't want to, I could . . ." Mia started.

"No, no, you're not taking it back. I want to design a meal. But what if no one buys it?" Christina looked at her in horror.

"What about it?" Mia wondered where the girl's mind was going now.

She sighed, exasperated. "If no one orders, I will have failed. What happens then?"

"We try something new the next week. Failure isn't fatal. And besides, if you lose, you have to go back to living by Mia's rules." Mia focused on her planner, ignoring Christina's shocked expression. It was going to be a fun day.

Mia called the break at eleven thirty so they could run upstairs and change into clean clothes. Cooking was fun, but because she'd themed the week Italian Night, the morning process of making sauce had been messy. She told Christina to be ready in ten and she ran through a quick shower, then pulled on some jeans and a cute top. Would Priscilla even be there for a lunch service? Mia didn't know, but she was taking a chance. If she failed, she'd try again later, for drinks. Maybe Trent would come with her.

At the thought of his name, she could see her face pinken in the bathroom mirror. Even though last night's date hadn't ended in fireworks, the rest of their dates had been exciting and full of promise. Maybe she's just been too tired or had too many things on her mind. She'd have to make it up to him next time.

Mia and Christina decided to walk to the winery even though it would add a few minutes to their lunch break. As they strolled, Christina chatted about upcoming events her school club had planned for the summer break. "I thought I'd be too busy to do any of these trips, but if I can keep up with my work here, is it okay if I go?"

"Of course. Just put it on the kitchen

calendar so I know how to plan if we get a catering event the same weekend. What are they looking at doing?"

She grinned. "A few fun road trips I don't want to miss. One to Seattle. I'd be gone four days for that one. And one to the Oregon coast."

Mia's first inclination was to wonder how she'd manage without her, but she shook it off. The girl wasn't going to stay around and be a sous chef forever. Besides, it would be a good lesson in time management for Christina, not to mention a fun time. "You'll have to bring me back sand from the beach. It's supposed to bring good luck in potions."

"As long as you're not drinking it, I guess." Christina pulled her hair up in a twist while they walked, securing it with a clip she'd had on her shirt. "It's warm today. Summer's going to be full blast soon."

"Yeah." Mia wanted to ask about Levi, but she let it go. "I met Trent's mother yesterday. Abigail's kind of a trip."

Christina burst into giggles. "She's a hoot. The last time I was over there we played cards until two in the morning. Abigail was killing the rest of us. She's sharp."

"I got that feeling." Mia pointed to the winery sign. "Clam chowder. Now that's

250

typically a Friday soup."

"So, either they haven't changed their sign or they still have leftover soup. I'm on a hard pass." Christina shuddered.

"I'll have to agree with your assessment. Too bad, though, I could have used a bowl."

Christina sighed. "I'll make you up a batch of soup when we get home. You can thank me for saving your life later."

"You're a complete food snob." Mia bumped Christina with her shoulder. "But I love that you're talking with other people about food. It's a shared experience. You need to expand your experiences and figure out what you don't know yet."

Christina was silent for a while. "Find out what I don't know: I like that. I should make it a bumper sticker. Or a T-shirt. 'Tell Me What I Don't Know.' It could be fun."

"It could get you a lot of interesting comments." Mia held open the door and they went inside, the sunny day disappearing and a dark, barlike atmosphere surrounding them. Not how she would have designed the winery. In her mind, it should be light and open, bringing in the new generations who wanted a bite or a glass before going off to their outside activity. Magic Springs was in the mountains, and most of the tourists who came into town were hikers or here for the fishing or rafting. Campers tended to stay out of town to get the full, roughing-it treatment.

"Two for lunch?" a young woman at the hostess stand greeted them.

Mia nodded. "Yes, please. And could you tell me if Priscilla is in? I'd love to chat with her for a few minutes."

"Ms. Powers is in her office, but I'm not sure if she's available to chat. I'll drop in after I seat you and let her know you're here. Can I get a name?" The girl picked up two menus and, without waiting for an answer, walked them over to a booth near the windows. It was in a corner, and Mia sat where she could see the entire restaurant.

"Sure, tell her Mia Malone wants to talk to her." Mia settled into the booth and opened the menu.

"I'll do that. Your server will be right over." The hostess left their table and made a beeline to the back of the restaurant that led to a hallway and Priscilla's office. Mia had visited Priscilla in her office before, when she'd had to hand out the chili cook-off flyers.

"I haven't been here since we did the chili cook-off." Christina glanced around the almost-empty dining room. It was early, but still.

"I was just thinking the same thing. Which is kind of weird. The winery is close to the school. I don't know why I haven't popped in for a meal or a drink." Mia glanced at the menu. Instead of the light, healthy food she'd expected, it was fried bar food. "I thought Priscilla said she served an upscale clientele when we were here before."

"She did. But the menu looks like this could be a bar and grill, not a winery. I took a class where we talked about restaurant themes last semester. My professor would use this menu and décor as a missed opportunity to brand the winery." Christina glanced at the menu, then pushed it away. "Fish and chips it is. I hope the fries are good."

"I think I'll have the same." She studied Christina. "So, you're liking your classes."

"I'm loving them. I can't believe there's so much to learn about the business side of restaurants. Isaac always made it seem like it was all about the food." She examined a fork and, finding it less than clean, moved it toward the side of the table for the server. "The front of the house has a lot to do with how people view a place. This place needs to wow us with the food in order to bring us back, because the rest just feels so 1970s."

Mia laughed. "Like you'd know."

"I've seen pictures." Christina nodded to the waitress coming toward them. "Black shirt, black pants, black shoes, and hair slicked back into a bun. Typical Robert Palmer minus the miniskirts."

"True. But you're surprising me with your knowledge." Mia smiled at the waitress, who noticed the fork and grabbed it to tuck into her apron.

"OMG, I'm so sorry. I'll bring you out a clean fork. Can I get you some drinks while I'm in the kitchen?" The waitress must have been just out of high school.

"Iced tea for me." Mia glanced at Christina.

"Same." She pushed the menu toward the girl. "You might as well take our order too. We're on a lunch break from work and we're expected back soon."

"No worries. I'll have food out to you fast. Thanks for telling me." She pulled out a pad. "What can I get for you?"

After the waitress left Mia wanted to talk more about the feel of restaurants. Maybe she needed to have Christina's help with the lobby area at Mia's Morsels. Or even the sign. She had her notebook in her tote.

"Hey, can you look at this for me?"

"Why are you here? Spying on me for your grandmother?" Priscilla had come up from the kitchen, but Mia hadn't noticed.

Still holding an old grudge for a guy who was already dead. No way was this chat going to give her anything useful. "Priscilla, I'm so glad you could make time for us. Actually, I'm here to ask you if you called the office this last week. I got a call from the winery, but it was disconnected before I could find out how I could help. Did you need takeout menus? I think I have one here in my purse." Mia opened her tote and started digging.

"I don't know what you're talking about," Priscilla said, but her gaze went to the door. She must have been hoping no one would see her talking to Mia.

Alarm bells went off and Mia had a thought. "Please tell me you're not the one spreading rumors about me packing up and leaving town."

"I would never," Priscilla said, then focused on Mia. "But while you're here, are you moving your operation to Boise?"

She'd lied. Mia had felt it. And from the look on Christina's face, she'd realized it too. "No, Priscilla, I'm not leaving Magic Springs. Mia's Morsels is doing great and there's no reason for me to leave. I have to think you know we aren't in competition with each other's businesses, so I'm not sure why you feel threatened by me."

"Who said I was threatened?" Priscilla's voice rose, and a few diners glanced over toward them. She turned and smiled at them, trying to calm them before they walked out without eating. She lowered her voice. "Look, you and your grandmother are not my favorite people. But I'm not going after your business. You will succeed or fail all on your own. And I've got to get back to work. Thank you for coming in today."

"Priscilla, someone called me from the winery. If it wasn't you, who else could it be?" Mia said quickly before she could stomp away to her office.

Priscilla turned and studied Mia. "I'm afraid I have no idea."

CHAPTER 18

Mia tried to call Baldwin for an update several times, but he was avoiding her. Or he was busy. She tried to push Denny's death out of her mind. She had work to do. She and Christina got the week's delivery orders ready by six that night. Grans had dinner on the table when they trudged upstairs to the apartment. "Thanks for doing this. I'm not sure I could cook one more meal tonight if I'd wanted to. I'm going to have to add an extra order into the mix so I can just bring it upstairs and reheat it when you go back to your place."

"Probably a good idea. Or have one from last week in the freezer; that way you don't have to eat the same thing you've been cooking all day. I bet it will taste better." Grans filled the water glasses on the table as they sat to eat.

Cindy shook her head as she looked at Mia and Christina. "You guys look wiped. I don't understand why anyone would cook for a living. Especially if they didn't have to. I order in all my meals if I'm not going out or they aren't provided on set."

"You have food. That means someone is cooking," Mia pointed out.

"I know. But why would someone choose to actually cook for a living? I thought only people with limited opportunities for their future went into the service fields." Cindy pushed back her perfectly highlighted hair — that someone else had done.

She was impossible. Mia could feel Christina's annoyance rising.

"You sound like my mother. According to her, if you're not a professional like a doctor or lawyer, you're wasting your life. I'm pretty sure she'd feel that acting, like dancing, is a total waste of brain cells." Christina didn't even look up at Cindy while she spoke. "So, I guess it all depends on what you enjoy doing for a living. Have you ever had a real job?"

"Acting is a real job," Cindy responded.

"Okay, fine, we'll just have to disagree on this." Mia was too tired to mediate a truce between the two women, especially when she thought Christina was right.

Christina picked up her plate and glass. "I'm going to finish eating in my room. I've got a study group chat coming up in a few minutes."

"Thanks for your help today. You were awesome," Mia said to Christina's back before she disappeared.

She paused and turned, throwing a smirking look at Cindy. "It's easy when you love your work."

The kitchen was quiet for a few minutes while the other three ate. Then Cindy stood up and announced, "I'm going into town to meet with my Realtor. He has an offer on Father's property. Mike has already greenlighted it, so I should be out of here sooner rather than later."

"If we can clear the spell work you did," Grans reminded her.

Cindy shrugged. "Maybe I should just let it stand. I've gotten three new parts scheduled in the last month. Maybe the repercussions won't be so bad."

"Like getting someone killed?" Mia said.

Cindy shook her head. "There is no evidence that it was my spell that killed Denny. It could have just been a random murder for his wallet or something. Like that guy who broke into your house. He was after money. There has to be more of that type around this backward town."

"We can't make you stay, but there are a

few more lessons you need to complete before I think you're ready to have the grimoire." Grans stared at Cindy. Mia had seen that look before and wondered if Cindy could withstand it. Mia never could.

Cindy dropped her gaze, but Mia still felt the defiance. Man, Dorian had messed up raising this child. She was totally out for one person: herself.

"I could leave the book here with you. Then I wouldn't need the lessons," Cindy offered.

Grans paused, thinking. "It doesn't work that way. You need to accept your inheritance."

"What if I don't? Mike might be better at this. He's better at everything. And Father was a witch, so it means it doesn't have to be a female, right?" Cindy looked like she was trying to convince herself more than Grans or Mia. "I'll just send him here to pick it up, and then it will be on his conscience. And I can be free to go back to my life without worrying about doing something stupid again."

"Mike may not have the power," Grans pointed out.

"If I don't want it, you can't make me take it." Cindy picked up her plate and put it in the sink. "Thank you for dinner, but I need to get to this meeting."

Mia and Grans didn't speak until the door shut behind Cindy as she left the apartment. Even then, Dorian was the first to express his displeasure with a loud and long meow.

Grans reached her hands down to the floor where he sat, watching her. "I know, Dorian, but I'm doing my best. Sometimes people just aren't ready to pick up the mantle."

Mia knew she was talking about her mom. The power in her family had skipped a generation because Mom had decided that being any kind of witch just wasn't in the cards for her. By contrast, Mia couldn't wait once she'd found out about her talent. She wouldn't ever give it up willingly or turn away from it.

It just wasn't in her DNA.

Grans pushed her plate aside. "I was wondering if you'd help me. I might have found a spell in Dorian's grimoire that might free him from Mr. Darcy's body."

"Should we copy it just in case Cindy decides to leave and take the spell book with her before we can get it perfected?" Mia glanced over at the front door. It was apparent their hospitality was all but over for her.

"Probably." Grans looked down at Mr.

Darcy. "Okay if we appropriate one of your spells? I know in life you were really tight with them."

The cat rubbed his head against Grans's leg, then looked up at the cat treats sitting on the cabinet. The box floated down to him and he took his paw to grab a treat out from the opening on top.

"You've got to be kidding me." Mia looked from Grans to Mr. Darcy and back to Grans. "When did he learn that?"

"Dorian is teaching your cat bad habits." She picked up the box and put it back on the counter. "You shouldn't just take treats. They should be freely given."

Mr. Darcy, or maybe Dorian, meowed and ran out to the hallway. He pawed at Christina's door, and Mia heard it open and close for him. Hopefully, Christina had been listening for him and he hadn't just opened that door too.

"Well, let's get started, then." Mia stood and started clearing the kitchen table to get ready to work on the spell that might just free Mr. Darcy from his guest. Before Dorian decided to stay around for a while.

The next morning Grans and Mia were at the table again. They'd cleaned up from several failed attempts at working the spell late last night. Mia had spent more time carefully copying the spell into a notebook. She wouldn't put it into the grimoire until she actually got it to work. She studied her grandmother over the top of her coffee cup.

"You look tired. Maybe you should have slept a little longer." Mia didn't like seeing her this way.

"I'll just be glad when I'm home. Muffy and I love visiting you, but I fear we're wearing out our welcome." Grans put a hand down to rub Muffy's ears. The little dog leaned into the contact.

"You know you're welcome as long as you want to be here." Mia set down her cup and went to check on the strata. "I've never had all four bedrooms filled with people before. The apartment feels like home, doesn't it?"

"A little crowded for my taste. I'm afraid Cindy isn't going to be leaving after all. Mark Baldwin called before you got up and asked if I'd bring her down to the station for another round of questioning." Grans glanced toward the hallway that led to the bedrooms. "She's not going to be happy about that."

"I take it he doesn't have any other suspects." Mia thought about what she'd found out about Denny and realized if she was in law enforcement, she'd go with the person she could prove knew the victim. Otherwise, the murder was just random. And she didn't feel like that was true.

The house phone rang. Mia stood and went to answer it. The lines were attached to the business line downstairs. So if someone desperately needed to talk to a live person at Mia's Morsels, the phone would transfer the call to the house phone. It was a little early for a business call, but it could be about the delivery schedule today. Mia refilled her cup as she answered. "This is Mia, how can I help you?"

"This is Priscilla. Look, I was thinking about what you said yesterday."

Mia blinked, surprised. "What part?"

"The phone call? Duh?" Priscilla's tone was sarcastic, but Mia let it ride. It was too early in the morning to play games.

"Oh yeah. What did you realize?"

"What time did the call come in?" Priscilla asked. "That was on Saturday, right?"

Mia thought about the day. She'd finished picking up things from the party, so it was after lunch. But not long after. "Maybe one, two at the latest. Why?"

"We're weren't open for lunch last Saturday. My chef needed a personal day, so I just closed up the kitchen. And the winery doesn't open until five on days when the kitchen is closed."

"So no one was at your restaurant?" Mia leaned against the wall. Now she was getting random calls from an empty building. Great. Sometimes magic was a real pain in the butt.

"I didn't say that. My day manager was here. You can call Heather at this number." Priscilla rattled it off.

"Thanks." Mia didn't know why Priscilla was being helpful, but she did appreciate it. "Look, I know we didn't get off on the right foot, but . . ."

"Save your apology. I'm only telling you because it makes me mad when someone does something wrong and uses my place to do it. If Heather called you that day, she needs to be held accountable. If it's really bad, tell me and I'll fire her."

"I don't know yet," Mia hedged.

"Well, let me know. I need to get rid of her anyway, I'm paying her way too much for what she does. I can get a kid out of high school for a lot cheaper."

Mia hung up the phone and stared at the notepad where she'd written the number.

"What was that about?" Grans asked. Muffy now was sitting on her lap, and they were both watching Mia.

"I'm not sure, but Priscilla might have just

given us a lead." She glanced at the clock. "I need to go wake up Christina and get the deliveries going."

"What about the call?"

Mia tucked the paper on which she'd written Heather's number and tucked it into her jeans. "I'll call her when we're loaded and on the way. Maybe we'll be making an extra stop today."

It was almost ten by the time they got the van packed. Christina had mapped out all the stops, so they had a plan. Mia let her drive while she pulled out the scrap of paper and dialed the number. When the phone was answered, she dove right in. "Hi, my name is Mia Malone. I believe you or someone who was with you at the winery called me on Saturday."

There was a pause, then the girl on the other end told her everything. When Mia hung up, Christina glanced over as she pulled into the first driveway for delivery. "What was that and do I want to know?"

"I need to talk to Bethanie. Can you call her and have her come over to the school this afternoon? Maybe at about two?"

"It's Tuesday; she's probably working." Christina picked up the clipboard and took off the first order sheet.

"Well, whenever she can get off. We need

to talk." Mia piled out of the van and headed to the back to grab the first delivery. She packed it into a Mia's Morsel's delivery bag, then tucked in the receipt Christina had used to pull the correct foods. She added next week's menu and a pen and headed to the door. "And tell her it's important. I'll handle this delivery. You call Bethanie."

When Mia came back, an order for next week in her hand, Christina was sitting in the driver's seat watching her walk toward the van. "She'll be at the house at two thirty. She didn't even ask what you wanted to talk about. So, what's going on?"

"Let's just say I have a hunch." She dropped the order into the plastic tote they kept upfront for orders and checks. "Where to next?"

By the time they were finished with deliveries and the totes were cleaned and back in the kitchen, it was almost two thirty. Christina glanced around, looking for something to do to keep her downstairs until Bethanie showed.

Mia glanced around the kitchen, then headed to the door. "Let's lock up for the night. Tomorrow we start on the luncheon for the library. I want everything to be special, so we'll have a lot of detail work to do. You go upstairs and relax."

"I was just going to say hi to Bethanie." She followed Mia out of the kitchen and paused as she locked the door.

"I'll let her know you said hi. I'd rather talk to her alone, if you don't mind." Mia grabbed her laptop from the office desk and sat at the couch in the lobby. "I'll see you at dinner."

Christina left and headed upstairs. As soon as the door to the apartment closed, Mia heard the front door open.

"Hello? Is anyone here?" Bethanie called out, still standing outside.

Mia stood and walked over to the door. "Come on in. I've been expecting you. I've got cold water in the office if you need something."

"Actually, I'm fine. Christina said you needed to talk to me? I hope this isn't about that prank I pulled on her with Levi. I know he's crazy about her and he really didn't even give me the time of day." Bethanie sat on one of the chairs facing the couch, her Coach purse tucked on her lap. Mia assumed the stylish boots the girl wore were probably designer as well, but she didn't know for sure.

"No, not about that. Honestly, Christina and Levi's relationship is in their hands.

Although it wasn't very nice to do, especially for someone who calls herself Christina's friend." Mia let that statement soak in a bit. She could see Bethanie was uncomfortable. Her left foot tapped nervously on the area rug under her chair.

"Then why am I here?" She glanced around the room.

Mia closed her laptop and sat on the couch, watching Bethanie. "I wanted to ask you why you called the school last Saturday." She held up her hand as Bethanie tried to deny it.

"Heather already told me what you did, she just didn't know why." Mia tilted her head, showing her confusion. "So, why did you call the school and hang up just as someone was trying to break in?"

She blew out a breath. "I didn't want you to be hurt. And I wanted to warn you. I hoped, by calling you, you would see him trying to break in."

"But Bethanie, one thing confuses me. How did you know he was going to break in? You and he definitely don't run in the same circles," Mia said, pointing out the obvious.

"Look, I overheard John talking to this guy. He'd send me for muffins, then he'd leave. Then, a few days later, he'd do it again. I thought maybe he had a girlfriend, and I was going to tell Carol. She's a really nice lady. He doesn't deserve her."

Mia thought Bethanie might actually have been looking for some blackmail evidence to use against her boss, but she'd give her the dignity story. "You overheard John telling the guy to rob my house?"

"No, he just kept telling him about the money. He never said he should break in, just that there was money laying around. Then the guy called him 'the muffin man,' and started singing this song. From like a nursery rhyme, you know?" Bethanie shuddered. "It was totally weird, but I knew this guy was going to try to break in. I could see it in his eyes when he asked John about the money. So I called you to let you know."

"Except you didn't let me know, you just hung up," Mia reminded her.

"I know; that was brilliant, right? That way it got you thinking about what was happening. So you could figure out the problem yourself." Bethanie grinned. "And I won't get fired for saying anything."

CHAPTER 19

"All you have is evidence that maybe John Louis tried to fool this guy into breaking into your house. And he's probably behind the rumors that you're closing. I'll admit, he wants this property. But there's no evidence, circumstantial or not, that he hired Denny Blake to kill you." Mark Baldwin sat at the table upstairs in the apartment with Grans and Christina. Cindy was missing from the discussion. She'd told them she had a headache and had gone to bed when Baldwin arrived.

Mia didn't blame her; talking to Baldwin was giving her a headache too. "Look, I know it's not much. But you know Cindy didn't kill Denny and you don't have another suspect. Why not look into John Louis?"

Baldwin sighed, took off his hat, and rubbed his hand through what appeared to be thinning hair. The job was stressing him out. She needed to make him a potion to reverse the process before all he had was memories of hair. "You're going to give him reasons for a harassment suit if you don't watch out. I know he attacked you, trying to get you to sell the school, but in the eyes of the law, he's done his time for that. Not that I agree with that."

"He did part of his sentence, not the full one. And the judge gave him a slap on the wrist. You know if it had been anyone else, they would have gone to prison for a long time." Mia took a breath and held up a hand. "Anyway, this isn't harassment, I just have a feeling it's John. Again."

"Well, I have a feeling it's your new roommate who got into a lover's spat with her wild online boyfriend, and she set him straight. If it was an accident, all she has to do is say that, and the judge will take it into consideration in the sentencing." Mark Baldwin stood and put his hat back on. "I've got to go. Sarah's having the church board over for dinner tonight, and if I'm late, she's going to have my hide."

"Thanks for coming by to talk to me." Mia stood and picked up Muffy and his leash. "I'll walk you out. It's about time for Muffy to go outside anyway."

"Look, I'll keep my eye out, and I'm

definitely talking to him about this home-less guy. If someone else besides Bethanie saw them talking together, it would go a long way in the DA's eyes. Bethanie has a bit of baggage with her dad and brother, you realize." He nodded to Grans. "Mrs. Carpenter."

"Give Sarah my best," Grans said as Baldwin and Mia walked out of the kitchen.

"I will, ma'am." He opened the door for Mia and they went downstairs.

When they reached the lower level, she put a hand on his sleeve. "You really aren't going to charge Cindy in this, right? There's no way she could have killed someone."

"You wouldn't believe how many times I hear that about people who really did kill someone. Especially over matters of the heart." He tipped his hat and went to his cruiser.

Mia walked Muffy for a while, then looked back at the house. "The only problem with your theory," she said to the now-absent police chief, "is Cindy doesn't have a heart to break."

She and Muffy went back to the house, but instead of going inside, Mia went to a bench she'd set up in the backyard for students taking breaks during classes. She settled into the space, opened up her hands, and quietly announced, "I'm here if you want to talk to me. We need to know who killed you. Baldwin is going to charge Cindy if we don't."

Muffy let out a long growl, and Mia opened her eyes to see — nothing. No one stood in front of her. She turned to the left, then the right. No one there at all. She frowned at Muffy. "Now what are you doing, scaring me like that?"

A pile of fur jumped into her lap from the left side, and Mia tried not to let out a scream. She glanced down and saw Mr. Darcy staring at her with an amused look on his face. Or at least as amused as a cat could get. Lately, his look seemed to be one of long-suffering patience. Probably the cat dealing with Dorian's sharing his body with him. He meowed and rubbed up against Mia's arm.

"Sorry, buddy, but you scared me. I'm trying to reach out to the other side and having no luck at all." She glanced around the empty backyard. If Denny was still around, avenging his death wasn't on his mind. She stood and nodded to the house. "Let's go inside. Grans will be wondering what happened to us."

Mr. Darcy jumped from her lap and ran to the edge of the yard. Right where she had planned to put the herb garden. She followed him over. "Look, we need to go inside. I don't like you running around all night. It's not safe."

He looked at her, then darted to the other side of the tree, where Denny's body had been found.

"What's going on, Mr. Darcy?"

A loud meow told her she'd guessed wrong. Dorian was in charge of tonight's adventure.

"Sorry, Dorian, but we need to go in." She crossed the rest of the way over the lawn and paused at the tree. She put a hand on it and felt a faint pulse. "What the heck?"

She leaned down and looked at the area Mr. Darcy, or Dorian, was patting.

"It's just dirt." She brushed off the loose dirt on top to show him, and her hand caught on a St. Christopher's medal. She pulled it out of the dirt and frowned. The only person she knew who wore this medal was Trent. She'd teased him about his divided loyalty for his gods, but he'd shut her down. What had he said again?

The words came back in a rush. She could hear him as he'd told her, "Being a witch is what I do; what I believe is my own personal business."

She pulled her phone out of her jeans and

keyed in a number. When the call was answered, she didn't introduce herself. She just asked one question. "Do you know where your St. Christopher's medal is?"

Trent met her outside the school a few minutes later. He'd still been at the grocery store, working on next week's order, when she'd called. Mia showed him the dirt-encrusted medal. He swore aloud as he glanced at it, his other hand raising in an unconscious movement to double-check that the medallion wasn't on his chest. It wasn't. "I don't understand why this is here, unless I lost it the day we were measuring out for the garden."

"That's possible." She sat back down on the bench and watched emotion run through his body, and the stages. "When did you notice it was missing?"

He sighed. "Yesterday. I thought the Goddess had taken it as payment for how well the training for new staff at the store had gone."

"Someone's trying to get me not to trust you. First the shoe prints and the open door at the library. Now your medal shows up right where the dead man was found? It's awfully coincidental, right?" She glanced up at him, but he was still staring at the medal.

"Trent?"

He tucked it into his jeans pocket. "You know I didn't have anything to do with Denny's death, right?"

"Of course you didn't." She glanced around the empty backyard. Mr. Darcy had gone inside when she'd taken Muffy back upstairs. "I'm just getting tired of someone messing with me. Baldwin says he knows John is spreading the rumors that I'm closing, but there's nothing that points him to this murder."

"He's still focused on Cindy?" Trent leaned back against the tree. He was watching the edges of the yard as well. Both of them were on edge over finding this trinket.

"Yeah. I'm afraid he's going to arrest her. And so is Dorian. He's the one who led me to the St. Christopher's."

"That's great, but one, I didn't do it. And two, Mr. Darcy, or Dorian, can't speak up and tell us what he's thinking." Trent's phone buzzed and he glanced at the text. "This is why I like running the store and staying out of the magic stuff. It keeps me from having to deal with things like proving a cat right."

"Well, if Dorian's the one who's trying to prove Cindy's innocence, it's not really a cat or Mr. Darcy you have to prove right.

It's the ghost inside him," Mia explained, but then stopped when she saw Trent's face. "And that's what you're trying to tell me."

"Exactly. I like my peaceful life, Mia. The less it's about magic, the better for me." He pulled her into a hug. "And yet I'm here with you. You're making things complicated for me."

"Sorry?" Mia rested her cheek against his chest. She wasn't sorry at all. She liked him in her life. And the magic was a part of her. She'd hidden that side of her for too long when she had been with Isaac. She wouldn't, no, couldn't do it again.

He pulled back and met her eyes. "Don't be. I'm more alive since you moved back. And if that means I have to deal with messy magic, I'll take the hit. Dorian must think this medal will help prove that Cindy's innocent. Any idea why?"

"Maybe he was saying that there are things we don't know. Or that Baldwin hasn't taken into account." Mia turned and walked toward the front door.

"As long as the answer isn't that I killed the guy, I'm fine with the new explanation." He paused at the front door. "I've got to run back to the store. Bakery emergency."

"Too many cooks in the kitchen?" She

reached up and touched his face. "You look tired."

He took her hand and kissed it. "Not sleeping well. I'm worried about what other surprises your school has for us. We found a library we didn't know existed. What's next?"

"I'm hoping a pile of cash, so I can pay off the remodel loan and get this company in the black." She checked the time on her watch. "Sorry to cut this short, but I'm going upstairs. Call me if you want to talk on your way home."

"Not sure when that will be, but I'll text first. If you don't respond, I'll know you're asleep and I'll just come by in the morning. Maybe we can figure out something to help Cindy." He leaned in and kissed her. "Thanks for returning the medal. It was my grandfather's. I would have been heartbroken if it had been lost for good. Thank Mr. Darcy and Dorian for me as well."

She nodded, then went into the building. She watched as Trent jumped into the delivery van and started the vehicle. Then she double-checked the locks and headed upstairs. Better to be overly cautious about the locks than too relaxed. She needed some time to think about how to clear Cindy from being suspect number one in Denny's death.

When she reached the third floor and her apartment door, her gaze was diverted to the door that led to the library. She hadn't had time to even think about what she was going to do with the area or what was in store for her if she did. The house already had two ghosts coming and going, her guardian and Dorothy. Did she need to open up the house to a third? And one that apparently had a grudge against the local coven for killing her.

History would have to stay in the past. At least until she figured out the current mystery and got Cindy cleared from the suspect pool. The woman wasn't the nicest person, but she was Dorian's daughter, and he'd been important to her grandmother. She ignored the pull from the library and unlocked the apartment door. She was going to make a timeline with Cindy. Maybe things would start to make sense after that.

Two hours later Mia had her timeline done, but she still hadn't heard from Trent. Cindy hadn't come out of her room after Baldwin left, so Mia decided she'd finish up the project tomorrow, when she could get her input. She didn't see any glaring red flags that would lead her to the killer's identity. But then again, she was certain John Louis was involved. Somehow. The lyrics to the muffin man nursery rhyme kept running through her head. It was a clue, maybe the one that would finally lock John Louis up for good.

At least she hoped so.

"Sorry about not calling last night. We had an oven go down and I was trying to get it back up without calling the emergency repair guys. In the end I had to call anyway. So, not only did I pay double time for a repair, I lost four hours of sleep." Trent poured his second cup of coffee. "I'm not sure I'm going to be much help in the creative thinking department today."

Mia glanced at the empty hallway. "Well, Cindy is still in her room, so I haven't made much progress either. But I did get a time-line written out last night."

"Let me see it." Trent reached for the notebook. After studying it for a while he set it down. "You're kind of good at this. Details like dates, times, who was there, it's all on this one list."

"I'm an event planner as well as a chef. I have to have everything on the plan or I'll forget something." She glanced at her schedule. "Which also means I need to get into the kitchen today and make a shopping list for next week. I don't have another catering event on the books, so I need to do some marketing and maybe plan another class. The business can't survive on just the home deliveries."

"And I thought managing the store was twenty-four seven." He tapped the paper. "You know, this all started with your house-guest. Are you sure Baldwin isn't right?"

Mia had entertained that thought too. "All I know is, Grans trusts her. My grand-mother has a knack for reading people."

"On the other hand, she's here at the apartment with you rather than in her own house with this Cindy person. Maybe she felt she needed some backup." Trent finished his coffee and put the cup in the sink. "I'm heading to the store to check on the ovens; then I'm going home. Call me if you need me."

"And wake you?" Mia shook her head. "I don't think I'll need you that bad. Go get some sleep. You look beat."

After Trent left Mia sat in the kitchen for a while. But no one else joined her. Apparently, the rest of the house was sleeping in this morning. She grabbed Muffy's lead. "Do you want to go for a walk before I get busy? Then you can sleep in the office while I work."

Muffy did a dance when he saw the lead.

At least someone besides her was ready to start the day. Mr. Darcy looked over at her, yawned, then laid his head back down. He was in the sleeping-in camp.

They'd just finished their walk around the small park when a woman with a Great Dane turned up their path. Mia hadn't seen the dog before, but Muffy apparently knew him and barked out a quick greeting. She pulled the leash closer, just in case the bigger dog didn't share the idea of friendship. She was surprised to look up into the woman's face and see she knew her. "Priscilla? What are you doing here?"

"Walking Elvis, what else? Sit, boy." She reached down and scratched the dog's ears, and he sat quickly, watching Muffy strain at the lead to get near the larger dog. She shot a look at Muffy. "Why are you walking Mary Alice's dog? Is she all right?"

"She's fine. She and Muffy are staying in the apartment with me for a few days, and I was the first one up, so I got puppy patrol." Mia pulled Muffy back a few inches, but he wasn't going to sit like Elvis had on command. Maybe Grans needed obedience classes for Christmas. "I didn't realize you lived nearby."

"In the subdivision on the other side of the park. I've got a three-bedroom ranch

I've had forever. It's my retirement savings, because once I sell, I'll be set up, but for right now, I'm stuck running the winery." She glanced over toward St. Catherine's. "I was happy you bought the school for your little cottage industry. Having a strip mall with a grocery store would have cut my land value."

"At least someone's happy I bought the building." Mia reached down and tried to push Muffy into a seated position. "Sit. No one likes a pushy puppy."

Priscilla nodded to Muffy. "You can let him have some lead. They're friends. Elvis won't eat him."

Mia let out the lead and Muffy went directly to the sitting Elvis and licked his legs. She smiled as the dog sat between the Dane's two front feet and grinned at her. "I guess you're right."

"I'm not a bad person, Mia. Your grand-mother and I just have a history." Priscilla paused, then looked toward the school again. "I heard someone was killed on the grounds. Did they find out who he was?"

"Some guy from out of town." Mia didn't want to say "hit man," because . . . well, she didn't know why he'd even come to town.

"I saw the picture in the newspaper. He was at the winery with your new friend."

Priscilla was still looking in the direction of the school. "I don't want to say anything negative, but what do you know about Dorian's daughter?"

With that, she snapped her fingers, and Elvis gave Muffy a sniff on the head, then turned and followed her on the path away from Mia. Muffy gave out a small whine, then looked up at Mia.

"I guess it's time to go back to the house and talk to Cindy." Mia turned back toward the house. Something wasn't adding up, and if she didn't get the answers she wanted, Mia was kicking Cindy out of the house, with or without Grans's approval.

When she got back to the apartment, Grans and Cindy were at the kitchen table.

"Good news — we fixed the spell. I've reversed the bad karma and now Cindy is clear again," Grans chattered, then she looked up at Mia and paused. "So why do you look like you have bad news?"

"I just have a few questions." Mia unclipped the lead and Muffy ran to his water dish. She sat at the table and opened her notebook. "Cindy? Tell me exactly when you got into town? And when did you have lunch with Denny?"

"I didn't have lunch with Denny." Cindy dropped her gaze and her face went white.

"Yes, he came over to the hotel, but we were working on the new part."

Mia pointed to the time frame on the page. "Seriously, cut the crap. Someone saw you at the winery. What haven't you been telling us about your relationship with Denny?"

Cindy swallowed hard. "Okay, fine. Look, I told him I was coming here to finalize my father's estate. I had some papers to sign and the lawyer was getting pressure from that real estate guy to sell the property cheap. Denny said he knew the guy and would help me out. We met the same day I arrived from California. He was supposed to come take me to dinner a few nights later, but he never showed up. Then I saw the news."

"When Grans came to visit you at the Lodge, that's when you decided to come stay with us?" Mia shook her head. "That doesn't make sense at all."

"It does if you killed him. I wanted to find out more about you. He died here, but no one was even looking at any of you as his killers," Cindy responded. "Besides, I did want to correct this spell, so I thought it was a win-win."

"You came here because you thought one of us killed Denny?" Mia couldn't believe what she was hearing.

"Yes. But Baldwin just laughed when I brought up the idea. I told him I'd find proof, but I didn't."

"Because we didn't kill him." Mia leaned back in her chair, frustrated. They'd been protecting Cindy all this time and she'd been trying to pin the murder on Mia or Grans or Christina.

"I know that now." Cindy met Mia's gaze. "But my plan backfired. Baldwin still thinks I killed Denny. And being here has just made things worse."

CHAPTER 20

Mr. Darcy jumped on Cindy's lap and patted her cheek, where tears had begun to fall. She reached out almost without thought to pet him. She smiled down at the cat. "I don't know why, but he always seems to know what I'm feeling."

"Cindy, you need to know something." Grans turned toward her.

"I'm not sure this is the right time," Mia warned.

"Pishposh, she's an adult, and she just cleared her karma in more ways than one. It's time we came clean with her." Grans turned back toward Mia and waited for her nod of approval.

"I knew it — you guys *did* kill Denny. Why? Did he see some magic ritual you needed kept secret? Or did you just need the blood?" Cindy's eyes widened as she stared at Mia and Grans.

"Seriously? I've just spent the last week

teaching you about magic and you bring up that old stereotype? Neither my granddaughter nor I killed your friend. And this isn't about Denny at all. This is about Dorian." Grans reached out and rubbed Mr. Darcy's ears.

"What about my father? I know the two of you were dating. That wasn't a secret. He called both me and Mike and told us." Cindy absently reached out and touched her grimoire, the one physical object she had from her father close by.

"Go ahead. This is your party." Mia leaned back to watch the conversation. She didn't have any part in this. Grans had put Dorian's essence into Mr. Darcy; she needed to explain the problem.

"It's not about us dating either, but thank you for telling me you knew about our relationship; that was so sweet of him." Grans pressed a hand to her heart.

"Get to the point, Grans," Mia pushed.

Sighing, she turned back to Cindy. "After your father was killed we didn't know who had murdered him. So I tried to talk to his spirit to find out."

Cindy didn't say anything, just stroked Mr. Darcy's back.

"Anyway," Grans continued, "your father came to me after my spell and I was trying to talk to him, and then, well, the cat jumped on the table and your father's essence went into his body."

"Father's body? You mean his spirit is stuck in his body?" Cindy's face winced, as if she was thinking about what that might mean.

"No, dear, Mr. Darcy's body. Your father's spirit is in the cat."

Mia was in the new-to-her library, looking at the space and the massive amount of junk in between her and a usable room. She walked over to where Christina had seen the picture of the girl, but there was nothing there that could have made the projection or was even close. She heard a noise in the hallway and looked up to see Grans coming into the room.

She paused and touched one of the old student desks. "Oh my, I haven't seen things like this for years. I didn't attend school here, but as you know, I sent your mother here for a while."

Mia crossed the room to stand next to her. She pointed to a far wall. "It's a lovely room. I'll be able to break out part of the kitchen wall to make a doorway right there. As long as the school is going to let me use the room."

"I don't think it would have opened the door if it didn't want you here." She glanced around the room, seeking out something. "I don't feel any negative vibes here. Maybe there's a ghost, but it's not angry, or at least not right now. Moving things around can upset them, so we'll have to be gentle with what we do with the stuff in here."

"I was thinking a yard sale. Maybe a call to an antique shop? These desks have to be old." Mia thought about the story about the school that Abigail Majors had told her. Maybe the story was somewhere in between that story and the one Gran knew. She rubbed the wood on the top of a desk that had an attached seat. The top flipped open, and she could imagine a child storing their books and school supplies in the desk. "I want to keep a few for the library, though, too. Just for decoration."

"You could have a section for cookbooks too. I think you have a couple of boxes still downstairs that need to be unpacked." Grans sank into a chair. "I needed to get out of the apartment for a minute. Cindy's still in her room. She's having trouble dealing with Dorian's current state."

"She took it better than I expected. Although I can't believe she thought we'd kill someone." Mia leaned against a table. "I guess it's not any different from us thinking she killed the man."

"True. But Cindy has trust issues. Dorian didn't do her any favors by walking away from the children when he divorced their mother. Children need both parents." She waved a hand at Mia. "I'm not saying they should have stayed together. But parents need to keep active in the children's lives, even if it's difficult. Dorian was a weekend, now-and-then dad. Not a solid force in their lives."

Mia let that sit a while. It was hard to judge someone who couldn't defend himself. "Okay, so we're back at square one. Just some random killing that happened to be in my backyard?"

"Maybe you're just going to have to trust that Baldwin will figure out who killed Denny without your input."

"Maybe." But Mia wasn't done. Not by a long shot. "I've got to go into town to check on something. Do you mind starting dinner?"

"Of course not, but where are you going?" Grans pulled herself up and followed Mia out of the room and into the hallway.

"I need to talk to Barney Mann about some legal work for the business." She made the idea sound dull, like it was just about the paperwork. Hopefully, Grans wouldn't catch on.

"Okay, dear. Tell Sheila I still need a tennis partner for my doubles league next week." Grans paused at the door as Mia headed downstairs. "Are you driving?"

"No, I think I'll walk. See you in a few." Mia left the house and headed toward the business section of town.

When she got to the second-floor office that held Barney Mann's law offices, she had a plan. It wasn't a great one, but it was a step in the right direction. She knocked on the door.

"Come in," Sheila called out. "No need to wait in the hallway."

"Sheila? Is Barney in?" Mia stepped inside, and a strong coffee smell made her wake up a bit.

"No, sorry, dear. Barney's in Boise for the week. He had a trial that got moved out of the county to get a clean jury." She nodded to the chair in front of her desk. "Have a seat. Can I get you some coffee or water?"

"No, I'm fine. I need to get back home. When will he get back?"

Sheila glanced at the file on her desk. "Looks like they're seating a jury today. So Friday at the earliest. Maybe sometime this weekend, if the jury gets sequestered. Can I

293

help you with something?"

"You've been around a while in Magic Springs, right?" Mia held out the paper that showed a mug shot of Denny. "Have you ever seen this guy? Denny Blake?"

When Sheila nodded, Mia asked, "I need to know what Denny was doing in town but, more importantly, who would have seen him."

"I didn't know that was his name until the paper came out. But yes, we both had seen the guy. Both Barney and me." Sheila frowned at her over her glasses. "The guy showed up wanting to know if Mr. Mann knew what the legal process for getting married was in Idaho. That's all I got before they went inside his office and closed the door. I thought it was a little strange, because he wasn't a resident and all, but you know how the rich are. They just come up here for a visit and the next thing you know, they're trying to put down roots. But roots don't grow overnight. And now that poor man is dead."

Mia pushed away the antinewcomer sentiment that Sheila's words held and tried to go back to the marriage thing. Maybe Denny had been here for another reason. Not related to John Louis. "So when he came in, you just thought he was visiting?"

294

"He told me he was in town for the week and had a proposal he wanted to take care of while he was here." Sheila smiled sadly. "I wonder if he ever got to ask the girl to marry him before he died. I don't know what would be sadder for the woman. Not to know how he felt or to know and lose him right afterward to a random mugging."

"You think it was a mugging?" Mia watched Sheila's reaction.

A frown came over her face. "I guess I'm not sure how he died. I just assumed from what the paper said that he'd been killed when he was on a walk through the trail system. He was found on the trail behind your house, right? You may want to make sure that big house is locked up at night. You're just far enough out of town that it could look like an easy place to break in to."

"Yeah, I'm very careful." Mia stood and put the paper back into her tote. "Thanks for your time. If you think of another time you saw Denny before he died, please call me. I'm trying to do some follow-up work for the family to clear up some missing time in his travels here."

"Oh well, isn't that sweet of you? I thought maybe you were just worried about the murder being so close to your home. I mean, St. Catherine's has a reputation for some strange goings-on there. Have you had any bumps in the night or seen any apparitions?"

Mia smiled, shook her head, and lied. Sheila wasn't part of the local coven culture. "Not a one. I'd heard the rumors too before I bought it, but it must have been just kids messing with one another when the place was vacant. No ghosts hanging out at the school now. Maybe they don't like all the cooking I do. It must make them frustrated that they can't eat."

Sheila laughed. "Well, that might just be why. I've been meaning to order one of your takeout meals, but it's just me, so it's a lot of food."

"I should make some one- or two-person serving choices. Actually, that's a great idea. I'll stop by next week with a free sample for you, if you don't mind. And one for Mr. Mann, of course." Mia started toward the door. "Thanks for chatting with me."

"No problem." She paused, tapping the desk. "You know, I did see that man one other time."

"Denny? Where?" Mia dropped her hand from the doorknob and turned back to focus on Sheila.

"I think it was that same night. Or the

296

next night? Days mix together at my age. Anyway, I was shopping for groceries, so it must have been a Monday night. I came out of Majors and he was standing by a car, talking to someone. I walked by and was shocked to see it was John Louis, but then again, it made sense because John is a Realtor. I think Denny was talking about a house, and John, well, he said something weird."

Mia could feel the muscles in her body tense. Would this be the missing piece that put the two of them together for Baldwin? "What did he say?"

"Something about it not being why he was in town. I guess John was having trouble getting him focused at looking at a house. Realtors are like that. They really want the sale." The phone rang and she sighed. "Sorry, work calls. Literally."

Mia walked out of the office and shut the door behind her. So, not a smoking gun, but another flashing arrow, at least in her mind, pointing toward John as the killer.

She really needed to focus her cover story. If Sheila hadn't been just lonely enough to want to talk, she might not have given Mia as much as she had. So now Mia had two questions. Why was Denny here? And who was he planning on popping the question to?

Cindy had made it seem like it was just work between the two of them. She'd been grilling him for a part. But maybe that wasn't how Denny had seen it. Maybe she'd reacted to the proposal by — what, strangling him? That was idiotic. But if Denny was going to propose, that gave Cindy another plus in her I-didn't-kill-Denny list of excuses and reasons. One that maybe even Baldwin couldn't ignore.

Mia decided to hit one more place before she headed home. She already knew he'd been at the winery with Cindy. Maybe he'd also visited the coffee shop bakery in the mornings? She might have to come back to talk to an earlier staff member, but she was here in town and she wasn't going to give up on finding Cindy an alibi, at least not just yet.

She headed west down Main Street and went past Majors on the other side. The Sunshine Bakery was across the street, and the lights were still on. Glancing at the door, she found the sign showing the place was open from six to six, every day but Sunday.

A bell rang as she came into the brightly decorated dining room area. It was small, holding maybe six tables, but the floors were shiny clean and the tables all gleamed. The bakery case was up near the coffee bar and held several cakes and pies. Her stomach growled as she considered taking the Deep Cocoa devil's food cake home for dessert.

"I'll be right out. I'm just taking out the last batch of cupcakes for tomorrow's sales," a happy voice called from the back.

"No worries. Take your time." Mia pulled out a chair and picked up one of the flyers for the bakery's takeout. It didn't mention catering, so maybe she could use the bakery as a source rather than as competition. Either way, it was long past time that she'd introduced herself to the owner.

"Sorry about that." The woman who came out of the bakery brushed off her hands on a black, tie-dyed apron. She wore a matching headband that pulled back cornrows. The woman smiled as she took in Mia at her table. "Welcome, Mia Malone, it's about time we met."

CHAPTER 21

The woman in the bakery poured two cups of coffee, paused, and looked at Mia. "Black, correct?"

"Yes, thank you." Mia still didn't know who the woman was, but if she was offering coffee, she was willing to find out. "I'm sorry, but should I know you?"

"I'm Nellie Market. I went to school with your mother. We were friends." Nellie set down the coffee, then sat across from Mia. "I heard she was in town a few months ago. I'm sorry I missed her."

"She came in for the St. Catherine's reunion. Did you attend school there?"

Nellie shook her head. "Sadly, I attended the public schools. Your mom attended Sun Valley High with me. We were both in flag corps together, as well as other clubs. That's the great thing about going to a small school — you really get to know the kids in your class. Both your mom and I were outsiders because we started in our freshman year rather than kindergarten. Kids can be a little cliquey."

"I've noticed that." Mia sipped her coffee. Good, strong, and fresh. "Your cakes look lovely. Do you cater?"

Nellie shook her head. "I have all I can deal with by supplying the winery and the Lodge their desserts. Catering for this group is a whole 'nother can of worms I don't even want to get into. I hear you're in that business, though."

"I do some desserts. Although outsourcing some of the items wouldn't be unusual. Maybe we can come to an agreement." Mia hadn't wanted to jump into negotiations quite this quickly.

"It's definitely something we can talk about." Nellie handed her a business card. "But you're not here to talk about catering jobs. What's on your mind?"

"Are you psychic?" Mia tucked the card and flyer into her purse.

Nellie laughed. "You don't have to be part of the local coven to know when someone is itching to ask questions. And it *is* Magic Springs, dear. Isn't everyone in this town a little special? At least the locals. Well, besides the local law enforcement troops. I swear, the magic and the common sense gene left those boys' bodies as soon as they put on that blue shirt. They're all nice, but they just seem to have certain blind spots."

"Baldwin is a little focused. But I believe he's got the community's good in mind," Mia added quickly.

"Oh, stop worrying. I'm not going to tell anyone you think Baldwin's an idiot. Mostly because I have the same feeling." She sipped her coffee. "So, what does have you out on a cold day where you could be cuddled up by a fire drinking hot cocoa?"

"As things are going lately, make that a spiked hot cocoa." Mia took a quick sip of her coffee and reached over to pull out Denny's picture. "Have you seen this man around? I'm trying to find out what happened in his last few hours. I'm working for the family."

Nellie snorted. "Keep working on that excuse. Even someone without talent could see through that weak explanation." She pointed toward the door. "I don't have time for games."

"Okay, here's the truth: My houseguest is going to be charged with his murder if I don't figure out who killed him." Mia tapped the picture again. "So, had you seen this man in the last week or so? And, if so, was he with someone?"

Nellie smiled and picked up the paper. "Now, was that so hard? Sometimes it's good to put your cards on the table."

Mia waited as the other woman studied the paper.

She set it down and picked up her coffee. "He was in here early last week. With a woman."

"Fortyish, blond, underweight for her height?" Mia tried to describe Cindy without mentioning the show Cindy was famous for acting in a few years before.

Nellie shook her head. "No, it was one of our locals. A much younger woman. She's always dressed like she's a New York fashion model. What is her name? Her father and brother had some issues with the police last year. Quite the scandal in town."

"You're talking about Bethanie?" Mia sighed and leaned back in her chair. If Bethanie was involved in this situation, it wouldn't be good.

"Yeah, that was her name." A bell went off in the kitchen and Nellie stood. "Look, I've got baking to do for tomorrow. Come by anytime to chat. And I'll consider doing some work for your next event. Just let me know the details and we'll work something out. It was nice meeting you. You look like your mother did at your age, did you know that?"

Mia reached up to touch her cheek. "I thought I more resembled my dad."

Nellie paused at the table. "It's in the shape of your eyes and your chin. You look just like her."

And with that, Nellie retreated to the kitchen. Mia blinked and wondered what the heck had just happened. She'd talk to Grans about Mom's friendship with Nellie when she got home. It seemed as if they'd been very close, yet Mom hadn't ever told her anything about knowing anyone in town.

Mia decided to take the hiking trail to the house instead of going the long way through town. She thought about what she'd learned about Denny as she walked home. He'd been interested in marriage law, he'd been talking to John Louis at least once, even though Sheila had thought it had been about buying local property. And he'd been in the bakery with Bethanie when he'd first come to town.

Maybe she was going to have to bite the bullet and go talk to John Louis tomorrow. She hated the scum and had good reason to, after what he'd done to her, but if she went to his office, where she'd be in public view, at least he couldn't pull a gun on her.

And he was still on probation from the last incident, so she had that protection.

Which didn't help if he actually killed her this time.

Pushing the thought away, she hurried the last bit of path to home. The woods, usually so warm and welcoming, felt unsafe. As if there was a killer hiding at each and every twist of the path. She felt her body relax when she saw the lights of the school just up ahead.

"What the heck are you doing out here?" a man's voice asked as she felt his hand on her arm.

She turned quickly and got into a fight stance and then saw it was Trent. She let out a breath and her body untensed as the fear ran out of her. "What are *you* doing out here? You scared me."

"I asked the question first."

Mia nodded to the house they were approaching. "I was on my way back home from town. I thought the path would be faster and safer than walking on the road because it doesn't have sidewalks."

"The path where a dead man was found? Your idea of safer is a little off." Trent aimed her toward the back door going into the kitchen. "I've got that door open for us."

"Technically, he was found in my backyard, off the path. And why were you in the kitchen?" She peered up at him in the gathering darkness. "And you never answered me about what you were doing on the path."

"I was looking for you. I was getting into my truck to drive to town to see where you'd taken off to. I heard someone coming down the path. Your grandmother is worried. She thought she saw a negative energy around you." He nodded to the door. "Christina's in the downstairs kitchen, working on a new dish for dinner. She says your grandmother gets too involved when she's trying to cook."

"Well, I have to agree with her there. Grans thinks there's only one way to cook something and that's her way." Mia reached up and kissed Trent on the cheek. "Thanks for coming to look for me. I'm sorry she worried you."

"I wasn't too worried." He opened the door for her. "I have my own spidey sense when it comes to your safety and I didn't feel a thing. Who were you talking with?"

"First, Sheila over at the law office. Crap, I forgot to give her Grans's message." Mia stopped in the doorway and took in the aromas that were filling the kitchen. It must be some kind of chicken dish that Christina was working with. "Then I ran over to Sunshine Bakery and met Nellie."

"Nellie? That woman's a hoot and a half." Trent grinned and turned back to lock the door behind them. "We have an agreement on pastry items. She doesn't do doughnuts and the store bakery doesn't do cakes. I'm always sending customers her way."

"About time you two showed up," Christina said from the stove. "Your grandmother is fit to be tied. She's called me upstairs three times."

"Sorry. I didn't think I was that late." Mia glanced at the kitchen clock. "And I was right. I told her I'd be home before dinner and it's only five."

"You need to go talk to her." Christina took a spoonful of the sauce she was working on and offered it to Mia. "So I'm thinking about this for next week's menu. Either that or I could save it for when school starts. We're supposed to bring a new recipe to the first class in my Innovations class. I talked to my study group and they've all been trying different recipes already. We don't meet until late August. I thought I had time, but I guess I'm behind. Taste this."

Mia tasted the sauce. She frowned as she thought about it. "It's okay. A little bland, and yet it tastes like garlic. I don't know

307

how you could do both of those things at the same time."

Christina's shoulders sagged. "That's exactly what I thought. It was one of the recipes my family cook used to make when I was growing up."

"You have a good story behind it, the flavor's just not there. Maybe another recipe you liked from your childhood, or maybe from one of your trips. Did you eat anything in Bermuda that you loved?"

"Yes, but I'm not sure that's the type of food I want to cook." Christina reached for the salt and added a sprinkle.

"I didn't say your signature dish. I just said something you thought would be good for the menu. If you decided to make this one your own, what would you do differently with the recipe?" Mia glanced at Christina's phone as it went off again. She could see the caller ID. It was Grans. "Don't answer that; I'm running upstairs right now. Is this dinner?"

"Yes, I said I'd cook."

Mia waved Trent over. "Help her make that white sauce that you made last month when we were cooking, will you?"

"Of course. I've got a few ideas." He walked over to the sink. "Let me taste what you have before you dump that one. Maybe

I can see where you're going off the rails."

Mia left Christina and Trent to finish dinner and headed upstairs to talk to her grandmother. The door to the apartment flew open before she even tried to open it.

"Thank the Goddess you're all right." Grans pulled her into a hug. "I've been so worried."

"Why? I told you where I was going." Mia moved her grandmother to the couch, where they both sat. "What's going on?"

Grans touched Mia's face as if she hadn't seen her in years, not just hours. "I had a dream, or a premonition or something. You were in trouble and no one could save you."

"Nothing like that happened. I talked to Sheila for a bit, then I went to the bakery."

Grans's hand dropped to her lap. "Oh. You met Nellie. That explains it."

Mia froze. "What do you mean? Nellie at the bakery? I thought she was Mom's friend."

Grans shook her head. " 'Friend' isn't the word I'd use to describe her relationship with your mother. Rivalry, anger, hatred. Whatever Theresa wanted, Nellie went after. She tried to break up your mom and dad when they met. She was captain of the flag corps and your mom was head of the debate team. Constant competition with those two.

I think Nellie even tried to join the coven, although she doesn't have a speck of magic in her body and your mother had already given that part of her life away."

"She read my mind." Mia wondered how long it had taken a nonmagical person to learn those tricks.

"Did she? Or did she just put pieces together? She's very intelligent. I should have warned you about her and her strength. Maybe that would have kept you from running into her, at least for a while." Grans ran her hands over the air around Mia, feeling out her aura. "It feels like you're intact, but maybe we should do a cleansing, just in case."

"Grans, just because Mom had issues with the woman doesn't mean I'm going to have the same type of competition with her. In fact, we're talking about collaborating on the next catering gig."

"Please reconsider. She's just not healthy to be around. It was one of the reasons your mom moved to Boise. She wanted to get Larry out of Nellie's reach. The woman is a complete mess. She'd do anything to win the game with Theresa."

Mia took both her grandmother's hands in her own, then focused on holding her gaze. "Nothing bad is going to happen to either you or me. Especially not from Nellie."

The door to the apartment opened, and Trent came inside, delivering dinner.

"Let's move this discussion to the kitchen. Where's Cindy?" Mia glanced around just as Cindy came out of the hallway.

"I'm here. I was waiting for you to finish your conversation." Cindy blushed as she entered the living room.

Mia assumed the blush was because Cindy had been listening in on their conversation. "Let's sit down for dinner. I've got some questions for you."

Cindy nodded, then stole a quick glance at Mr. Darcy. "You were serious when you said my father's ghost is living in the cat?"

"Yes. I thought it was time you knew. Especially because you're going to leave and take your family's grimoire with you soon. It's a heavy burden, holding all your family's history in one book. Have you thought about what you're going to do when you get home?" Mia helped Grans out of the chair and then took her arm to move toward the kitchen. "You need training."

Cindy nodded. "I know. I guess I could come here and train with Mary Alice, but my shooting schedule is so busy. Once I get back, I don't know when I'll be able to visit again."

Trent set the food on the table and then helped Christina get out plates and silverware. "There's a teaching coven in LA. I could put you in touch with the people who manage the entrance process. I think you'd have to show some proof of magic, but I'm sure we could get you enrolled."

"I've got the spell I worked from the book. I made my agent lose all her hair. And everyone thought she had cancer." Cindy glanced at Mary Alice. "And, with help, we reversed the spell. So she should have eyebrows growing back soon. Her long, blond hair, on the other hand, will take some time. And a good dye job again, because Belle's real hair color is jet-black."

"That would probably be enough. And they're local, so they can verify the results." He patted her shoulder as he set a bottle of soda in front of her. "And the reversal. Sometimes you have to break a few eggs, right, Mia?"

"That's what they say." Mia didn't want Cindy to feel anything but lucky that they were able to reverse the spell without the major rule of three Karmas coming down on the caster. She thought that perhaps because it was Cindy's first spell, the Goddess had given her a pass. "Anyway, I need to ask you something. Was fixing the spell the only reason you came to Magic Springs?"

Cindy looked confused. "We just talked about it. I needed to settle my father's estate. And I knew Mary Alice was a witch from my conversations with my father. I thought she could help after I did that to Belle. I just wanted her to have a really bad hair day. Not have a no-hair day."

"So why was Denny here?"

"You must have realized he was more than just my source for the part." Cindy smiled as she ladled chicken and sauce over the noodles she'd just put on her plate. For someone who didn't eat carbs when she arrived, she didn't seem to hesitate now. "We talked a lot. He was funny and I liked him. When I told him I was coming here, he agreed to meet me. We'd been talking for months and he wanted to take it to the next level. He wanted to see me in person."

"That's it?" Mia pushed as she took the bowl of pasta from Grans. "Just your first date?"

"Oh, it wasn't a date." Cindy put down her fork. "Okay, so it was a date. I'd been feeling something for him for weeks, but I didn't know if he felt the same way. Until the day at the winery, when he said he loved me and wanted to spend his life with me. I was shocked. I mean, I knew he'd done some bad things in his life."

"So were you going to date?" Mia could see Trent and Christina's gazes on her, wanting to know what was behind all the questions, but she shook her head slightly. She needed to let this play out, just to make sure Cindy was going to tell her the truth. The woman was an actor, after all.

"Yes, but I said he had to clean up his act. I didn't want to know what he'd done before we met, but from that point on, he was going to stop doing bad things. No matter what. No excuses. No secrets. Just be a law-abiding citizen." Cindy laughed as she remembered the discussion. "You should have seen his face. You would have thought I was telling him to give up water or air. But he swallowed and agreed to my terms. He said the next night he'd have a surprise for me. I never saw him again."

Mia nodded. "He was going to ask you to marry him. I heard that from Sheila at the law office. Did you know that?"

"I suspected. Denny was a go-big-or-go-home type of guy. That, and he took one of my rings that night. He said he'd give it back, but I asked the officer if they found

314

my ring on him. No one has."

"What type of ring was it?" Mia asked.

"A blue sapphire my father gave me when I moved away to LA." Cindy rubbed her left hand. "I wore it on my left ring finger, which kept the creeps from hitting on me."

Chapter 22

"Now we have a dead guy and a missing ring," Trent said as he dried the last plate as he helped Mia clean up the kitchen. They were the only two left in the main part of the apartment. All the others had retired to their rooms. Christina was working with her study group. Grans was reading a mystery with Mr. Darcy cuddled beside her. And Cindy was studying her lines for her new role. A role she needed to get back to Hollywood to get to work on, which was why she had to leave Magic Springs soon. "I feel like we're going around in circles here. Maybe Baldwin is having better luck solving this puzzle. We just keep adding more layers."

"I don't think so. I think Cindy gave us a clue tonight. If Denny took her ring to size an engagement ring, maybe hers is at the jeweler's. I'm going to run by there tomorrow to see if there are any packages waiting to be picked up. I know his pending proposal doesn't mean Cindy couldn't have killed him, but I don't see any motivation saying she did."

"In an odd way I think it's sweet she was willing to let all the past go if he promised to go clean from that moment forward. That shows real love." He dried the last cup and put it away. He glanced around the kitchen. "My work here is done."

"Thanks for helping Christina out with that sauce. Grans would have gone off on her if she'd served what she was planning." Mia took the cup from him. "You want some tea?"

"I take it you don't have a beer?"

When she shook her head, he nodded. "Then tea would be great. I'm going to have to stock your kitchen with some more manly drinks and snacks if I'm going to be visiting here a lot."

Mia smiled as she filled the tea pot and set up the tea bags in the cups. "I like the sound of that."

He came up behind her and put his arms around her. "I need to be here to keep you out of trouble."

He kissed her neck, which made her retort disappear. She leaned against him. "I don't try to get into trouble. It's just my curious nature, I guess."

"Curiosity killed the cat." He kissed the top of her head and stepped away to go sit at the table. He glanced under the table. "Good thing Mr. Darcy is with your grandmother. I think he might have swatted at me for that cliché."

"More likely that Dorian would take offense." She sat at the table with him. "I feel bad for Denny and Cindy. It's kind of a love-lost story."

"It's a love that never could have been. He was a hit man. Someday a job that was just too big to pass up would have come along and he would have broken his promise and her heart. It's an addiction. Those guys like the thrill of getting away with it." He glanced at his watch. "Levi's on duty now. He's working nights this week."

"You keep close tabs on your brother."

Trent shrugged. "There was an incident a couple of months ago in Sun Valley. Some dopehead looking to score drugs called in a fake emergency to an out-of-the-way cabin. One of the responders, a kid who'd just joined the crew, was killed, and the other guy was shot and left for dead at the cabin. They got a bottle of high-powered Aleve and a few EpiPens. The good drugs were locked in a safe behind a fake wall in the rig." He rubbed his face. "One life lost because of drugs. Two more, if you count the kids who shot the EMTs. They were almost seventeen. And now they'll go to prison for life."

"So you keep an eye out for Levi." Mia put her hand over his. "I'll do protection spells for him with the Goddess as well."

"It can't hurt." He squeezed her hand. "He's a good kid. He'll be a good man someday."

Mia watched Trent's gaze go toward the hallway, where Christina had gone when she left the kitchen. "I think they're good together."

He nodded. "So do I."

"When is he off nights?" Mia glanced at her calendar.

"Saturday is his first day off. Why?" Trent smiled at her. "You have a plan."

"I think we need a game night. Saturday at seven? You bring the margaritas?" She smiled and glanced around the kitchen. "And I'll make a nacho bar for us."

"You're amazing." He leaned over and kissed her again.

The next morning Mia headed to town again. First stop, Magic Springs Jewelry. The bell above the door rang, announcing her arrival to an older man in a white dress shirt and black dress pants. He wore black dress shoes that matched his belt. There was a pair of glasses hanging on a chain around his neck.

"Good morning; you're my first customer of the day. What special thing can I find for you? Or maybe you'd like a custom-made item? I'm very talented with Idaho opals. You'd have something original, made only for you." He stepped out from behind the desk to greet Mia. "I'm Charlie Parker."

"Nice to meet you, Charlie. Unfortunately, I'm not a customer. I'm Mia Malone. I just bought the old school and I'm turning it into a catering spot."

"From what I hear from my wife, you're doing more than that. She signed up for one of your classes next month and we had your chicken pot pie for dinner the other night. It was very good, young lady. You have quite the talent." He took her arm and moved her over to the rings. "Now, why are you here this fine day?"

"Actually, I was wondering if you happened to have a package that hadn't been picked up yet. An engagement ring, and a sapphire that was given to you to size the engagement ring by."

Charlie stopped and took a step back.

"Don't tell me you're a mind reader as well."

"I'm not. I can assure you of that." She felt the excitement. "So, you do have the package?"

"Yes. It's all paid for and waiting for that man to come back." He focused on something in Mia's eyes. "But he's not coming back, now, is he? What a shame. I've never seen a man so deeply in love. When Bethanie brought him into the store, he was just about to pop out of his skin, he was so excited to be choosing a ring."

"Wait, Bethanie brought him here?" A tingle scooted up Mia's spine. Maybe this was the clue she'd been waiting for.

"Yes. She likes bringing me business. Bethanie Miller was my best customer for a long time. Now she's selling those pieces back to me to pay for her college costs. Such a shame what her father did to her life. Anyway, she brought her friend in so he could pick out a ring for his girlfriend. As I said, I've never seen a man so in love." Charlie brought out a small bag and set it on the counter. "The ring is paid for. If you know who the owner of the sapphire is, have them come in and claim it. I'll have her put it on for me. I'll know. Then I'll give her the other ring. Unless you think it will make her sad."

"I think it would be perfect." Mia nodded to the bag. "Can you show me the ring?"

"Of course. All the pretty ladies enjoy seeing rings. Mr. Blake did a good job choosing this design. He was very much in love. And the band is inscribed with his name and his love."

Mia held her breath as he opened the box. He held up the ring, then pointed to the engraving.

"You know this Cindy?" He handed her the ring.

After seeing it Mia gave it back and thanked Charlie for his time. "The ring is beautiful. You did an amazing job."

Outside the shop, she punched in Baldwin's number. When he answered, she told him about the almost-engagement. "Cindy couldn't have killed Denny."

"Love story gone wrong. It's playing all the right notes, Mia," Baldwin replied. "What am I missing here?"

"She wanted a future with the guy. A future she told him they wouldn't have if he continued his current ways. Maybe he was here not just to meet Cindy. Maybe he was here to do a job for our local convict Realtor." Mia started walking toward the real estate office.

"Look, you're treading on thin ice here. I'll go talk to Charlie to get his take on it. And I'll talk to John again, but we don't know for sure that he even knew Denny." Baldwin sounded tired.

"Actually, there is. Sheila saw Denny talking to John. She thought he was looking to buy a house due to the upcoming nuptials." Mia paused and decided to tell Baldwin everything. "And Charlie said Bethanie was the one who brought Denny into the store. Why would Bethanie know Denny unless she was doing a favor for one of John's clients?"

"Okay, I'll talk to her too, but don't get your hopes up." He paused, and Mia could hear the clicking of his keyboard. His sharp intake of breath told her he'd found something. "Well, I'll be. I may have found a connection between Denny and John."

"Besides Bethanie?" Mia could hear her heart pounding in her ears.

"Yep. I just got a full report on Denny. He and John were cellmates for the short time John was in prison. I guess the state pen rented out space to other jurisdictions when their numbers were low." He quickly added, "Of course, that doesn't mean John killed Denny. But it does mean he lied. I need to go talk to him about that little discrepancy."

"That's awesome." Mia could hear Baldwin moving around his office. "You might want to head to John's office first. I'm right outside and I'm going in to talk to Bethanie. I'm hoping John's not in this afternoon."

"Are you crazy? He's going to file a restraining order against . . ."

Mia didn't hear the rest of the rant because she'd ended the call and tucked her phone into her tote. Baldwin knew where she was. John wouldn't have time to kidnap her or kill her and hide the body before he got here. She just hoped she would be alone with Bethanie. She said a prayer of protection for herself as she pulled open the office door.

Bethanie was sitting at the reception desk and looked up with a smile when she heard the door open. Then the smile dropped from her face. "Ms. Malone, what are you doing here? John's expected back from a showing any time."

"Good, then we have a few minutes to talk." Mia leaned on the desk and pulled out the picture of Denny. "Do you know him?"

Bethanie glanced at the photo, then swallowed. "I don't know what happened to him, I swear."

"I just want to confirm that he was one of John's clients." Mia put the picture away. "And you did him a favor."

Now Bethanie smiled softly. "You know about me taking him to the jewelry store. He wanted to buy an engagement ring for his girl. That's what he called her, his girl. So I took him to see Charlie. Full disclosure, I got a referral fee from Charlie for the sale. It was super nice of him. I don't make much here and the referral — well, it paid my rent for a couple of months. I guess the ring he bought was pretty big."

"Okay, you need to tell Baldwin all this when he shows up. So, Denny was looking at property with John?" This was the part Mia held her breath for. The answer would at least give Baldwin a starting point to question John.

"No, Denny wasn't a client. I asked if he was looking at property and he said they'd need to live in California, where his girl worked. He said he had been here to do a favor for John, but he'd had to cancel the contract. I heard them talking in John's office. Man, John was mad. I've never heard him yell like that." Bethanie looked behind Mia to the door. "Uh-oh."

Mia steeled herself. Apparently, John had just walked back into the office. She smiled at Bethanie, trying to calm the girl. Mia pulled out a flyer with next month's cooking classes on it and handed it to her. "I'm so glad you were able to take a class. I wanted to let you know I'll give a ten-percent discount on a second class as long as you schedule this month. Call me if you have questions."

"What are you doing in my office?" John's voice was calm, but cold as ice. "Did you come to tell me you're selling?"

Mia turned and let shock fill her face. "Oh, John, I didn't think you'd be in the office this late. I was just trying to round up some repeat business. I guess you wouldn't want a flyer for your wife to support the cooking school considering you want me to close down."

"I don't care about your stupid school. But if you wanted to look successful in the business, I'm sure we could make an arrangement and get you into something new. Maybe even closer to Sun Valley, so you could get clients with a little money rather than these hicks from Magic Springs." John walked past her and paused at his office door.

"I'm not interested in selling."

He sneered at her. "For now. Please refrain from marketing your business in my office. I'd hate to have to sue you."

He slammed the door behind him and Mia took a deep breath. She looked at Bethanie. "I hope I didn't get you in trouble."

She shrugged. "So what if he's mad. He can't fire me for talking to you. I know that, and he knows I know a lot of people around here. He doesn't want to get on my bad side. I'll remind him of that later today."

"Thanks." Mia hurried out the door and almost ran into Mark Baldwin, who had just parked his cruiser on the street in front of the building.

"At least you're alive." He put his hands on her arms to stop her from crashing into him. "But you're shaking. I take it John is inside?"

"He is now. And Bethanie has some interesting news." She filled him in on what Bethanie had said. She swallowed. "I think John killed Denny."

"I know that, but like we've said, there has to be proof." Baldwin looked at her. "Are you all right?"

Mia wiped a lone tear from her cheek. "I'm fine. I guess I didn't really believe John would do something like that, but after talking to him just now, I know he killed him."

Baldwin pulled her to the edge of the sidewalk and nodded at an older woman, who was walking her toy poodle. "Good afternoon, Mabel."

The woman nodded a greeting, staring at Mia. "Officer Baldwin."

He waited for her to get out of earshot. "Great, now Sarah's going to get a call about how I was flirting with some woman on the street."

"You call this flirting?" Mia laughed, and with the release of emotion, she suddenly felt stronger. "Just tell Sarah I was on one of my conspiracy rants about John Louis. I'm sure you've complained enough about me for it to sound believable."

Mia saw his face pinken and knew she'd hit a nerve.

"I'm going to go talk to him. Why don't you just go home and stay out of trouble? Can you do that? Just for a day or two? If John killed Denny, there has to be some sort of evidence linking him to the crime. Something I must have missed."

Mia thought about the St. Christopher's medal she'd found. What if Trent hadn't lost it when they'd been working on the garden? Maybe John had planted it there to implicate Trent. If so, he might just bring it up when he talked to Baldwin. "Hey, let me know if he mentions a religious medallion that would put someone else at the scene.

I'm not sure how he'd bring it up, but call me if he does, okay?"

"That's weirdly random and specific at the same time." Baldwin studied her. "Want to tell me why?"

"It might not be anything." Mia turned to head home. "Just call me and I'll explain then."

"Mia, you are the most frustrating woman I've ever met," he called after her.

She turned and smiled at him. "Now, Mark, you sound like you're flirting."

When she got back to the school, she decided to work in the office for a while rather than go upstairs to the apartment. She had plans to make and lists to do for the next three months. It worried her that they didn't have a catering job this weekend, but then again, she appreciated the break. Which meant she needed to figure out how many weekends she really wanted to cater and block off the others for her time off. She wasn't going to work twenty-four seven for this business the way she had when she worked for Isaac.

This time, she was going to have a life.

CHAPTER 23

Mia didn't have to wait long for Baldwin's call. Her cell rang less than two hours after she'd left the real estate office. "Long time no talk. I was kidding about the flirting thing. I'm kind of in a relationship."

"Funny girl," Baldwin said. "Where are you? Did you go home like I asked?"

"Yes, Dad. I'm in my office on the first floor. Why?" She already knew why he was asking. She'd seen his car pull into the parking lot on the video feed. Mia headed to the door to meet him.

"Let me in." Baldwin hung up on her.

He looked surprised when she opened the door a few seconds later. He glanced up at the security camera. "You upgraded the system."

"Last week, after finding the dead guy on my lawn. Of course, after Ronnie started trying to break in, I realized I still have some blind spots on the campus. Between the heating and cooling bill and the security systems I'm putting in, I'm going to have to sell a lot of mac and cheese." Mia locked the door after him.

"Who's down there?" Grans called over the railing.

"Mark Baldwin came to chat, Grans. We're going to talk in my office, okay?" Mia called back up.

"I'm sending Christina down to walk Muffy. Don't lock her out."

"Okay." Mia nodded toward the office. "What did he say?"

Mark sat in one of the visitor chairs and glanced at the tiny fridge. "You got a root beer in there?"

"Oddly enough, I do." Mia pulled out two locally brewed root beers and opened them with a bottle opener. "The company owner wants to do a pairing of his handcrafted sodas with a few of my dishes. I'm still working out the recipes."

"Steve's a good guy. This brand is my favorite. It's pricey as heck, but Sarah buys me a six pack every now and then." He sipped the soda, then set it down. "How did you know he'd bring up Trent's St. Christopher's medal?"

"What did he say?" Mia hadn't thought he'd be that direct, but she guessed if John thought he could take Trent out along with her, he'd get the building that Majors was in as well as St. Catherine's.

"He said that his client, Denny Blake, was agitated when he came to see him about buying a condo. He said Denny was looking for a bachelor pad to come up and ski every now and then without the Sun Valley prices." Baldwin sipped his root beer.

"Wow. I guess he didn't know about Bethanie taking him to the jewelry store to buy a ring." Mia shook her head. When people lied, their stories just kept getting bigger.

"Nope. John said he'd been in a bar, saying something about you and what he'd like to do with you. Then John left, and Trent ambushed him in the parking lot. John took him down and ripped off the St. Christopher's."

"So much wrong with that story, I don't know where to start. One, he said he took Trent in a fight? Then kept his St. Christopher's as a trophy?" Mia played with the label on the root beer bottle. "And how did I get involved in the story?"

"You had been coming on to him earlier when he'd stopped by the school to check out the classes. John confessed to being a closet foodie." Baldwin held up his hand. "Don't say what you're thinking, but did he

332

come to the school?"

Mia thought about the last week. "Trent found his business card outside when he came over last week."

"I'm assuming you threw it away?"

"Of course. He'd written a message on the back that said if I wanted to sell, he'd pay me a bonus. But I don't want to sell. And besides, having something he touched in my home kind of messes with my head. Okay, back to his story. If he took Trent in a fight, which I doubt, wouldn't having the medal be a flashing neon arrow straight to John killing Denny?" Mia wasn't following the logic.

Now Baldwin did grin. "Yeah, but it took him a while to realize that. Then he started backpedaling and told me he'd given the necklace back the day Denny died."

"Long way for a story." Mia grabbed a water from the fridge. "Do you want another root beer?"

Baldwin shook his head. "No, I'm still nursing this one. So, why did you know he'd bring it up?"

"I found the medal by the tree just off the trail a few days ago. Where Denny's body was found." Mia sipped her water and waited for Baldwin's reaction.

"He planted it." He leaned back in his

chair and sipped his soda. "Huh. I wouldn't have given him enough credit for setting up the scene."

"I think it was an afterthought. From the last time Trent saw the medal, I think his necklace was stolen from the store on the day that John was there to try to convince him to sell."

Baldwin stood. "Okay, then. I need to get to the station to see if I can find a gun registered to John."

"You might want to check registrations to Bethanie, or her dad or brother too. According to Charlie, she's been selling a lot of her jewelry to survive. If she knew the gun was valuable, she'd sell it just to get it out of her house. Christina says she's not fond of guns." Mia followed him out. "Thanks for stopping by. I'd like to get this wrapped up soon."

"It's all circumstantial unless someone saw John kill Denny," Baldwin reminded her. "Or we can find the smoking gun."

Mia leaned against the doorway as Baldwin paused at the step. "Well, thanks for trying."

"It's not impossible, so don't give up yet." Baldwin glanced around the step. "You have a home to fight for. That makes all the difference in my mind."

When she got upstairs, Cindy stood at the door, her suitcases nearby. "You're leaving?"

"I talked to Officer Baldwin. There have been some developments that I guess have cleared me." She glanced at her phone. "It's time for me to go back to my real life. Or as real as Hollywood ever gets."

"How are you getting to Boise?" Mia asked.

"Oh, I rented a car."

"Trent's coming to take Cindy to the car rental lot," Grans said as she came into the living room. "And she's leaving her grimoire here until she can find a school in California."

"Can you ship those things?" Cindy touched the book in Gran's hands.

"Probably. Or Mia and Trent could bring it to you." Grans smiled at Mia. "They haven't ever been on a road trip together. It would help cement their relationship."

"Or destroy it." Mia took the book from Grans. "Don't worry, we'll get it to you when you need it."

Cindy leaned down to pick up Mr. Darcy. "Dad, if you're in there, I love you and I'm sorry about everything."

Mr. Darcy — or Dorian — reached up and patted Cindy's cheek with his paw and softly meowed.

"Now there, isn't that nice?" Grans smiled at the two.

"Grans, call Trent and tell him I'm taking Cindy to get her car." Mia put the book on the fireplace mantel. "Whenever you're ready."

"Thanks." Cindy gave Dorian a quick hug, then set him down on the floor. "I'm ready now. If I don't leave soon, I'm going to miss my first day on set."

"Can't have that happening." Mia held open the door and waited.

Cindy turned and hugged Grans. "Thanks for everything. I know why my dad was so taken with you. You're amazing."

Grans's eyes misted as she patted Cindy on the back. "You're a lot like your father, you know. Have a safe trip."

"That's the nicest thing anyone's ever said to me. I'll talk to you soon." Cindy picked up her bags and nodded to Mia. "Thanks for taking me."

"No problem." Mia went ahead of Cindy and opened the door for her. When they got in the van, Mia put on her seat belt. "We have one stop to make."

They found a parking spot right in front of the jewelry store, and Cindy glanced out the window at it. "Don't tell me you found my ring?"

"Okay, I won't tell you. Come on in — you've got a surprise coming." Mia hurried into the store and gestured for Cindy to follow her. When they got inside, Mia pointed at Cindy and stepped back.

"So glad you could come. I've cleared this with the police station, so we are free to do our transaction." Charlie motioned Cindy over to the display case. "Please sit down. Mia tells me your name is Cindy. And you might recognize this ring."

He pulled out the sapphire, and Cindy choked up, tears falling down her cheeks. "I didn't think I'd ever see this again. It was a gift from my father. Thank you so much."

"It was my pleasure. Please put it on, so we can verify it's yours." Charlie watched as Cindy slipped the ring on her left hand. "Okay, then, I guess it is."

"Thank you so much. I appreciate you taking good care of it." Cindy went to stand, but he waved her down again.

"We aren't done." He smiled and took out the other ring box. "I believe this was also supposed to be yours. The police say that there is no family of record, so I can give it to the person it was made for. Your name is in the engraving, and he bought insurance and put the ring in your name. Therefore, you own it."

"I don't understand." Cindy looked at Mia, confused.

"Open the box; you will." Mia smiled encouragingly. Inside, she wanted to rip open the box herself and show Cindy the ring.

Cindy opened it and took out the ring. She glanced inside at the engraving and cried as she read the inscription: " 'Cindy and Denny, Forever.' "

"I guess it was his forever," Mia said, feeling sadness at the lack of time the couple had had to enjoy life together.

"Yes, it was." Cindy switched over the sapphire to her right hand and put the diamond on the left. "I'll treasure this always."

Mia met Charlie's gaze. The man had tears in his eyes. So, he was a romantic, which explained why he owned a jewelry shop. "Are you ready to get your car? I know you're on a schedule."

Cindy wiped her face with her hands and blinked away more tears. "You bet. Thank you again for holding on to both rings," she said to Charlie.

"My pleasure, dear girl. My pleasure." He patted Cindy on the back, then handed her a few tissues.

When they got back into the car, Cindy

stared at the ring. "I guess he'd decided that he was going to follow my rules. I'm sorry he didn't have the chance."

"Me too." Mia started the engine and drove Cindy to the rental car agency. She parked and got out with Cindy.

"Thank you for everything. I know I was a bit of a pill, but I'm so glad I got to meet you and your family. We could have been kind of sisters." Cindy pulled her into a hug, and Mia thought her face must have looked like Grans's had when Cindy hugged her.

"Make sure to keep in touch. I want to know how you're doing." Mia gave her a little squeeze when she hugged her.

"You got it." Cindy took her suitcases into the agency's front door and disappeared.

Mia sighed in relief. The house should be back to normal when she returned. Grans would be staying for a few more days and was heading back to her house to get more clothes. Mia could hear Gloria laughing and knew it was a warning signal. Nothing was that easy.

CHAPTER 24

It was a sunny Saturday morning and Trent and Mia were out in the backyard, finishing the herb garden planting. It had taken another week to get the underground utilities marked and the permission to dig completed. And then another week to make sure the plantings were all where they needed to be. Grans had vetoed several plan drafts and had sent Mia looking for a book in the newly discovered St. Catherine's library. But once Mia had found and read the book on magical herb growing, the next draft plan was accepted. Grans was back home with Muffy. Mia and Christina had Mr. Darcy and Dorian. The world of Magic Springs wasn't perfect, but it was a little more normal than it had been.

"So, we're doing the yard sale next week? When are the antique dealers coming?" Trent leaned on his shovel, taking in the completed garden.

"What, we get one project done and you want to jump into the next one?" Mia teased as she took a sip from her water bottle. "I may put you on paint patrol. The second floor needs a lot of remodeling."

"Yes, but you haven't decided what to do with it yet, so I'm safe there." He pointed to the parking lot, where Baldwin's police cruiser had just pulled in. "Good news or bad? Want to take a guess?"

"I'm feeling pretty chipper today even with the planting, so I'm going with good." She watched his face. "Am I wrong?"

"What? You think I can read people through the steel body of a Charger?" He gathered up the tools and took them to the back shed.

"Is there really steel in car bodies these days?" Mia mused.

"That's what you got out of that statement?" He tucked his gloves into his pocket and put an arm around her shoulders. "No more stalling. Let's go see what Baldwin wants."

They met about halfway in the middle, where there were a couple of benches. "Do you mind if we sit? It's been a long morning." Baldwin took off his hat and leaned his forearms on his thighs.

"This doesn't sound good." Mia sat down

and leaned into Trent, who sat next to her. "Go ahead, tell us the bad news."

"I was called to the station this morning at five." Baldwin yawned. "Saturdays are my only days to sleep in. Sarah drags us to early services on Sunday."

They just watched him. And waited.

"Anyway, when I got there, I was surprised to see Carol Louis with a shiner of a black eye and something wrapped in a towel. When I asked her what had happened, she shoved the towel at me."

Mia leaned forward. She had a feeling where this was going.

"She didn't say anything. Just stared at me. Then I asked what was in the towel, but I had a feeling. Guns have a certain weight." He massaged his temples. "She tells me it's the gun used to kill Denny Blake. That her husband had it hidden in the garage. And there was no way she would ever go back to that — well, let's just say she used some colorful adjectives."

"You have the gun that shot Denny?" Mia's breath caught on the name. She'd hoped. She'd prayed. She'd even tried to make a locating spell, but it hadn't panned out. Carol Louis just walking into the place and handing it over wasn't a possibility that had ever crossed her mind. "I can't believe she just turned it in."

"I doubt she'll testify by the time the trial happens, but we may not need her. If there are fingerprints on the gun, we might have a slam dunk." Baldwin grinned like he'd been given a lollipop. "She'll probably regret coming to the station after she calms down, but she did the one thing she couldn't take back. She brought the smoking gun."

"It's the one he bought from Bethanie and told you was stolen from his office, right?" Mia tried to remember John's story when Baldwin had questioned him regarding the missing gun.

Baldwin nodded. "It looks like it. I've got to go back to the station. There's going to be hell to pay when we bring him in, but I think we've got him this time. At least I'm going to hope. Sometimes right needs to win out over wrong, doesn't it?"

Mia and Trent sat on the benches long after Baldwin had left.

"I can't believe this is over." Mia's gaze went over to the tree where Denny's body had been found.

"I can't believe Cindy didn't whack him." Trent pulled her closer. "You know it's always the spouse, right?"

"Except they weren't married." She made a mental note to email Cindy later to let her know that John had been arrested for the deed.

"Hey, you two. I thought you were busy planting a garden. Or was that just the excuse you used to get out of doing inventory this morning?" Levi and Christina walked up the path from the street.

"Any excuse will work. And I am the boss. I take it Mom called you in?" Trent kissed her on the top of the head. "However, now that the garden is planted, Mia has a new honey-do list for me."

"I learned the idea from Baldwin. He was complaining that Sarah has a running one for him. I didn't want Trent to feel left out." She nodded to Christina. "I wondered where you'd taken off to so early this morning. I was going to ask you to help."

"I hate gardening. Even more than counting boxes of cereal." She leaned into Levi. "Besides, I like spending time with his mother."

Mia smiled. "So, you're telling me you had a better offer?"

"I'd say so." Christina tapped Levi's chest. "And now he's taking me out for a make-up date. Dinner, dancing, fun. He owes me."

"Hey, now," Levi started, but his brother shook his head.

"Just feel lucky you got back into her good

graces and leave the details behind. Or are you that stupid?" Trent asked his brother.

"No, man, I'm not stupid at all." He squeezed Christina's waist. "I'm right where I need to be. Oh, by the way, Mia, your sign out front is perfect. Reminds me of a down-home Southern restaurant."

"Well, hopefully they'll know we're only takeout." Mia smiled. The sign was installed late yesterday and Mia had already taken a few pictures to add to their website page.

"It's wonderful. I'm sending a picture of it to all my college friends to let them know we're here. Some of them have family in the area." Christina nodded to the door. "I've got to go in to change for dinner. See you all later."

Christina and Levi disappeared into the kitchen.

"Maybe we should go to the Lodge tonight for dinner." She glanced at the backyard. It was all coming together. And she couldn't have been happier. "I'm feeling a little less worried about losing the place after Baldwin's visit."

"There was no way John Louis could have forced you out of your home." Trent stood and held out his hand to help her up.

Mia stood and they walked hand in hand, following Christina and Levi into the building. "Yeah, you're right. But now I don't have to worry about what he's going to do next. He's out of my hair and I can focus on building the business."

Gloria laughed from her window perch in the apartment kitchen.

Trent glanced around the commercial kitchen. "This building makes the weirdest sounds. I could have sworn I just heard a little girl laugh. Did you hear it?"

"I didn't hear anything." Mia took his arm and led him to the stairs. She didn't want to lie, but there was plenty enough time to introduce him to Gloria, and to explain that most witches can't hear another witch's kitchen friend. It just meant that Trent was special. For this reason and oh, so many others. Some Mia hadn't even realized yet.

But they had time. Time to learn each other's secrets.

Magic Springs was full of secrets. Was it any wonder that St. Catherine's Prep held its own? Grans held the secrets that her guardian wanted her to know. But for today, at least one secret had been solved: Denny's murder.

"So, dinner at the Lodge? Are you in?" Mia asked as they made their way up the stairs to the apartment. And to the next chapter of their lives.

TWO WICKED DESSERTS

Dear Readers,

Cheesecake wasn't made or served at my house until I left for my own place. Then my mom tried a few at Easter. I'm pretty sure they used some sort of Jell-O. I didn't make my first cheesecake until a few years ago. In fact, I'd told several people I didn't like cheesecake. I think I was crazy or thinking of something else at the time.

If I'd known they were this easy, I would have tried making one earlier. Anyway, once I made my first cheesecake, I was hooked.

The chocolate version below was on my Christmas menu for a lot of years. It's very chocolaty, so make sure you serve it with lots of whipped cream.

The pumpkin version was my Thanksgiving recipe. I love both.

Enjoy.
Lynn

PUMPKIN CHEESECAKE

Pre-heat your oven to 350 degrees.
In a large bowl, cream the following

2 pkgs. cream cheese
3/4 cup sugar
1 tsp. vanilla

Then mix in

3 eggs

Beat after each addition.
Add

1 cup pumpkin
3/4 tsp. cinnamon
1/4 tsp. nutmeg

Pour mixture into a graham cracker crust
(premade).

Bake for 55 minutes.
Cool and chill. Serve with whipped cream.

DARK CHOCOLATE
CHRISTMAS CHEESECAKE

Pre-heat oven to 300 degrees.

1 1/2 cups chocolate cookie crumbs
3 tbsp. melted butter

NOTE: You can replace the above items with a premade graham cracker crust.
Mix butter into the cookie crumbs, then push into a greased pan (springform or pie plate).

2 8-oz. packages of cream cheese, room temperature or softened

In a large mixing bowl, beat cream cheese until fluffy.

1 14-oz. can of chocolate sweetened con-densed milk

Gradually beat in the sweetened con-densed milk.

3 eggs
3 tbsps. cornstarch
1 tsp. peppermint extract (or almond if you want a different flavor)

Add the eggs, cornstarch, and extract, beating until well mixed.

Pour mixture into the prepared pan.

Bake 55 minutes or until center is set.

Cool and chill. Decorate the edge of the cheesecake with crushed peppermint candies (if you used the mint extract, slivered almonds if not). Serve with whipped cream.

ABOUT THE AUTHOR

Lynn Cahoon is the *New York Times* and *USA Today* bestselling author of the Kitchen Witch Mysteries, the Cat Latimer Mystery series, the Tourist Trap Mysteries, and the Farm-to-Fork series. Originally from Idaho, she grew up living the small-town life she now loves to feature in her novels. A member of Sisters in Crime, Mystery Writers of America, and International Thriller Writers, she lives with her husband and two fur babies in a small historic town on the banks of the Mississippi River. Visit her at Lynn Cahoon.com.

The employees of Thorndike Press hope you have enjoyed this Large Print book. All our Thorndike, Wheeler, and Kennebec Large Print titles are designed for easy reading, and all our books are made to last. Other Thorndike Press Large Print books are available at your library, through selected bookstores, or directly from us.

For information about titles, please call:
(800) 223-1244

or visit our website at:
gale.com/thorndike

To share your comments, please write:
Publisher
Thorndike Press
10 Water St., Suite 310
Waterville, ME 04901

CPSIA information can be obtained
at www.ICGtesting.com
Printed in the USA
BVHW082225150222
629149BV00007B/30